Mountain Journey Home

A J Hawke

Mountain Quest Publishing
ISBN: 978-0-9834505-4-2
Copyright © 2012 Barbara A Kee
Cover copyright © Barbara A Kee
Layout design © by Barbara A Kee

ISBN: 0-9834-5054-4
ISBN-13: 9780983450542

Dedication

This book is dedicated to my family who continue to stand beside me on this journey.

As always, To God Be The Glory

Acknowledges

A big thank you for the continued encouragement of Janet Grimes, Barbara (Bobbie) Kee, and Teresa Hanger for their help and encouragement toward the publication of this novel.

Chapter 1
Rock Corner, Texas, 1877

Dave Kimbrough struggled to keep breathing. Jenny, his wife, his love, his world, couldn't be dead. Glancing around at the small crowd around the open grave and listening to the soft sobs, he wanted to scream at the suddenness and unreasonableness of her loss. Jenny was dead. He couldn't accept it. His light and his joy had ended, buried in a pine box in the nearly frozen ground. As Jenny's brothers shoveled clumps of dirt mixed with snow into her grave, Dave saw nothing but blackness to come.

Mr. and Mrs. Harrod clung together across the grave from Dave hugging Jenny's little twelve year old sister Rachel. He needed to say something to them. After all, they were burying their twenty-four year old daughter, but he had no words with which to comfort them.

He couldn't look at Jenny's sister Mary, not with her holding his two-year-old son. It hurt too much even to look at Jonathan.

The preacher stepped around the grave and took Dave's hand. "You have my deepest sympathy, Dave. May God be with you in the days to come."

God? Where had He been when the fever had taken his beautiful wife and left a two year old motherless?

"Let's go to the house and get out of this cold." Mr. Harrod walked toward the buggy supporting his wife on one arm and his youngest daughter with the other. Dave almost envied the tears that the Harrod family shed so easily. The ache in his chest felt as if it would consume him if he didn't release the tears that flooded his soul. But he couldn't cry.

Everyone had left except for Jesse and Wayne, Jenny's brothers. Dave couldn't leave the grave now mounded with fresh dirt. How could they expect him to leave his bride here in this cold ground? Jenny didn't like the cold. Dave wanted to howl his refusal to accept that he would never hold her again and feel her arms around him.

Darkness would soon be upon them. Wayne put his arm around Dave's shoulders. "We have to leave. You can come back tomorrow but for now let's go home and get warm."

"I can't...I can't leave her...she doesn't like the cold."

Jesse led their horses up. "Wayne, we got to go." Jenny's oldest brother seemed to be choking as he spoke.

Wayne nodded. "Come on Dave. Let's go check on Jonathan."

Dave allowed Wayne to guide him to the horses. He wanted to get on his horse and ride until he could outdistance the tearing pain of his loss. But he had no strength to even turn toward his own ranch and allowed Jesse and Wayne guide him to the warmth and caring of the Harrod's ranch.

His agony was so great that even to look at his son, Jonathan, was more than he could bear.

The Harrod family gathered around him even in their own grief, but Dave couldn't go on with the life that so remained him of Jenny.

Two days after he buried his beloved Jenny, he rode out from the Harrods' place where he and Jonathan had been staying and returned to his ranch. He sat on his horse and stared at the little ranch house that had been so full of hope and dreams. He dismounted and tied the horse's reins to the hitching post in front of the house. Taking a deep breath, he slowly climbed the steps onto the porch and opened the front door. The house already smelled abandoned and cold had crept into every corner of the now empty rooms. The furniture was still there, but without Jenny there was no life in the place anymore. The ache within was so great that he couldn't even release his tears. Everywhere he looked, he saw her.

He gathered up a few things, including all of the baby's clothes and flannels, and put them into a valise. Taking a last look around at his life with Jenny, he then walked out of the house without a backward glance. He rode back to the Harrod's ranch with a sense that all sounds and feelings had been deafened.

Dave put his horse in the barn and carried the valise into the kitchen.

Mrs. Harrod stood at the dry sink washing bottles used for the baby. "Dave, I'm glad you're back. Are you all right?"

"I'm all right." It amazed him how easily and how much he lied these days. He wasn't all right. He would never be all right again. "Here are the baby's things from the house." He couldn't bear to say his son's name.

Mr. Harrod came into the kitchen from the back porch. He walked up to Dave and put his hand on his shoulder. "What have you got there, son?"

The kindness of these people only made him feel worse. He had to get away. "I want to ask you to do something for me."

Mrs. Harrod dried her hands on a towel and came to stand next to her husband. "Anything we can do, you know that."

"I need to get away for awhile. Can you take care of the baby? And maybe, look after my place?" He looked down at the valise on the table.

Mr. Harrod moved around to look at Dave. "What are you asking? For a few days, weeks, or longer?"

"No, Dave, don't go away. Stay here with us, with Jonathan. Don't leave us." Mrs. Harrod raised her apron to her face as she cried.

Dave felt he was drowning in sorrow, his sorrow, the Harrod's sorrow, the sorrow of the world. He had to get away.

"Is it the memories of Jenny?" Mr. Harrod asked in a soft, sad voice.

Dave couldn't answer. He could only nod as he continued to look the table.

Placing his hand on Dave's shoulder, he asked, "When will you leave?"

He took a deep breath before he could speak. "I'll leave in the morning."

A year later, Dave met Mr. Harrod and Jesse at the cafe in town.

"Son, it's good to see you." Mr. Harrod gave him a hug.

Jesse also gave him a bear hug. "You look awful. Haven't you been eating?"

"How are you all doing?" Dave tried to grin at them but it came out as a grimace. He was glad to see them. They were good men, but he could see Jenny in Mr. Harrod's eyes and Jesse had the same color of hair as his wife.

Mr. Harrod and Jesse told him about the ranches and the family as they sat together over a meal that Dave couldn't eat.

Mr. Harrod leaned forward. "Johnny is the liveliest three-year-old you ever saw, always running and curious about everything. He's a happy little fellow. You'll see when you come out to the ranch."

Dave turned his attention to Jesse to avoid answering Mr. Harrod. "Jesse, I understand that you've been taking care of my ranch."

"Yes, Pa has had too much to do on his own place. It just naturally worked for me to take responsibility for your ranch." Jesse shifted in his chair.

"I'm glad. You're a good rancher. There's no reason for you not to run the ranch. Would you like to buy it from me?" Dave leaned forward toward Jesse.

"Don't you want to come back and run the ranch yourself?" Jesse looked at his father and then back at Dave.

Dave rubbed his hand over his face. He felt beyond weary. It wasn't a fatigue of the body but of his spirit. "I don't plan to move back here. I'd like for you to have the ranch if you want it."

"I would rather you come back, but if you aren't, then yes, I want the ranch."

"You've been doing the work anyway. I've already written a bill of sale for you." Dave wanted to get it over. He handed the bill of sale to Jesse.

"Dave, come back to the ranch with us. Ma will want to see you, and Wayne, Mary, and Rachel. And you need to see your son." Mr. Harrod implored.

Dave could only shake his head. It had taken all the courage he had to return to the town where he and Jenny had met. He felt guilty about not seeing his son, and feared that Jenny didn't approve of what he was doing. In dealing with the loss of Jenny, he felt out of control and it wasn't really Dave Kimbrough making the decisions. The Harrods didn't understand, but they would care for their grandson. If Dave thought the child had not been well cared for and loved, he knew he would have done differently.

"Jesse, I don't want anything for me from the ranch. I want you to pay your father the money for my son's care."

"Now, we can take care of Jonathan. You need to take the money for yourself." Mr. Harrod put his hand on Dave's arm.

"I'll send you money when I can." Dave reached for his hat.

"Don't you know that we would rather have you back with us?" Mr. Harrod looked close to tears.

Dave could only look at his feet. Giving the money from the ranch to Mr. Harrod wasn't much, but at least his son wouldn't lack for the essentials.

As he left Jesse and Mr. Harrod, he felt Mr. Harrod put something in his pocket. It wasn't until he was camped that evening that he remembered to look to see what it was. In a little pouch was a locket with two pictures, one of Jenny taken the year before she married and one of a serious round-faced little boy of three looking out at him with Jenny's eyes.

For the first time since his wife's death, he cried that evening by the campfire. Deep wrenching sobs that felt as if they would tear him apart. He didn't know if he cried for his own loss, or for the little boy who would never even remember his mother.

Chapter 2
Colorado

Five years later, 1883

Dave Kimbrough held his horse and body still—in order to blend in with his surroundings and detect anything out of harmony with the countryside—he slowly looked in all directions. Nothing was out of the ordinary and he could hear birds from several directions. He drooped in the saddle as the daylight faded. Besides being grungy and travel worn, he was tired to the bones. He glanced down at his clothes, rough and stained from long wear and hard use. From a distance, he supposed he looked like a hard case that rode the back trails of these high mountains.

Dave dismounted and let his thirsty horse drink from the little stream descending from a small spring that bubbled up from the hillside. With a caution bred of long years of being aware of sounds and movement around him, he lifted his cupped left hand to his mouth and slowly drank, while his eyes constantly searched the top of the nearby ridges.

Only after he stripped the saddle and blanket from his horse, rubbed him down with extra care, and staked out the mare under some trees, did he turn his hand to prepare a simple meal. As he ate, he sat on the horse blanket with his back against the saddle and looked out over the foothills.

What had his life become in the six years since he lost Jenny? He thought about their son and wondered how he fared with his in-laws. Jonathan's round baby face entered Dave's mind and he wrestled with the guilt that threatened to consume him for having abandoned him. Dave reasoned that Jonathan was better off with the Harrods while he ran from the murder charges that loomed over him. A couple had been found dead in their ranch house. Dave had been a convenient stranger passing through, in the wrong place at the wrong time. It had pushed him further away from returning to see his son. Though he originally left his son because he couldn't handle Jenny's death, he refused to let that reason rest in his mind.

Dave sighed and focused his attention on his search for Terrill, the one man who could clear his name. Five years he'd been on the run from the law. He feared he'd never completely escape the outlaw trail. Deal with Terrill first, and then worry about the rest—if he could just manage to stay alive long enough.

He heard Terrill was in the town of Clearwater, to the west. The need to end the chase pushed Dave to cross the mountains this late in the fall, even though the snows would come soon.

The clear sky encouraged him to continue, though the air held a hint of sharpness that promised a cold winter waiting to descend on the land.

Before he pulled his hat over his face to sleep, he checked his horse one last time. It munched contentedly on the high mountain grass with no sign that it heard anything but normal night sounds. With a sigh that was close to contentment, Dave allowed himself to drift into a dream-filled sleep.

Just before daylight, Dave jerked upright and searched for what had startled him awake. The brown mare, a dark shadow among the trees, stood still, ears forward, listening. Not hearing anything out of the ordinary, Dave trusted his horse. Gathering up his things, he quickly saddled the mare. He climbed into the saddle just as the sun broke through the trees down the small valley. As he swung the brown mare around to settle her down, he looked toward the east. A line of horsemen dotted the horizon, obviously sweeping the valley floor in a search. The glint of the sun off a rifle barrel was the next sight that caught his eye. No idea whom the men were or what they searched for, but he'd learned from hard experience not to be in the path of men on a hunt.

Dave kicked his heels into the flanks of the horse and urged the mare up the mountain slope. A yell went up behind him and drifted on the morning air. Glancing over his shoulder, he spotted several of the horsemen swinging their rifles in his direction. He guided his horse through the trees with a reckless speed as bullets chipped at the branches close by. Not only were the horsemen within rifle range, but some of them could shoot from a running horse. Because of the quickness with which they had taken up the chase and fired, he guessed they were in no mood to capture their prey alive. Evidently, he was their prey.

When he came to an open glade, Dave turned in his saddle to see how much they had gained on him. A tremendous blow hit his left side followed by an agony that mounted and grew without stopping. Clinging to the saddle horn, he managed to hang on, but the edges of his mind darkened and faded.

The horse ran flat out among the trees with tree branches almost hitting Dave in the face and arms. As the mare topped the ridge, a small ravine opened up to the left; and Dave urged the galloping horse in that direction.

The horse stumbled and lurched. Dave found himself flying through the air.

The sun glowed through swirling clouds and stood directly overhead when Dave came to himself. It had been just daylight when the horsemen had appeared. It had to be close to mid-day. As he moved, the breath left his body from a pain so intense that he bit his lip to keep from crying out. Remaining absolutely still, he waited for the agony to recede. Twisted at an odd angle just above the elbow, his left arm throbbed in rhyme with his heartbeat. Every shallow breath brought up a stabbing pain from his left side. He lay there not wanting to move.

Slowly he took the glove off his right hand by pulling at it with his teeth. With a caution created by the fear of the stab of agony, he slowly felt under his coat and felt along his left side. The wetness of blood-soaked clothing surrounded an injury that was too sensitive to want to explore. Only one wound and that meant the bullet was still in him. Dave untied the bandana from his neck, wadded it up, and pressed it into the wound to slow the bleeding. Gasping from the searing pain and sweat breaking out on his forehead, he tried to catch his breath. It was just a taste of what setting the arm would cause, but he had to do it if he was to survive. He looked around to see what he could do about his arm. Leaving it in the sleeve of the leather coat would help, but he needed a stick or something to act as a splint.

He slowly pushed himself up with his right hand with as little movement to his left arm as possible. Even so, he gritted his teeth until he thought his jaw would break to keep from crying out his protest at the pain that threatened to consume the left side of his body. With his whole body breaking out in a sweat and his head beginning to spin, he made it to his knees.

The brown mare lay about eight feet away and from the angle of the neck Dave knew it was dead. Holding his left arm tight against his side, Dave crawled over and grabbed the canteen off the saddle. Making himself drink slowly, he glanced around the small clearing. He could see now why the horsemen hadn't followed. The area where they had entered the ravine appeared as a solid wall of trees and brush. Dave pried his saddlebags from the saddle. With the shape he was in there was no way he could pull his saddle off the horse.

He retrieved pieces of rawhide strips that he carried to repair his equipment. The one pan he carried had a long handle that was broken off, and it would work as a splint.

How to straighten the arm was a problem; but he sensed that if he could pull on the arm, the two ends of the bone would slip back into place. He spotted a small tree with two branches growing out low to the ground in a way that formed a tight v-shape. Taking the handle and the rawhide strips, he carefully moved over to the tree.

With a stick between his teeth, he gently wedged his hand in the small fork of the tree branches. He took a deep breath and planted his feet more securely; he forced himself to lean back with his full weight on the broken arm. The agony was a living thing that slowly took over his whole being. When the pain reached an intensity that he couldn't stand much more before he screamed, or escaped into the blessed relief of unconsciousness, he heard a snap and grating sound and felt the two ends of the bone slip back into place.

Even though the pain was still a driving force, it subsided enough that he could deal with it. Keeping the pressure on the arm by leaning back, he spit out the stick. With his teeth and a trembling right hand, he put the handle of the pan along the break, held it with his chin, then wrapped the strips around the left arm and tied them off. He then released the arm from the tree fork and tightly immobilized it against his side with more leather strips tied around his body. If the arm was to heal, he had to keep the broken ends of the bones together.

He allowed himself to sit and lean against the tree to build up a little energy for what he must do next. His body communicated pain from the broken bone, but the wound in his side wasn't far behind, with the pain in his head a close third. With only a few hours before sunset, he had to get what he could carry from his horse and try to put some distance between himself and the ravine. Dizzy and sick, Dave sorted through the saddlebags. He kept his flint, tin box of Barber Matches, lye soap, and a piece of honing stone to sharpen his knife. He couldn't find either rifle, a serious loss. However, he still had a knife, his revolver, and extra bullets. Putting the two canteens and bedroll around his back and his saddlebags over his right shoulder, it was all he could do to put one foot in front of the other. He had no choice but to try to survive. From the horsemen's instant reaction when they spotted him, Dave had no illusions that they had intended to kill him. The best choice was distance from the ravine.

Darkness surrounded him as he awoke in the shelter of a large fallen tree trunk against some boulders forming a natural barrier. How long had he been there? He had no memory of crawling into the space against the rocks. Looking between the dead limbs of the tree, he saw only a few stars. To the east, the sky was growing light with the rising of the sun.

As he made himself take only a couple of swallows of water from the half-empty canteen, he became more aware of the fever and it scared him. Finding a stick to lean on, he began a slow trek up the mountainside.

His broken arm throbbed more with the motion of walking. The wound in his side took on a life of its own, sending out arrows of pain that made him stop and steel himself until they passed. Soon he must find a place where he could take his coat off, and attend to the wound. By the middle of the afternoon, he found that the rest periods got more frequent than the time of moving. He found no place to refill his canteen and no place that would provide shelter for the night. Shivering Dave buttoned his coat against the air that turned sharper with falling temperature. This night would be much colder.

For the first time, the claws of desperation closed in on him. He had been in some tough spots before, but with a way out. Would surviving now take more than he had in him? The dropping temperature sent a chill down his spine. He tried to hug the warmth in his body and forced himself to stop thinking about the future.

Why he was crying? He couldn't remember, but he must be crying because tears moistened his cheeks. He blinked several times. No, not tears. Snowflakes melted on his face. The darkened sky released a blanket of snow. For a moment, he quivered inside, and he recognized it as panic. With snow, his tracks would now be easy to follow, and he didn't know but what this was the beginning of several days of bad weather. In the mountains, it started snowing early, and sometimes didn't stop until spring. Desperation pushed him to find some kind of shelter.

The terrain got more rugged and rocky. The higher he climbed the colder it got, but the alternative meant the risk of running into the horsemen. It snowed gently off and on for hours, but not enough to accumulate much. The mountains were reminding him of the coming winter.

Dave stumbled upon a stream about three feet wide and running at least a foot and a half deep. With relief, he filled the empty canteen. Looking up the rocky streambed, he made the decision to continue going up. The climb became difficult as the sides of the ravine closed in on the stream that made a quiet, cheerful gurgling sound as it flowed down the mountain. With a determination that came more from stubbornness than sense, he kept climbing up the narrow streambed.

He'd almost given up hope of getting out of the ravine before darkness impaired him more than his injuries, then he came to a small cave with an entrance hidden by fallen trees and brush from which the little stream flowed.

The entrance was large enough for him to enter if he stooped down a little to allow for his six foot plus height. Dave didn't know where the cave led, nor if some critter already called it home. A dry tree branch lay just inside the entrance. Taking the piece of flint from his vest pocket, he struck it against the rock wall until a spark lit the branch. He held it in front of him and stepped into the cave. Beyond the opening, the ceiling rose until he could stand upright. The narrow walls were about twelve feet apart and the back wall was much farther than the light of the torch would carry. Compared to the temperature outside, Dave grew warmer as he moved farther into the cave.

Small animal tracks dotted the dust-covered floor, but no signs of any large animals appeared. About twelve feet into the cave a ring of stones held the remains of an old fire. Beside the fire ring, there was a hollow bowl-like place in the rock floor. The little stream originated somewhere in the recesses of the cave. Where it had flowed, it cut a streambed that was smooth and even.

Energy surged through Dave as he looked around. The cave was exactly the kind of place he needed to stop for a few days. He secured the torch into a small hole in the side of the cave near the entrance. With the torch giving out a flickering light, that he suspected would not last long, he put down the saddlebags, canteens and bedroll.

Just outside the cave's entrance, he gathered dry wood. He went back into the cave and started a fire. With relief, he saw that fresh air entered the cave from somewhere in its interior; the smoke pulled up to the ceiling and then disappeared.

The light faded fast even though it was only late afternoon. It stopped snowing for a time, but the heavy gray clouds held the promise of more to come. He gathered branches that would do for torches to have light in addition to the fire. With armloads of pine needles, he made a bed. With the luxury of a fire and roof, he might as well have a soft bed.

On his last trip out, he stopped and looked slowly and carefully in the direction of the cave. He could faintly smell the wood burning, but no smoke appeared above the cave.

Feeling almost secure for the first time in days, he went back into the cave to settle down for the night. He built up the fire, and took the small beat-up pan that he used for a cup, filled it with water, and put it on the flames. Even though he had nothing to put in it, just drinking the hot water helped warm him. His head drooped and the cup fell from his hand. He needed to attend to his side, but the pain had subsided to a dull ache and the surge of energy he'd felt when he found the cave was gone. Feeding more wood to the fire, he decided to lie down for a few minutes, and then he would take care of the wound. The fatigue and the effect of the warm fire were too much, and he drifted into a sound sleep.

He reached for the covers as he was cold, but other than his thin blanket there were none. Blinking into the cold darkness, it took a moment for him to remember that he was in a cave. The fire had died down to a few embers, and cold air seeped in from the cave entrance. Dave tossed a few dry twigs on the embers, and then more logs to keep it going for a while.

The skin on his face felt stretched and dry and his lips were cracked. The fever had returned. He sat up and put some water on to heat. Was it the second or third day since he'd been shot? Trying to think through what he needed to do was hard because his mind wouldn't hold a thought long enough to deal with it. The wound in his side had to be cared for, or it would eventually kill him.

The bandana he'd used to stop the bleeding had dried onto the wound and would have to be soaked off. Taking one of the canteens, he filled the hollow place beside the fire with water. Using two sticks, he rolled several of the smaller rocks from the fire into the bowl. The hot rocks hit the cold water and made a sizzling sound and quicker than he thought possible the water was hot to the touch.

He hated to sacrifice his other undershirt, but he had nothing else to use as a bandage. With his knife heated in the fire, Dave readied the piece of lye soap to wash the wound. Seated cross-legged on the floor, he carefully released his left arm from its splint and slipped out of his coat and vest. Even though he was extremely gentle, the movement increased the slow throbbing from the broken bone. The shirt had to come off next and then his problems really started. His undershirt, caked with dried blood, stuck to the wound.

Taking the hot water, he began slowly to soak the undershirt and bandana away from the wound. It took longer than he wanted to remove the cloth, and his arm began to protest in earnest. He cut off one of the sleeves of the undershirt and used it to wrap around his left arm just above the elbow where the bone was broken. He then took the metal strip, and using his right hand and teeth, managed to put the splint back on the arm. It relieved some of the pain and the weird sensation that his arm was falling off.

The warm water finally loosened the blood soaked handkerchief and undershirt. Dave washed the infected wound the best he could. A solid lump poked out just under the swollen hot skin below the rib bone about six inches above the entry wound. The bullet. And the cause of the infection. He sat there in the soft glow of the fire with his head hanging down for a moment, almost in defeat, and felt like giving up. If he didn't get the bullet out the wound would just continue to fester until it killed him.

Taking the knife he cleansed in the flame of the fire, he dipped it into the water to cool it. Before he let himself think more about what he needed to do, he cut into his skin directly across the hard lump. Drawing in his breathe against the pain, he cut a bit deeper and the bullet popped from his flesh. The new wound drained blood and pus in a steady stream. When the wound seeped fresh blood, he cleaned and bandaged it as best he could.

Putting his shirt, vest and coat back on left him cold, weak, and sick. Several gulps of water from the canteen quenched his thirst. He then added more wood to the fire, exerting his last ounce of energy. Lying down and pulling the blanket up over his shoulder, Dave drifted into a twilight world of pain and sickness.

The dreaming was the worst part. Or was that reality? The fever ebbed and flowed, and at times, he came to enough to feed the fire, drink some water, and even chew a strip of beef jerky. Then he slipped back into the shadowy world of the fever. In the dark cave, time blended into time.

Chapter 3

Dave opened his eyes to a dim-world of shadows. His mind was clear and his body felt almost whole; the fever was gone. Light came in from the cave entrance. The fire had died out and a cool dampness filled the cave. Dave sensed the coldness outside and was thankful that caves maintained a constant temperature regardless of the weather. At this altitude in the mountains, the cave would be cool but not freezing. A few small pieces of wood remained, and he put some dry twigs together with some of the moss to start a fire. He then leaned back to catch his breath, sensing his weakness. However, he had to go out and bring in more wood soon.

He set a cup of water on the fire, and as it heated, he surveyed his injuries and found the area around the wound in his side still red and tender, but no longer inflamed with infection.

As he sipped the hot water, he reflected on his major problem—food. He only had two pieces of beef jerky and one tin of peaches left. His clothes were much looser on his body, and as he stroked the growth of beard on his face, the outline of the jawbone felt sharper than before. Just when he needed all the flesh on his body, he seemed to be losing it fast. The day the horsemen shot him, Dave had been clean-shaven. Knowing how fast his whiskers grew allowed him to calculate that it had been at least three days since he'd removed the bullet from his side.

Food had to be a priority. He had his revolver and twenty-four bullets. A rifle would have been better for hunting, but he would make do with what he had.

He ate both pieces of jerky and hoped he could find a rabbit or squirrel at least. Dave bundled up and braced himself to meet the cold. Brilliant sunlight assaulted his eyes after spending so much time in the dim interior of the cave. He had to stop at the entrance, close his eyes, and then slowly open them to a narrow squint. Freshly fallen snow covered everything. It stood about a foot deep in the ravine. Dave breathed in the crisp air and judged the temperature to be just below freezing.

As he looked out on the world of white framed with a clear blue sky, he noticed small animal tracks leading up the side of the ravine to the left of the cave. Deciding to see where they would lead, he slowly made his way out of the ravine and onto an area that wasn't as rocky and rugged. When he saw rabbit tracks, he stopped a couple of times and made simple rabbit snares.

He didn't go far and gathered wood as he returned to the cave. It took several trips to bring in enough wood. Because he had to stop and rest so often, it was already approaching late afternoon and all he'd done was to set a few snares and bring in some wood. An old man could have beat him in a game of arm wrestling, he was sure. He checked the snares, but found them still empty. Returning to the cave, he faced another night without much in his belly.

At least he had shelter, fire, and water. As his hunger had increased throughout the day, the last tin of peaches had taken on the guise of a banquet. As he slowly ate—taking small bites to make them last as long as possible—he thought through his predicament. Even if he escaped anyone still searching for him, he was in no shape to walk out of the mountains. Just setting the snares and collecting wood had used up all his strength.

Staying in the cave for a while would be endurable if he could get the food he needed. He could trap enough meat, and he knew enough about some of the plants that grew under the trees to help provide some variety in his diet. Could he survive in the mountains until spring? He was mindful of mountain men who had done it, but with a little more readiness than he had.

He took stock of exactly what he had to use to stay alive through a mountain winter. He had his coat, vest, chaps, and gloves, but they were not heavy enough for the extreme weather coming in the next few months. However, furs from the animals he'd catch could add the warmth he needed to his wardrobe.

His boots were in good shape, but he would need to make some snowshoes to get around when the snow became deeper.

Dave carefully laid out everything from his saddlebag. He had an extra shirt, pants, socks, and long johns. His extra undershirt served as a bandage, but he could wash it after that need was over. Dave ran his thumb over the ivory comb that had belonged to his mother. The little Bible that she'd always read to him would come in handy when the cold days grew shorter. He had a little bag of salt, the piece of soap, tin of Barber matches, his flint, hunting knife, the revolver and bullets, and his bedroll. A cup, two empty tin cans, and a spoon made up his only utensils.

With the fire burning warmly and his stomach protesting, he lay down on his hard bed for what he hoped would be a solid night of sleep. It was more difficult to get comfortable because his body was losing flesh and his bones had less padding to protect them from the cave's hard floor.

The next several days passed in a blur. Everyday Dave went out to check the snares and to build more, but he wasn't successful at trapping anything. Reluctant to use his gun because of the noise, he had no choice. It was better to take the chance of discovery than to continue to starve to death

Chapter 4

As Dave approached one of the snares, he saw a rabbit feeding up ahead. Taking out his revolver, he carefully aimed at the head. He squeezed the trigger, and the loudness of the blast shocked him. Other than the normal sounds of the forest, it was the first noise he'd heard in several days. The rabbit was a fair sized one, and he'd hit it exactly where he'd aimed.

The desire to start tearing at the flesh and eating it raw was strong, but he would not let himself. He skinned and gutted the rabbit and, leaving the rest for the carrion, wrapped the meat in the skin. The trip back to the cave seemed to take forever; but once inside, he stoked up the fire. With a forked branch, he started roasting the rabbit. His jaws hurt from his mouth salivating from the smell. As the meat cooked, he slowly cut off little pieces. Enjoying the aroma as much as the taste of the cooked meat, he made himself chew slowly and ate only half of the rabbit. With a sharp rock, Dave scraped the inside of the rabbit fur and started the process of curing the hide.

With adequate food in his belly for the first time in days, he sensed how despondent he'd been. Having some meat not only would strengthen his body, but also was a sign that he could survive on the mountain. He wrapped the other half of the rabbit in the piece of oilcloth that he'd used for the beef jerky. Then he enjoyed the luxury of falling to sleep without the pain of hunger.

The next day he discovered a sort of ledge toward the back of the cave. It was about three feet deep and head height. He hoped it would be out of reach of any critter wandering into the cave. There he put his saddlebag, bedroll, and the rabbit fur that he was in the process of curing.

The rest of the day was spent checking the snares and gathering material to make a barrier for the cave entrance. Toward evening when he found rabbits in two different snares, his heart soared with joy like a rich man about to have a banquet.

Taking a couple of oak branches, he spent several hours stripping them into very thin, long strips to tie branches together to make a sort of barrier for the cave entrance. He used the same process to braid a rope together.

The next morning he constructed a barrier at the entrance. It would only repel small animals, but it was better than no barrier at all. When his arm healed, he would make a much stronger one; and as he studied the cave entrance, he decided that two barriers would be even better. He could make an outer barrier with spiked sticks pointing outward. The barrier itself might not have to be so strong if he could construct it in a way that would discourage animals from wanting to get too near it.

Taking a piece of charcoal from the fire, he started marking the days on a rock. Scratching his head, he tried to figure out what day it was. He thought it was into the third week since he was shot, which was the last of November and that made it the middle of December. Putting the piece of charcoal on the ledge above his rough calendar, he rubbed his left arm where it seemed to maintain a constant ache. It was better but to be on the safe side, he gave his arm another week in the splint. In the meantime, he continued to bathe the area around the gunshot wound. Though still red and tender, it continued to heal without a problem.

The rabbits and other small game he trapped kept him fed, but yet, he still was constantly wanting more to eat. The days fell into a routine of going out every morning looking for food, and returning to the cave just before dark to bring in more wood.

One morning he awoke with a sense that something was different outside the cave. Pulling on his boots, he went to the entrance and removed the inner barrier. As he did, cold air—much colder than the night before—rushed to greet him. He shivered at the full blast of cold, driven by a wind that came up in the night. The temperature dropped noticeably as he stood there and looked at the dirty gray sky.

Dave had endured enough winters to recognize that the weather was in the process of changing drastically, and only a few hours remained to prepare before it descended on him.

He pulled on his hat and gloves, and went up the trail out of the ravine to check his snares. If a real northern storm came, he might never find them again, and he needed the meat.

Once out of the ravine, another gush of cold wind hit him and almost took his breath away. The urgency in his bones quickened his steps. He moved against the wind, making his rounds. Only one snare held any game, but it was a fair-sized rabbit.

As he headed back to the cave, snow and ice pelted him. The icy arrows stung his face and made seeing difficult. He needed to get back to the cave before he became hopelessly lost. Stopping long enough to remove the meat cache he had in a tree, he moved down to the ravine. Guided more by instinct than sight, Dave made it back to the cave.

While he made do with the meat he'd been able to collect beforehand, a good meal and someone to talk to would have made Dave's confinement more bearable. He had never been much of a talker, but he liked people and was not adverse to their company. Choosing not to be around people was one thing, but to have no choice made him feel more isolated. He admitted to himself that he was a little lonely.

As the storm and intense cold continued, Dave kept himself busy in the cave making snowshoes, and some soft, warm moccasins. He also carved some bowls and plates and started whittling arrows to go with the bow he made.

As he looked around the cave, he'd come to regard it as a permanent place for the winter. He wasn't even thinking of trying to make it out of the mountains before spring. With patience, he could trap enough game to stay alive, and the water source of the little stream came from somewhere deep in the mountain, and gave no evidence of freezing up. As soon as he decided to take his arm out of the splint, he intended to start making a bed frame Indian-style, which would make him about as comfortable as he'd been in many a bunkhouse.

The next morning, he opened the first barrier, but it was blowing snow. If he left the cave, he wouldn't be able to see his way. The temperature had dropped until it was bitter cold. The cold penetrated through his body just the few minutes he had the barrier open. He quickly decided that a couple of days rest wasn't a bad idea.

Going back into the cave to build up the fire, he noticed that the air inside was rank compared to the outside air. His own unwashed body and clothes were the problems. In the normal course of things, he bathed often. He put water on to heat in the tin can and cup, filled the natural stone bowl by the fire with water, and put several of the hot rocks from the fire into it to heat the water. If he was going to bathe, at least he could use hot water.

As he removed his clothes, he was shocked at how much flesh he'd lost in the last month. His ribs were so defined he could have played a tune on them. His left arm had shrunk, almost to a point of alarm. However, removing the splint, he was relieved to see the arm was hanging straight. The elbow was stiff from lack of movement, but he could still bend it. Using the small piece of soap, he washed his body, hair, and beard. He used the cup to pour water over himself to rinse off. After dressing in his clean extra pants and shirt, he felt better.

The storm finally blew itself out on the third day. He opened the barrier to a fantasy world of deep white drifts and bitter cold. He needed to find a deer, or even a bear, in order to stock up enough meat for the duration of the winter. The blizzard was just the first of many that could descend on the mountains, and he had to take advantage of the break in the weather. With the bow and arrows, he worked his way up out of the ravine. It was slow going on the snowshoes.

Most of the snares he'd set were either gone or buried beneath the snow. Resetting the few he did find, he kept searching for signs of deer. He came upon a bowl-shaped upper valley just after noon. Deer tracks had been thick for some distance. The wind had blown one side of the valley almost clear of snow. Several deer pawed through what snow there was and found winter grass.

The deer needed to be brought down with one arrow so he worked his way as close as he dared. He chose a fair-sized doe and aimed at the animal's broad chest. Using all the strength he could muster in his arms, he drew the bowstring taut and released the arrow. It struck true and deep. The doe took a few faltering steps before collapsing. The rest of the herd immediately fled with such speed, Dave had trouble following their flight.

By the time he dressed out the deer, the meat was already starting to freeze. If the carcass had not added warmth to his hands as he worked, his fingers would have suffered frostbite. Hefting the gutted deer across his shoulders, he figured he had a good seventy pounds of meat. It was already getting dark when he finally made it into the cave.

With the weather holding cold and clear for another week, he dried and stored the deer meat, and he almost filled the cave with wood. Each day he checked the snares and added a few rabbits to his food stock. The cave provided enough warmth to survive, but Dave never felt warm enough. The temperature in the cave stayed around fifty-five degrees. When he went out, an overshirt made from the rabbit furs added protection from the cold.

Seven days after killing the first deer, he returned to the same area and spent most of the day hidden and waiting. Toward the middle of the afternoon, he spotted a big buck. He aimed carefully then released the arrow. It flew just as the buck started to move. The arrow penetrated the buck's chest and it collapsed in a heap. Sadness tugged at Dave for killing the beautiful animal, but his own survival kept him realistic about the necessity of the kill.

Deep savage growls sliced the air. The hairs on the back of Dave's neck rose as two wolves advanced. They sprang at him and one of the wolves fastened his teeth into Dave's left hand just as he drew his revolver. Two shots quickly brought down both wild animals. As one wolf collapsed, his front claws ranked Dave's leg. After wrapping his bleeding hand with his bandana and putting snow on his leg to stop the bleeding, he skinned the wolves quickly as the pelts would be useful.

The combined weight of the meat and wolf pelts were too much to carry on his back in one trip, but it was too far to the cave to make two trips in one day. Taking some branches and one of the wolf pelts, Dave quickly tied together a travois to pull his load through the snow.

Exhausted from the struggle through the snow and dragging the travois, the cave never looked more like home. After building a fire—and while chewing on some dried meat—he unloaded the travois. It relieved Dave to find the meat and wolf pelts were frozen; he didn't want to deal with them tonight. After securing the barrier, he surveyed his own condition.

Soaking the bandana off his left hand, he found a deep laceration, but his hand didn't appear to be broken. He cleaned the wounds the best he could, then lay down on his bed. The fire burned warmly and he allowed himself to drift into a deep sleep.

He spent four days dealing with the infection in his hand and tending the wounds on his leg, but they healed, leaving behind another set of fresh scars.

While he'd tended to his hand, the weather had closed in again. The temperature rose somewhat, but brought several days of snowfall. The path he'd made up the side of the ravine filled completely with snow again. He stood at the entrance of the cave and looked out at the falling snow. It looked like a white curtain that surrounded him. He could only see a few feet down the ravine until a veil of mist, and falling snow completely filled his view. With the amount of snow that had already fallen, and continued to fall, he would not be able to move about outside the cave for several days.

Still feeling weak and tired after his encounter with the wolves and dealing with his hand, he was glad for a day to lie around and rest. One day of inactivity was about all he could cope with, and the next day he began to work on curing the wolf pelts.

By his marks on the rock wall, it was two months since he was shot, making it somewhere near the end of January, or the first week of February. If there should be an early spring in the mountains, he figured he still had at least six weeks before he would be able to safely leave the cave and walk out of the mountains. While scraping on the wolf pelts, he found himself thinking beyond day-to-day survival. Moreover, to consider what he was going to do when he left the mountains.

He talked aloud just to hear his own voice bounce off the cave walls. From disuse, his voice carried a gravelly sound. As time passed, he wanted to hear another voice answering. It wasn't being alone that bothered him, but that he had no choice.

In some ways, he feared leaving the mountains and going back into the towns, but he couldn't spend his life away from people. With no one seeing him for the months of winter, it was possible they would assume something had happened to him; and the law might not be as actively looking for him.

With a sigh, he added fuel to the fire and made a rack to stretch the wolf's pelt. As he worked, he continued to think about leaving the mountains. He needed to replace his equipment and buy a horse. As he looked at the wolf pelts and other furs he'd trapped so far, he realized he already had a source of money. If he trapped more, he might accumulate enough furs to provide what he would need to get started. A surge of energy coursed through him at having a purpose during the time left until spring rather than just being a prisoner of the weather.

As he used the knife that he had carried with him for the last twelve years, he thought of Indian Charlie for the first time in a long time. Dave had learned to hunt from an old Indian who had worked on one of the spreads where he had spent some time when he was sixteen. Being the youngest rider and Indian Charlie as the men called him being the oldest, they ended up with all of the chores that the cowhands didn't want to do such as chopping wood and making fence posts. Every few weeks they spent a day gathering a wagonload of wood for the ranch for the coming winter.

Chopping firewood in the deep forest away from the other cowhands was relaxing for Dave. That was when he started developing his broad muscular shoulders and strong arms. Charlie taught him much about the forest, how to snare a rabbit or trap a deer with nothing but a hunting knife. He had taught him how to read the signs. Another useful thing that Charlie had taught him was how to wrestle Indian style. Through the years it had helped him defend himself and to survive some rough ranch crews.

It was not until years later that he realized what he added to Charlie's life. After his folks had died, Dave had withdrawn into a silent observing kid that did what he was told without arguing. He had no interest in the drinking and carousing of the younger men who would spend all month working for $15 or $20 and then blow it in one evening in town. Dave was careful with his money and managed to put a little in a sock each month that he kept hidden from the other hands.

For Charlie he was like a son to be taught how to grow up and survive, but he was also someone to listen to Charlie's stories of a life and world that were now lost to him. Never commenting about it, Dave was always amazed at how quiet Charlie was around the other men on the crew; but how Charlie would talk all day while he and Dave chopped the wood or mended the fences.

Charlie was getting too old and frail to do the sort of work that was expected of him on the ranch. Dave quietly went about taking up the slack for the old man, whether it was carrying wood and water or digging postholes.

The second spring he had worked at the J-Bar, Dave was bigger, stronger, and working out on the range with the other cowhands, but he still managed to help Charlie in the mornings and evenings with his chores. The old man was getting slower with the passing of time. Charlie had seemed intent on telling Dave things that would help him deal with life. He realized later that Charlie was trying to leave some of his own wisdom to smooth Dave's way in life.

He was up early one morning to help Charlie get his chores done and get the horses ready for the day. When the old man wasn't at work in the barn as usual, Dave checked his bunk in the storeroom of the barn but he wasn't there. Looking for him, he spotted him up on a hill slumped by a tree facing west with a peaceful look on his face. Death had released the stress of living from his face and he looked much younger. As Dave looked at Charlie, he felt the same pain and emptiness that he felt with the death of his mother. Being almost a grown man, he pushed down the pain and went back to tell his boss of Charlie's death.

The boss had known Charlie for many years and felt his death enough to have the hands gather around for a short service beside the grave that Dave dug on the hillside. The only thing of value that Charlie had was his hunting knife, and the boss let Dave keep it. Until Charlie died, Dave had not realized that he was the only thing that kept him at the J-Bar. That evening he drew his pay and left on a horse that the boss gave him as a bonus. When he first arrived at the ranch, he had been a scrawny hungry kid. When he rode out after a year and half he was almost a grown man. He owed much of it to Charlie. And now what Charlie had taught him was saving his life.

The snow continued for several days almost filling the ravine. When the weather finally broke, as did his invisible chains, Dave faced a world of white. A wall of snow stared back at him as he tried to look down the ravine. The wind eddied the snow around the entrance to the cave until there was a clear space of about five feet, but then had blown it into a solid wall along the side of the mountain. It took most of the morning to dig a path from the cave to the top of the ravine.

As Dave spent the afternoon setting traps, he enjoyed the beauty of the world of snow and ice. The blanket of snow quieted the forest; and except for a few snowbirds, no sounds penetrated the air that smelled fresh. The peacefulness of the snow-covered mountains made them seem friendly and safe.

The first pair of snowshoes he made were already coming apart, so he spent one day making a new pair that would stand up to hard walking. He also spent time thinking about how to build traps that would work with his limited tools. As he worked at building them, he was grateful to the old Indian Charlie who taught him so much.

This was just an interlude and within hours there could be a change of weather disturbing all this calm. Making sure that he didn't go so far from the cave that he could not get back before dark, he set his traps and watched for animal tracks. There were a few, but not many because most of the animals would find the snow too deep. However, he did spot fox tracks, and a few deer tracks. The deer were heavy enough that they would go through the crust of the snow and leave wide swaths in their paths. Some of the smaller animals only left the paw tracks on top of the snow.

Dave fell into a routine over the next several weeks of working the trap line, hunting with the bow and arrow, and keeping the cave replenished with firewood.

On the days when the weather closed in, he spent the time curing the pelts he'd trapped or drying meat.

He'd devised a way of catching the fat as it dripped from the cooking meat by suspending a rock bowl between the fire and the meat. Taking small strips of venison and drying it slowly over a small smoky fire, he then beat and ground it between two flat rocks. Putting the meat into a hide pouch he made for the purpose, he poured the melted fat over it. The result was pemmican and was used by the Indians and mountain men as a way to preserve and carry meat. It wasn't his favorite; but when out on the mountain in the cold, the pemmican tasted better after several hours of hard walking in the snowshoes.

Although he didn't have much variety in his food, he was eating well enough that he even gained back some of the flesh he'd lost. A layer of fat on his body would help keep him warm. At least, he wasn't losing more fat. His body adjusted itself to the cold.

Chapter 5

When Dave first came to the cave, survival took every minute of every day and consumed his thoughts. As the weeks turned into months, he longed more and more for the sound of another human voice. He talked aloud for hours at a time, just to hear the sound. He had never been one to sit and tell stories but had always enjoyed listening. Now he told stories he'd heard, with only himself to listen.

The long days when the weather kept him from leaving the cave were the worst. He tried to remember long forgotten poems and Bible verses that his mother had taught him. Several times, he read the little Bible that had belonged to his mother.

As he scraped at the pelts, he sang songs from his childhood and hymns he learned from going to church with Jenny. The acoustics in the cave strengthened and broadened his voice until he almost thought at times that others sang with him. The problem was that when he stopped singing, he felt the silence like a physical blow.

As the long winter days and nights continued, he sensed Jenny's presence. He stared at her image for hours in the little locket that held a picture of both Jenny and his baby, Jonathan. He allowed Jenny's eyes to haunt him. A loud crackling from the fire brought him back to the darkness of the cave and his aloneness. Even six years later as he sat looking at the fire, the pain of his loss was still just too great.

As the winter days crept by, Jenny and his baby son were ghosts who kept Dave company. He couldn't shake the feeling that Jenny was unhappy with him, and it had to do with the boy.

He had deliberately kept on the move for the last six years to avoid having too much time to think about them. Now, he couldn't think of anything else. For the first time, he understood that his son would not only have no memory of his mother, but none of his father either. The boy had been three years old when Dave had left him with his grandparents. The difference was that Jonathan's mother had not chosen to leave him; his father had deliberately left him.

The cold day that he finally faced his cowardice toward his son was the most difficult of the long winter on the mountain.

He was taking Jenny's death out on the boy. What had his son done to deserve such treatment from his father, the very person from whom Jonathan had a right to expect care and protection? And Dave had promised Jenny he would take care of their son.

As he sat by the fire looking at his son's baby picture in the little locket, he understood that in a way he'd done the same thing to Jonathan that his father had done to him when he was twelve. His father had not left him physically during the two years after his mother had died, but he'd left him all the same. The deep feeling of aloneness had started when his mother had died. Later when he'd seen his father buried, it had been an end to what had really taken place two years earlier.

His son would be nine-years-old. What might be Jonathan's feelings about his father turning his back on him? Dave didn't like the thought of Jonathan's view of him as a father. He had physical courage, but it wasn't physical courage that he'd needed to cope after Jenny's death. It was a moral courage to do the right thing by his son. For the first time, Dave faced that he had made sure of his son's physical needs, but that he'd been more concerned with his own pain than what his son needed from him. His father had done the same thing to him.

By the fire that evening, he cried for the second time since Jenny's death. Deep wrenching sobs tore him apart. He didn't know if he cried for his own loss, or for the little boy who would never even remember his mother, nor his father.

The sun had barely risen the next morning as Dave put on his warm clothing and snowshoes to check his trap lines and hunt for whatever he found moving in the fresh snow. Disturbing dreams filled the previous night and he'd awakened with an uneasy feeling that spirits populated the cave and wanted something from him.

The physical effort of dealing with the cold and snow was a relief after the thoughts of the last couple of days. He walked fast and hard and put out much more effort than necessary. By the time the sun shone directly overhead, he forced himself to stop and eat a handful of pemmican. He then climbed a good thousand feet up the mountain and stopped to rest at the edge of a natural hanging valley.

With the snow-covered fir trees and the mountains rising higher beyond the valley, he looked out over one of the most beautiful areas he'd seen. There was no evidence that anyone had ever been there. Soon the cold penetrated his clothing, and he started back. He hadn't really accomplished anything by the long hike in the snow except to give his mind a chance to rest from all the memories that kept crowding in. The trap of snow and mountains closed in on him. As if he were a prisoner and the cave was his cell. When he approached the cave, he didn't want to face another long evening in the flickering light of the fire with the shadows around him. However, he had no choice if he wanted to survive. The cold was relentless all day and with night, it would fall on the mountains even more. Even with the rabbit fur vest and linings for his boots and gloves, he'd been cold most of the day.

Spring and the thaw had to come before he had a choice of what to do. What then? He had no idea where Terrill, the one man whose testimony could free him from the murder charge, might be now after all these months. Dave needed to get outfitted again and would need to find work somewhere. With his hair and beard grown so long over the winter months, he was not worried about being recognized.

One morning he awoke with a sense that something had changed. As he pushed the barrier aside, a moist warm breeze caressed his face. The drip of melting snow and ice echoed through the air like music.

He went to the top of the ravine without his coat or snowshoes for the first time in months and his spirits lifted. Soon he would leave the mountains. Through the bad winter months, he somehow regained his strength. He decided to carry a load of the prime furs up over the mountains to the town of Elkhead.

He packed his mother's Bible, his few ragged clothes, extra moccasins, and boots. After sorting through the pelts and hides, he gathered a pack that he tied onto a frame made by binding branches together with strips of hide. Even though it was almost April by his figuring, he wore his fur clothing.

Thankful he'd found the cave at all and had been able to survive the hard winter, the long months of solitude had caused him to think through his life. Now he felt better able to deal with what life would bring. In some ways, he felt more alive than he had in years.

Thinking through what he would do as he left the mountain, the first challenge was to make it over the mountains with the furs. Then he would go back to Rock Corner and face his son. The light filtered through the pines as he started up the mountain toward the upper valley and the pass beyond. He figured on two days to make it to the pass and there he had no idea what the terrain would be like or how far it was to Elkhead. The pemmican would last a week and then he would have to live off the land. Early spring flowers appeared in the open spaces where the sunlight penetrated the forest. Birds chirped in the trees and the fresh smell of new growth surrounded him.

After he passed the hanging valley, he stumbled upon a stream coming from the direction of the pass and followed it. The ravine had broadened somewhat, and as he hiked past some of the large boulders, a new region of mountains and valleys appeared suddenly in front of him. He soon found himself standing at the edge of a two-thousand foot drop looking out over the other side of the mountain range. He'd made it through to the top of the pass. Now he faced the challenge of getting down the other side.

Slipping out of the pack, he left it in the snow while he explored along the rim of the cliff. As the shadows closed with the coming of darkness, he spotted a faint pattern of small animal tracks in the snow. They led toward the rim of the cliff but hugged the mountainside as the granite wall continued to ascend above him. Soon it opened to a three-foot wide ledge that descended from the pass down the cliff wall toward the valley below.

The thought of starting on the trail carrying the pack caused him to break out in a sweat. It would take only a small misstep to slide over the edge, but he couldn't see any other way down the mountain.

Dave built a fire between two of the boulders that served as a protection from the wind, then set about making camp. In his mind, he kept looking at the little path descending the narrow ledge, and he was afraid to start on such a trail. He feared falling, getting stuck partway down, or the trail becoming so narrow he could neither descend nor turn back.

Drifting into a troubled sleep, his night was filled with dreams of falling and never reaching the bottom. Two hours before dawn, he finally gave up trying to sleep and lay gazing into the fire. Amassing as much courage as he could, he faced the descent down the cliff trail. He had faced other things in his life that held the danger of death, but the thought of falling off the cliff held a special fear.

A quick swig from the canteen, a pull on his gloves to make sure they were secure, and a prayer for protection, and he was ready to take the first steps down the trail. Using his left hand as a balance against the rock wall, he had just enough room to descend by placing the snowshoes carefully. He didn't allow himself to look up or down; he kept his gaze on his feet. The side of the pack scraped the wall of the cliff and threatened to catch on the sharp rocks that jutted out.

At each turn, it took more and more effort to let go of the cliff wall to make the next switchback. A couple of times he almost made the turns too quickly and felt the pull of the pack throwing him off balance. Only by grabbing at an outcrop of rock was he able to regain his balance. As the day progressed, he fell into the rhythm of the descending trail. He took his time, holding on to the rocks with a grip that caused his hands to hurt up to the elbows.

Without warning, a large brown bear was breathing in his face.

The bear appeared as startled as Dave. It swung at him as if batting an insect out of his way. The claws caught Dave on the neck and pushed him over the ledge in one sweep.

Falling and falling, he was in the midst of his worst nightmare. Unlike his dream, he soon slammed into the branches of some fir trees, which helped to partially break the speed of the fall. However, these didn't cushion the impact as he hit the snow-covered slope of the mountain below the granite wall. How far he slid and tumbled in the snow before he landed against a tree, he didn't know. By a miracle, he still had the pack and bedroll.

The bear, and the fall off the cliff, happened so quickly that Dave thought he must be dreaming. Sharp pains in his side helped force him back to reality. As his breathing eased, and his head stopped spinning, he examined his beaten and bruised body.

He wiped at the blood flowing down his neck where the bear clawed him. The cut ran from the back of his neck to about halfway toward his jaw. Putting a handful of snow against his neck to stop the bleeding, he looked up at the granite cliff.

Dave chuckled at the humor in it. He wanted to be off the cliff and on solid ground. It just happened quicker than he'd planned. The bear provided him a service. Having experienced his worse nightmare and lived exalted him. He didn't think he would ever be so fearful again.

He managed to pull himself up to a standing position by hugging the tree. He needed to find some shelter and get a fire going. He struggled through the two-foot deep snow.

A warm gentle breeze replaced the strong bitter wind that he experienced on top of the pass. As he slowly made his way down the slope of the mountainside, the trees became more dense and the snow wasn't as deep. The gurgling of a stream grew louder. Exhaustion that went beyond physical overwhelmed him. He finally came upon an outcropping of rocks and boulders that formed a sort of overhang that would do to make camp. After several tries, he finally started a fire and gathered enough reasonably dry wood to get through the night.

It was pure relief to stretch out on his bedroll with the pack as a back support. He hadn't eaten or had anything to drink other than a few handfuls of snow, since early morning. His tiredness overrode his desire to eat. After drinking a couple cans of hot water, he forced himself to munch on a handful of pemmican.

As his eyes drooped, he banked the fire, pulled the blanket around him, and drifted off sleep.

Chapter 6

Dave woke to the feel of sunshine on his face. He gauged the air to be warmer compared to the day before. Water dripped everywhere and the stream down the mountain slope below him flowed with a roar. The sound of birds filled the air. It was as if he'd fallen off the cliff into the land of springtime.

As he broke camp, he began to think about what lay ahead. The first thing was to get out of the mountains and get outfitted. Then he would make his way to the Harrod's ranch and visit with his son. For the first time in years, he actively thought of the future.

Terrill could be anywhere after all these months. To continue to track him was futile. Dave had been obsessed with the hunt, but something had happened over the winter, and now the chase didn't hold the same importance. Had he been using his chase of Terrill to keep from facing himself? Terrill could clear his name, but the probability that he would ever find him and make the man actually testify was remote. He didn't want to waste any more of his life.

When he thought of what he really wanted to do, the idea of returning to the mountains, starting a small herd of cattle, and developing a ranch that felt worthy of the effort, kept filtering through his mind. He could never go back to the joy and contentment of his time with Jenny. Maybe he could build something again that would be meaningful to him. He didn't know how, but maybe someday his son could be a part of that future.

Four days later, as evening approached, he followed a turn in the narrow road, and suddenly in the distance, buildings dotted the horizon. He left the road and found a place to camp by the stream where it met the river. The current had changed its streambed enough to leave a little beach of rocks and logs.

Dave bathed in a pool and washed his clothes by beating them between two rocks. The air was so arid that in a short time his clothes were dry enough to put back on. The beating had added to their tattered condition, but at least they were cleaner and he felt better.

The next morning brought mixed feelings of expectation and apprehension. He'd cleaned his gun the evening before and had loaded the last of his bullets. Not really expecting trouble when he went into town, he still wanted to be prepared.

After he hid the pack by covering it with some brush and rocks, he put on his long coat even though he knew the day would be warm and he didn't need it. The coat would cover some of the worst of the tears and holes in his clothes, but more importantly, it would conceal his gun.

As he passed the first buildings, he found that the town was bigger than he'd expected. He was on a side street with about thirty houses and stores. He had not reached the main road that ran through the town.

Hunger left Dave decidedly shaky this morning. He'd eaten the last of the pemmican two days ago. He swallowed with difficulty because he couldn't seem to drink enough water to relieve his dry mouth. He'd rehearsed in his mind what he would say and had a mental list of what he would purchase. The general store stood where the smaller road met the main road. He wanted to purchase some new clothes and food before he did anything else. Then he would find the local barber.

Dave got his first shock as he neared the front of the store. A young woman, leading a small child by the hand, came out laughing. It was the first human voice he'd heard other than his own in six months. The sheer beauty and delight of it left him standing looking after her with admiration. He was unprepared for the rush of emotions that suddenly flooded his mind. Part of that emotion was a longing as he remembered Jenny with their small son.

He shook his head and made himself walk casually into the store. Relief filled him to see only one other customer and the storekeeper busy helping him. This gave Dave a chance to calm himself and look around. He immediately spotted the stack of work pants and shirts on a counter. It only took him a couple of minutes to choose some to fit him. By this time, the customer left and the storekeeper greeted Dave with a smile.

"Howdy stranger, you find what you need?" The storekeeper's deep voice filled the store with the sound of good humor. The rotund man came up to Dave's shoulder. With a fringe of gray hair, the top of his head was as bald as a baby's behind.

For the first time in a long time, Dave found himself smiling.

"You got any boots?" His voice sounded strange to him.

"Sure do, right over here." The storekeeper led him over to a corner where several pairs sat on the floor.

Chuckling, the storekeeper looked at Dave's. "Yes, I'd say yours are about used up. Let's see, this pair looks about the right size." He handed a pair of plain brown boots to Dave.

It embarrassed him for the storekeeper to see the condition of his socks and feet. The socks had more holes than sock, and blisters covered his raw feet from the long climb over the mountains. But he couldn't buy new footgear without trying them on. Dave sat, pulled on the new boots, stood, and walked back and forth to determine that they were a good fit.

"How do they feel, mister?" The storekeeper bent slightly to examine the fit. "You know, new boots take breaking in, like a new horse." He chuckled at his own joke.

"Good, just what I need." Dave grinned. Some of the tension left his body as he realized that he could still interact with someone after months of solitude.

Dave removed the new boots and put his old ones back on. He handed the new ones to the storekeeper. "I need some food too. Do you have any canned peaches?"

"Right over here behind the counter."

Dave placed the clothes next to the boots. He picked out some cans of peaches, dried beef jerky, and a loaf of homemade bread. He would need to buy more food later, but he was too hungry to concentrate on anything else for the time being. Dave immediately opened a can of peaches with his knife and ate them.

After eating, he included a piece of soap to his purchases and at the last minute, added a hat similar to the one that he'd lost with his snowshoes. As the storekeeper added up the total, Dave asked where he could find a barber.

"Right here," the storekeeper answered. And turning toward the back of the store he yelled out, "Ma, come here, you got a customer."

He turned back to Dave. "My missus does all the barbering in this town."

A little woman that couldn't have been more than five feet tall came from the back rooms. She had the same cheery look as the storekeeper.

The storekeeper patted himself on the chest. "I'm Pop Frazier and most everybody calls the missus, Ma." He waved toward the little woman.

"Dave Matthews." He gave the little woman a slight bow. Matthews was his middle name and he'd used it as a last name often since the first wanted posters had gone out.

"Mercy, Dave Matthews, you do need a barber," Ma said in a manner that gave no offense while looking up at his six-foot three-inch height. "Follow me. I do my barbering on the back porch." She turned and led the way through the door at the back of the store without waiting for a response from Dave.

He followed her through a large busy-looking kitchen—that evidently also served as the living room for the family—to an oversized back porch that ran the length of the building. Canvas enclosed it on the north. Chickens pecked at insects in the backyard and a milk cow stood in a pen by the barn. The comfortable clutter of the place suited its inhabitants quite well.

"Take your coat off and hang it on the nail there," she said, then directed him to a small stool. After he sat down, she tied an old piece of cloth around his neck.

"Now tell me how you want it cut and what about the beard?" She eyed his hair as if eager to rearrange.

Dave hadn't really thought about it, but Ma waited expectantly with a comb in one hand and a pair of scissors in the other. "Cut the hair short and trim the beard close." He decided to keep the beard. The wanted posters described him as clean-shaven, and besides, it was simpler not to shave when traveling.

"Right, let's see what we got under all this hair." Ma Frazier began to cut and immediately big swatches of dark hair fell to the floor and circled the stool. As she worked, she kept up a barrage of talk that didn't require much response from Dave.

By asking a few questions, Dave found out some useful information without having to be direct about it.

Pop Frazier didn't deal much in furs for one thing, but Reilly over at the livery stable had, in his younger days, been one of the first mountain men and still enjoyed being associated with what was left of the fur trade. As Ma Frazier talked, Dave formed in his mind how best to deal with Reilly and get the prices he wanted for his furs.

The other bit of useful information that he gained as she chattered was that the town had no law. In times past, a marshal ruled in legal matters, but he'd moved on and the town hadn't gotten around to finding another authority figure. When disputes or trouble broke out, the men of the town met together and handled it. That indicated to Dave that they wouldn't be much interested in a wanted poster.

Dave was thinking about the beef jerky and bread and was only half listening to her talk when she stepped back to survey her work.

"You interested in a bath when I finish here?" she asked suddenly.

It took Dave a moment to respond to her, as he was so out of the habit of conversation. "Pardon, ma'am?"

"We have a tub over there at the end of the porch, and for ten cents Pop will heat you water for a hot bath. You can wash your hair when I finish cutting it," she added with a twinkle in her eyes. "You need to wash behind these ears."

Dave felt himself turn red. But she was right, he did need a good scrubbing with some soap, and a hot bath before putting on his new clothes would feel great. "Sure, ma'am, that would be fine."

She kept on clipping and called out to her husband, "Pop, put some water on to heat. Mr. Matthews is going to take a bath."

Pots banged around in the kitchen, and shortly after, Pop came through the door carrying a big pot of steaming water. He chuckled. "A hair cut and a bath all in the same day. You're going to feel like a new man." The older man went to the north end of the porch and pulled aside the canvas to reveal a galvanized bathtub big enough for a man to actually sit in and have a proper bath.

As Ma Frazier trimmed his beard close and put the finishing touches on his haircut, Pop made several more trips carrying pots of hot water. Then he came out onto the porch with the stack of new clothes that Dave had set aside to purchase.

"Don't want you to think me distrustful, but if you're going to put on these clothes after your bath, would you mind showing me that you can pay for them?" Pop's voice held a chuckle, but the blue eyes that looked intently into Dave's did not.

As Ma stepped back, Dave stood up and pulled out his worn wallet. He removed his last twenty dollars and handed it over.

Dave sat back on the low stool. "Sounds reasonable to me. Just add everything up including the bath and take it out of this." He purposely kept his voice quiet and neutral so they would understand that he took no offense.

They both relaxed, and Pop went back into the kitchen carrying the money.

Ma brushed the hair off Dave's shoulders and took away the piece of cloth. "Now you just go take a hot bath and soak as long as you want. There won't be anyone around to bother you." She grabbed a broom and swept up the hair.

Dave made his way to the tub. A big piece of soap and a scrub brush lay beside it. He pulled the piece of canvas down and undressed. Lowering himself into the hot water, a sense of well-being swept over him. He just wanted to sit there and let the warm feeling soak into his muscles. By bending his knees, he was able to soak his six-foot plus frame all the way to his neck.

He felt a little dazed and disoriented. After having spent so many months alone, he had trouble believing the reality of the day. The person who had spent all that time in the mountains seemed to drop off just as the hair had and a new person emerged.

When the water cooled down, he decided he'd better get busy with the washing part and soon was happily scrubbing every inch of his body with the soap and scrub brush. As Dave scrubbed away on his foot sticking up in the air, Pop pulled back the canvas curtain.

"Here's a bucket of hot water to rinse off with and a towel the missus reminded me to bring to you." Setting the bucket and towel down, he dropped the canvas back and left without waiting for a response.

Dave knew the proper reply should have been "thank you," but he was so out of practice, it took him a couple of minutes to think of it. He hated to end his first real tub bath in almost a year, but the cool water urged him to step out of the tub and towel off his clean body. Dressing in the new clothes felt strange. It would take a little time to get used to them, especially the boots. Dave gathered up his old clothes after combing through his hair with his fingers. He buckled on his holster holding his revolver.

As he stepped up to the kitchen door he heard Pop say, "That boy looks a sight different with all that hair gone and without them ragged clothes. Did you notice them scars on his neck? They don't look too old."

Dave pictured Pop seated in a chair at a kitchen table and Ma stirring something on the cook stove.

"They are new. They still have scabs on them. Where do you think he got them and where did he come from?" Ma asked.

"Don't know, but I'll tell you one thing, there weren't much food wherever he came from. He's as thin as a rail. His shoulders are built up like he's been doing a lot of hard work, but you could play piano on his ribs, they're sticking out so. He looks hungry."

Ma asked, "Want to ask him to eat stew and cornbread with us?"

Dave's stomach growled.

"That'll be fine with me as long as you got enough to feed me first." Pop chuckled.

A bell chimed from the direction of the store and Dave assumed that Pop had a customer. Pop got up and went into the store.

Dave knocked lightly on the back door, then stepped into the kitchen where the aroma of stew and baking cornbread almost physically assaulted him. His mouth watered and his stomach twisted with hunger pains.

Ma Frazier turned from the stove and looked him over. "My, my, Dave Matthews, but you do look a sight better," she exclaimed in delight as she surveyed her handiwork with the scissors. "Now just sit down at that table. Pop and I are about to have a bite to eat and we want you to join us."

After the relaxing bath, the odor of food cooking, and the warmth of these people, Dave felt himself swaying, and the room started to spin.

Suddenly Ma looked concerned, walked over, and guided him to a chair at the table. "What's the matter, son, you look ready to faint on me."

Dave let his bundle fall to the floor and gratefully sank into the chair. He held on to the table to stop the room from spinning and told her the truth. "I haven't been eating much lately, ma'am. I kind of ran out of food. I'll be all right in a minute."

"Well, why didn't you say something? We got all kinds of food. I never let anyone go hungry in my home." She quickly crossed to the stove, dished up a large bowl of stew, and put it down in front of him with a huge wedge of fresh hot cornbread.

"Now you just eat up. There's more in the pot." Ma poured a glass of milk from a jug on the table and put that beside his bowl. She dished up two more helpings of stew, placed them on the table along with the iron skillet of cornbread, and called out to Pop.

Dave knew it wasn't polite to start eating before Ma and Pop sat down at the table, but he couldn't help himself and dug into the stew like a starving man.

As Pop came in and sat down at the table, Ma said with concern, "Slow down son, you'll make yourself sick if you eat too fast. It's not going anywhere so take your time."

Embarrassment rose to Dave's cheeks. He forced himself to chew each spoonful slowly and thoroughly.

"That's better," Ma said with satisfaction as she joined them at the table.

Pop just looked at him with a grin and winked.

During the next several minutes, nothing was said as they each concentrated on eating. As soon as Dave emptied his bowl, Ma filled it again. When he'd first tasted the food, he thought he could eat the whole pot. By the time he'd almost finished the second bowl, he could feel that it was enough for now. His body wasn't used to such rich food, and he'd eaten more in this one meal than in the last two weeks. Out of politeness, he finished the last morsel in the bowl. When Ma started to get up to refill it, he politely told her no, but thanks.

"That was the best stew and cornbread I ever ate," he told her sincerely. Dave gathered up his bundle and stood up. "Thank you so much. I better get my stuff and get going." Dave walked toward the store with Pop and Ma following behind.

"I put your food in the gunnysack there on the counter and here's your change." Pop walked behind the counter and showed Dave the list of his purchases with the price by each one.

Everything totaled twelve dollars, leaving him with eight. Dave was tempted to pick out some other items but decided to wait until he sold the furs. He might need every penny to buy a horse and saddle. He noticed the meal hadn't been noted.

Both Pop and Ma chuckled when he pointed it out.

"We've never charged anyone for a meal at our table and we sure don't plan to start with you," Ma said with a twinkle in her eyes. "And you're welcome any time you're in town."

Gathering up his bundle and gunnysack, Dave left the store with both Ma and Pop Frazier waving after him. He walked back up the road with a lot less tension. His stomach was full for the first time in weeks, he felt fresh and clean after his bath, and there was no law around to ask questions. Life was good.

When he returned to his camp, he felt drowsy and lazy. He had planned to take the furs in that afternoon, but he decided to wait until the next morning. A spot of shade under some trees beckoned him, and he spread out his bedroll and napped the afternoon away. Toward dark, he decided to risk a fire as the warmth of the sun faded. Here on the edge of the high plains, it cooled down quickly at night this time of year.

He ate some of the beef jerky and half the round loaf of bread and sat looking into the fire. He poked it with a stick and mulled the day's events over. The casual friendliness and humor of the Fraziers reminded him that good people existed. It encouraged him that his first encounter with people had been a positive one.

Dave stared into the fire. The couple of hours of talk with the Fraziers had left him worn out. After so many months of solitude, his nerves seemed all sensitive. The barrage of sensation and words from being around people took some getting used to.

He would try to accomplish two things the next day and then be on his way. The first thing in the morning he planned to take the pack of furs in to the livery stable, and hopefully catch the man in an expansive mood. Dave wasn't sure of his ability to bargain for a good price, but he would just have to do his best. He then wanted to buy a horse and saddle. Ma Frazier had mentioned that someone had ridden in from the west and sold his gear for the price of a ticket on the stage going east. The liveryman might not have paid much for the gear and horse and be more open to bargaining.

Never far from his mind was his decision to head back to Rock Corner. Now that he'd made it this far, he was ready to visit Jonathan. After that, he didn't know what the next trail would bring. With his mind going around and around, Dave settled into his bedroll and slept.

The morning was again clear and promised warm sunshine. Taking his time, he ate the beef jerky, the rest of the loaf of bread and a can of peaches. Dave savored the taste of something besides the pemmican.

Dave shouldered the pack of furs and started back to town. He wasn't as nervous as the previous day, but he still moved with caution, keeping a watchful eye out for people. He relaxed a little when he spotted the livery stable on the road that led out of town to the east. Walking up to the big, wide-open doors, he found an older man inside pitching hay into a stall.

The man glanced up when he heard Dave walk into the livery stable. "Howdy stranger, something I can do for you?" He leaned the pitchfork against the wall.

"You Mr. Reilly?" Dave stood still in the open doorway.

"That's me." Suddenly he spotted the pack. "You got furs there?"

"Yes, I heard you might be interested in buying." Dave waited quietly, not wanting to appear too eager.

The man motioned Dave to follow him into a room used for storage and an office.

"I may or may not be interested. Depends on what you got." Dave saw that the older man could also play the game of not appearing too eager. "Put your pack on the table here and let's see what you have there."

Dave put the pack down and untied it. He laid out the pelts one by one.

Automatically, Reilly fingered the silky fur of the beaver, rabbit, and wolf pelts.

It took about half an hour of bargaining, but they finally agreed to a price of two hundred sixty dollars for the lot. It was more than Dave had hoped for and more than enough to buy a horse and saddle.

Dave put the money in his wallet. "You have any horses for sale?"

Reilly's face brightened considerably. "Sure, I got a couple of horses to sell. Let's go out back." He led the way through the livery stable to a fair-sized corral. Several horses looked up at them as they entered the gate.

"That brown mare over there and that gray are both for sale. The rest of these horses belong to folks in town." Reilly pointed out the two and waved his arms at all eight to get them moving around the corral.

Dave looked the horses over with an eagerness he could hardly contain. It had been six months since his horse had died under him and he was tired of walking. The gray barely lifted its hooves as it moved about the corral. It was swaybacked and old.

The brown mare, on the other hand, was a solid looking horse of about six years and big enough to carry his tall frame without effort. The look of it reminded him of his horse that had been killed on the mountain.

Dave walked up to the brown mare and patted her neck. The animal looked around at him with inquiring eyes.

"How much for the mare?" He tried to keep his voice neutral.

"What would you say to two hundred thirty dollars?" Reilly asked hopefully.

Dave just grinned at him. Only a tenderfoot would pay that much for an ordinary horse.

"All right, how about two hundred and I'll throw in the saddle and bridle that came with it." Evidently, Reilly was as eager to sell the horse, as Dave was to purchase one.

"Sounds more reasonable, but let me see the saddle first." Dave walked back toward the livery stable. He felt a nudge on his back and turned to find the brown mare following him.

Dave held out his hands. "You're out of luck, old girl. I don't have any sugar." The mare seemed to understand for she stopped and if a horse could, she looked disappointed.

Reilly laughed. "Looks like you two are already getting acquainted."

The saddle was used but still in good shape. The bridle had a few worn places that would need watching, but both would do fine.

"I'll take the horse if you can give me a bill of sale." Wanted by the law had made Dave extra careful about legal matters. It didn't help to ask for trouble.

"Sure, the fellow I bought the horse from gave me one and I can just sign it over to you." Reilly started to the office when he stopped and turned back to Dave. "You wouldn't want the saddlebags and camp gear that came with the horse, would you?"

Dave shrugged to appear less interested. "I might. What do you have?"

Reilly went into the office and picked up a couple of saddlebags and a haversack from the corner of the room. "There's a skillet, coffeepot, tin plate and cup plus some other stuff. I haven't really looked through it. You give me fifteen dollars and I'll let you have the whole lot. What do you say?" He stood there holding the haversack and saddlebags expectantly.

"Might as well take it." Dave handed over the money.

"While I look for that bill of sale you go get the mare and saddle her up." Reilly was already shifting through the clutter.

Dave felt like a kid at Christmas with a new toy as he picked up the saddle, horse blanket, and bridle. The mare was well broken and stood patiently as he saddled her. After he had the horse saddled, he led her back into the livery stable and tied on the haversack.

"Here's your bill of sale." Reilly handed him a rumpled piece of paper with a fresh signature and date on it. In a casual-sounding voice he asked, "You got any more furs? I might be interested if you do."

Dave folded the paper and slipped it into his pocket. "Not right now, but if I get any more I'll bring them by." He didn't expect to get any more furs trapped for a long time.

"You do that. I might be interested in buying some more if they're as good as these."

Dave shook hands with Reilly and led the mare out of the stable. He crossed the road to the general store. After tying the horse to the hitching post in front of the general store, he went in carrying the saddlebags.

Pop Frazier worked alone in the store, but pans banging from the kitchen echoed through the air.

"Howdy, Dave, I see you bought that brown mare that Reilly been wanting to get rid of."

Dave returned the greeting with a grin. He'd forgotten that everyone knew everyone else's business in a small town. In a couple of days, everyone in the countryside would know about the tall bearded man who had come into town with furs and bought a horse from Reilly. "I need some grub and a rifle." Dave could tell that Pop would have preferred some small talk before getting down to business, but Dave was too out of the habit of small talk to oblige him. After so many months of silence, it seemed to Dave that he had already used up a lot of words.

"Help yourself on the grub," Pop said. "What you see on these shelves is what we got."

Dave quickly picked out tins of beans, peaches, tomatoes, and baking powder. He then added small sacks of flour, sugar, coffee, and salt. Last, he picked up more beef jerky and a side of bacon. He soon had a pile of food that would last him about two weeks. He'd been a wanted man long enough to know that the more he could stay away from towns and stores on his journey to Rock Corner the better off he would be. He added a box of shells for his revolver to the pile.

Pop laid a rifle on the counter with a box of ammunition.

Buying the rifle reminded him of the reality that he was a hunted man. Mentally shaking himself, he asked what he owed.

"Well, it's a lot with that rifle added in to the total." Pop seemed reluctant to charge him. "A twenty should do it." He scratched his head and looked at Dave with concern. "You got that much, son?"

Dave didn't take offense at the question, remembering how Pop had first seen him the day before, and he didn't yet know of the sale of the furs. Dave was sure he would know by the end of the day.

"That's a good price for all of this. Thanks, Pop." Dave handed him the money.

As he packed the grub in the saddlebags and a gunnysack Pop had given him, Ma came into the store from the back wiping her flour-covered hands on her apron.

"I thought I heard your voice out here, son. You're just in time for dinner. We got fried chicken, potatoes, gravy, biscuits and dried apple cobbler. Now you won't get a better offer anywhere in Elkhead."

Dave looked at their cheery expectant faces and couldn't think of a reason to turn down the invitation. What Ma described was a meal that he wasn't likely to find anytime soon. Grinning he said, "You know just how to invite a man to dinner. I would be honored."

"Well, come on then, it's ready to dish up and I don't like to give the gravy time to sit." She walked back into the kitchen.

Pop directed him to a basin on the back porch to wash up.

Dave was glad for Pop's directions because he'd almost forgotten such niceties as washing up before a meal.

By the time they returned to the kitchen, Ma had set another place at the table.

Dave enjoyed the next couple of hours. Because of the food he'd had in the last twenty-four hours, the edge was off his hunger. He could eat slow enough to enjoy the taste of the food.

Ma and Pop carried on a running conversation throughout the meal without needing many responses from him.

Dave got a picture of an ordinary family who had built a happy life through the years of hard work. Envy and a sense of loss of his own family washed over him.

After the last bite of apple cobbler, which Pop and he'd totally finished at Ma's insistence, Dave felt a reluctance to leave the warmth of that kitchen, but he knew there was no permanent place for him there and he had something that needed doing. He couldn't do it standing there. Getting on to see Jonathan was his next order of business.

He took Ma's work-worn hand as he gave her a little bow. "Thanks so much, ma'am, for the meal. It was kind of you to invite me."

She patted his calloused hand. "You'll be leaving us. Heading on your way now that you have grub and a horse." She stated it more as a fact than as a question. Dave guessed that Ma and Pop had seen many riders passing through their town and knew Dave wasn't a stayer.

"Yes ma'am." He gathered up the saddlebags, gunnysack, and rifle. "I'll be heading out in the morning." He wanted to share with her that he was going to see his young son. He couldn't overcome the habit of keeping everything bottled up inside of him so easily, so he said nothing.

They followed him out to the porch where they watched him tie on the saddlebags and gunnysack, and slide the rifle into the scabbard that had come with the saddle.

Turning back to them, he took off his hat. "You folks have been very kind to a stranger. You'll never know what it meant to me. Thanks again."

Pop reached out and shook his hand. "No thanks needed, we've enjoyed your company. Next time you're through Elkhead, you know where you're welcome to stop."

Ma didn't say anything, but before Dave knew it, she gave him a hug and pulled his head down so she could plant a big kiss on his cheek. It was the first time he'd been kissed since leaving Jenny's folks almost six years ago. It so surprised him that he didn't know what to say, so he simply gave her a hug and kissed her back, and then turned and mounted his horse.

Dave felt that Pop and Ma Frazier in two days had gone a long way toward helping him feel a part of the human race again. The terrible sense of isolation that he'd experienced through the long winter receded somewhat. It wasn't completely gone, but Dave didn't expect to ever be at a point in his life where he didn't feel alone.

At his campsite, he repacked and loaded his stuff on his horse. If he'd had all this gear and supplies at the cave, he would have lived like a king. Dave decided to ride on until dark. As he tied the bedroll, the brown mare looked back at him with such big mournful eyes that he couldn't help but laugh.

"Do you feel mistreated already?" Dave had no idea how long the horse had been eating oats at the livery stable, but long enough to get fat and spoiled.

Dave mounted and started out with at least hours of daylight left. The sense of freedom at being mounted again was marvelous.

The journey over the mountains cast shadows in his mind like a fading dream. He felt so removed from it now and only looked forward. What the future would bring and what part could he have in his son's future? The closer he got to seeing Jonathan, the more concerned he was about what the boy's reaction would be to him. It scared him to think that he might be judged and found wanting by one whose opinion really mattered to him.

Chapter 7

Five days later Dave arrived at the Harrod ranch. He owed the Harrods the courtesy of letting them decide if they wanted him to see his son. By leaving the boy behind and allowing the Harrods to have responsibility for Jonathan, he lost any right to a say in his son's life.

Camped by a spring in the hills above the Harrod's place, he watched for someone working the cattle on the slope of the hills below him. He used a pencil, envelope, and piece of paper he found in the haversack. What should he say in the note? There was always a possibility that it would fall into the wrong hands. The last thing he wanted right now was a posse taking up the hunt for him. He finally decided on one line that he hoped Mr. Harrod could decipher. *Meet me before dark at the bubbler. Dave.*

Wayne, Mr. Harrod's son, had called the springs the bubbler. The term had evidently started when Wayne was a kid and had become a family joke that made sense only to the family.

Most of the day passed before Dave finally spotted someone on a far slope working their way through the cattle as if counting them. Dave had changed his place of concealment several times during the day. About a mile from the springs, he casually rode up to the rider. He half expected it to be Wayne or Mr. Harrod, but it was a stranger to him, a young Mexican.

"Howdy," Dave said.

"Hello, *Señor.*" The rider waited for Dave to speak.

"You work for Mr. Harrod? Are these his cattle?" He might as well find out quickly if the Harrod's had sold out and moved.

"Si, I work for *Señor* Harrod. You want work too?" the rider asked, evidently assuming that Dave was riding the grub line looking for work.

"No, but I got a letter for him. Would you take it to him?" Dave pulled the envelope out of his pocket.

The rider nodded his head without speaking and reached for the letter.

Dave handed over the note with a silver dollar. "You'll give it to him when you ride in this evening. You won't forget?" Dave wasn't too sure the note would be delivered.

"Si, *Señor*," the rider replied, "I give, I no forget." With that the rider turned his horse and continued on his way across the slope of the hill.

Dave would have to chance that Mr. Harold would get the note. He guided his horse back up the slope in the opposite direction of the springs until he was out of the rider's sight and then circled back. He wished for a pair of binoculars, but all he could do was wait. He respected what the Harrods had done for him and Jonathan. If they asked him to ride away without seeing the boy, he would do it. He fervently hoped they wouldn't feel that way. Seeing them again made his hands tremble.

In a grassy hollow behind the springs, he hobbled his horse to allow it to feed. He had enough of a view that if he saw anyone whom he didn't recognize riding up the slopes, he could quickly saddle up. If he had to leave quickly, he wanted the mare to be as fresh as possible.

After checking on the horse, he saw the rider heading back toward the ranch buildings in the distance. Dave didn't know if the rider had completed his chore, or if the responsibility of delivering the letter urged him to ride in early.

Dave didn't care which, he just hoped that Mr. Harrod was there and would ride up to the springs. The suspense was getting to a point Dave felt his heart wanted to jump out of his chest it was thumping so. He kept an eye toward the ranch.

Toward late afternoon, Dave spotted a rider leave the ranch buildings and head in his direction. Mr. Harrod rode directly toward the springs without seeming to make any effort to hide his movements.

Dave removed his hat and stood quietly for Mr. Harrod to speak first because he wasn't at all sure of the reception he would get from the older man.

Looking Dave over as if he too were not sure of his reception, Mr. Harrod dismounted. "I still can't believe it's you after all this time without a word." Mr. Harrod had genuine warmth in his voice. He threw his arms around Dave and gave him a bear hug. "We were so afraid you were lost to us. You don't know how good it is to see you." Releasing him he said, "Come on, let's go on down to the house. Everyone will want to see you."

Dave didn't know how to respond. Mr. Harrod acted as if it were the most normal thing in the world for him just to ride in after all these years.

"Mr. Harrod, it's good to see you too. But let's talk before we ride to the house."

"You got any coffee, son?" He tied his horse to a tree and walked over to where Dave had his pack. "Let's get a fire going, make some coffee, and talk if that's what you want."

For the next half hour, Mr. Harrod talked about the ranch and Dave's old place that now belonged to Jesse. Dave learned that both Jesse and Wayne were married to girls with whom they had grown up in the community. They each had two children.

Wayne and his family built a house not far from the main house and worked with Mr. Harrod. The family agreed that Wayne would some day have the ranch.

Mary, one of Jenny's younger sisters, lived in Rock Corner and taught school. She was betrothed to a young man who worked at the bank.

Rachel, the youngest, was now nineteen and still at home. Mr. Harrod talked about Rachel with a special fondness in his voice as he told Dave how much help she was to Mrs. Harrod who was getting on in years and having a problem with painful joints.

All the time that Mr. Harrod talked Dave waited to hear of his son. Almost as if he could read Dave's mind, Mr. Harrod grinned and poured himself another cup of coffee. "And that Johnny, now there's a great boy, one you can really be proud of. He's so smart. Why, you wouldn't believe the things he can think to ask questions about." He paused to drink some of the hot coffee. "And he has really missed you not being around."

Suddenly Mr. Harrod was very serious, "Where have you been, son? Why didn't you come home after Terrill confessed?"

Dave wasn't sure he'd heard correctly. "What do you mean? After Terrill confessed?"

Mr. Harrod looked at him with raised eyebrows. "Don't you know? Isn't that why you're back now?"

"What are you talking about?" Dave leaned forward and waited intensely for a response.

"You really don't know, do you?" Mr. Harrod slowly shook his head in disbelief. "Last October it was, Terrill got trampled bad by a horse over by Clearwater. Before he died, he wanted to clear his conscience. He cleared you, completely. The sheriff had someone take it all down as Terrill told it with the doctor and another man as witnesses. They dropped all the charges against you, and called back in all the wanted posters. You really hadn't heard?"

Dave had been prepared to hear almost anything from Mr. Harrod except that his name was cleared. A new world opened to him, and he had trouble realizing it was really there for him.

"You mean I'm free?" Dave couldn't keep the quiver out of his voice.

"Son, you've been free since last fall. What happened to you that you didn't hear about it?" Mr. Harrod looked at him intently. "You haven't gotten into any other trouble have you?"

"Not that I know of." Dave had more control in his voice. The shock of what Mr. Harrod told him passed, but the reality had yet to sink in.

"Tell me where you've been and what's been going on with you." Mr. Harrod settled more comfortably and poured another cup of coffee.

With the sun setting and darkness not far behind, Dave told of his trailing Terrill and being shot on the mountain, of the time in the cave and the long hard winter that had passed, of the fall from the cliff, and the selling of the furs.

As he told his story, Mr. Harrod shook his head in amazement. "It's a miracle you're alive, son. No wonder you didn't hear any news. So that's why you sent the note."

"I didn't want to cause a fuss, and I especially didn't want to bring the law on you folks."

"Well, there's no reason not to come on in now. Ma is probably putting supper on the table and I'm hungry. Let's go to the house and get something to eat." Mr. Harrod poured what was left of the coffee on the small fire.

Dave caught up his horse almost as if he were in a dream. He soon found himself riding up to the house. A ranch hand came out of the barn and took the horses from them.

Mr. Harrod was about to open the back door when he realized that Dave had not followed him up the steps of the back porch.

Dave stood at the bottom of the steps almost crushing his hat in his hands. He was terrified of going into the house and meeting his son. Could he stand it if Johnny rejected him?

As if sensing some of what was going on in Dave's mind and heart, Mr. Harrod came back down the steps, put his arm around Dave's shoulders, drew him up the steps, and into the house saying, "It'll be all right, son. Now that you're home, it'll be all right."

Without the warmth of that arm around his shoulder and the kindness of the older man, Dave didn't know if he could have entered the house on his own.

"I brought company." Mr. Harrod pushed a reluctant Dave through the kitchen doorway.

Dave stood in the bright light of the oil lamp in the kitchen and waited for a clue to what kind of welcome he would receive from Mrs. Harrod who was busy at the stove.

A look of wonder and joy spread over her face as she realized who stood in her kitchen. "Dave?" She hurried across the room to embrace him. Holding him tight, she gazed up into his eyes. "Dave, Dave, is it really you?"

Dave did the only thing he could. He embraced her back.

When she finally let go she looked up at him with tears streaming down her face. "The Lord does answer prayers. He brought you back at last." She wiped her face with her apron.

Mr. Harrod patted her on the shoulder. "Let the boy go, Ma, and go get some supper ready. We're hungry." There was a glint of tears in Mr. Harrod's eyes, too.

The obvious depth of their emotion at having him back surprised Dave. Feeling shaky inside, he allowed himself to be led across the kitchen and to the big oval table.

Mrs. Harrod was all flustered and excited. "Where did you find him, Pa? You're too thin, Dave. Haven't you been eating right? My goodness, the cornbread! I better get it out of the oven." She didn't wait for an answer from either man.

Sitting at the table with Dave, Mr. Harrod grinned at both of them. Finally, when Mrs. Harrod paused for breath he asked, "Don't you think we should call the kids to supper?"

Putting the iron skillet of fresh baked cornbread on the table next to the pot of stew, her face lit up even more, and Mrs. Harrod hurried out of the kitchen to the bottom of the stairs all the time calling out.

"Rachel, Johnny, come on down. Supper's ready."

Mr. Harrod must have noticed the look of panic on Dave's face for he began to talk quietly about ordinary things as if to distract him from the sounds of footsteps coming down the stairs.

"You know, Ma likes the kitchen to herself when she prepares supper. Therefore, Johnny and Rachel always do the washing up afterwards. Ma and I sit out on the back porch." He spoke in a casual voice that didn't require any answer.

Dave couldn't have answered anyway. His whole being cried out for him to run, to get out of there before Jonathan came into the room. But he held himself still and waited for what was to come. Whatever his son's reaction to him, Dave knew he deserved it.

Mrs. Harrod came back into the kitchen with a young woman following.

Dave had expected a twelve-year-old in pigtails with an upturned nose and freckles, but Rachel was a grown woman. She was small like her mother, but with uprightness in the way she walked that made her seem taller. With dark brown hair and eyes, she was even prettier than Jenny had been.

When she saw Dave, she stopped in the doorway as if waiting to find out whether this stranger was friend or foe.

Mr. Harrod stood up with Dave. "Rachel, don't you remember Dave, Johnny's pa?"

For a fleeting instant, Dave thought he saw fear cross her face. Then, she gave him a look of curiosity. Dave was aware that her response didn't hold the instant welcome of her parents.

"Hello, Rachel." Was all that Dave could get out and even that sounded odd to him.

"Hello," was all he got in response. She then turned toward the cabinet and took down another plate and bowl.

Just as the silence following her entry into the kitchen was about to become awkward, a thundering sound came from the stairway and a nine-year-old bundle of energy raced into the kitchen. He, too, stopped abruptly when he realized that a stranger was in the room.

Dave held his breath as he looked at the boy. Jonathan reminded him so much of Jenny. He had the same curly, sandy blond hair and the large brown eyes that were characteristic of the Harrod family. The eyebrows and silky, long eyelashes were dark brown, almost black, making a contrast to the blond hair. Dave thought him extremely handsome. He had Jenny's eyes.

Dave wished Jenny could have been there to see him. She would have been proud. Dave tried to swallow the lump in his throat, but it wouldn't go away.

Mr. Harrod walked over and put his arm around the boy's shoulders. "I have someone here for you to meet, Johnny." He walked with the boy over to where Dave stood. "Johnny, this is your pa, come to visit."

The boy put out his hand. "Hello."

Dave took the little hand into his big work-hardened hand and shook it, man to man.

"Hello, Jonathan," was all that Dave could manage.

Looking up at his six-foot-three frame, the boy blinked at him. "Wow, you're tall. Nobody told me you were so big."

Johnny's comment broke a tension in the room and the Harrods laughed.

Dave found himself grinning. Of all the things he'd expected the boy to say, it wasn't that.

"Come on everyone. Let's sit down and eat before the cornbread is stone cold," Mrs. Harrod admonished, being practical. "Dave, you sit down at that side of the table with Johnny."

Dave would have preferred to sit across from his son where he could look at him more easily, but he made no comment. He found himself instead gazing across at Rachel who looked back with a straight, intent gaze as if she were trying to read something in his face.

With everyone settled, Dave was caught off guard when both Johnny and Mr. Harrod, who was seated at the end of the table to his left, reached over and took his hands as they bowed for the blessing of the food. Dave had forgotten the Harrod's custom to hold hands during the prayer. It gave him an odd sensation to hold the boy's hand and that his son allowed it so confidently.

As Dave looked around at the bowed heads and heard Mr. Harrod's blessing of the food, the whole thing had a dream quality to him in comparison to the last six years. Dave almost expected to wake up at any moment. Mr. Harrod's prayer caught his attention.

"And last, but not least, thank you, O Lord, for answering our prayers in bringing Dave safely back to us. May we be the family for him you want us to be. In Jesus' name. Amen."

The instant the prayer was completed, Johnny let go of Dave's hand and reached for a piece of cornbread.

Amid the clatter of the dishes, Mr. and Mrs. Harrod carried on the talk around the table with Johnny joining in as if it were the most usual thing in the world for his father to visit.

Except to respond to a direct question, Dave had nothing to say. Questions crowded his mind, but they were not questions he wanted to ask in front of the whole family.

Rachel didn't join the talk of the ranch and family activities. Dave didn't know if this was just her way, or because of his presence. She made no effort to avoid looking at him across the table, and several times their eyes met. Each time she gave him the same intent, searching stare as if she looked for the answer to a question.

The rest of the evening passed in a blur for Dave. It was as if his mind was overloaded with too many sensations. He still couldn't comprehend that he was truly a free man. There was no longer a need for caution and fear at every new face he met. To have something that had dominated his life for so long suddenly gone left him almost anchorless. He felt almost frightened with no restrictions on his choices. He would have to find a way to get on with a normal life again, which was something he'd not had since Jenny's death. He wasn't sure he knew how.

All these thoughts kept going around in his head as he sat on the back porch with Mr. and Mrs. Harrod while Rachel and Johnny did the supper dishes.

He'd offered to help, but had been told firmly, but politely to go visit with the Harrods.

Both Rachel and Johnny had seemed relieved for him to get out of the kitchen. Dave wasn't sure, but that he felt relieved also.

Johnny made no protest about drying the dishes.

Dave realized that Mr. Harrod had asked him a question. His mind had been on the two in the kitchen, he wished he knew what they were thinking.

"Excuse me, what was that?" He tried to focus his mind on the conversation on the porch.

"I was just wondering about your plans. Ma and I want you to know that you are welcome to stay right here as long as you want."

Mrs. Harrod didn't say anything, but she nodded in agreement.

Mr. Harrod continued, "As far as we're concerned you're part of our family and always will be. And we would both like for Johnny to get a chance to know his father better."

Dave knew it was a reasonable question. Most folks had plans, but his situation had so changed in one day that he felt adrift in his life.

"I appreciate that, and if it's really all right, I plan to stay a few days. And Johnny's father would like a chance to get to know him too. You all have done a fine job with him. I don't know how to thank you."

Mrs. Harrod brushed that aside with a wave of her hand. "My goodness, Dave, you don't need to thank us. That boy has been a delight to our lives from the day he was born." She looked over at her husband and smiled. "Of course, you understand he's a normal little boy. He can get into mischief with the best of them. Why, we sometimes have to tell him he has to stay in for a while and not go roaming with his friends so we can get a rest from all the things he finds to get into around here."

"And Mary tells us that Johnny is far and away her best student." There was pride in Mr. Harrod's voice. "She says he soaks up learning and is always curious for more. I tell you, he keeps all of us on our toes. Usually he's a chatterbox at supper, coming up with more questions than you can imagine. He was sort of quiet tonight, which is to be expected, but you wait until he gets used to you and you'll see what we mean."

Having completed the washing up, Rachel and Johnny appeared in the back door.

"Ma, we're going on up to bed." Rachel told her mother without looking toward Dave who sat in the shadows on the porch with his hat in his hand.

Mrs. Harrod gave them each a kiss on the cheek. "My, it is getting late. Johnny, it's way past your bedtime even if it is summertime and no school. Now you go on up and go straight to bed without reading tonight. You can visit more with your Pa tomorrow. He's going to stay and visit a few days."

By the light from the kitchen, Dave saw a look cross Rachel's face, and he didn't think it was disappointment at going to bed. Here was one member of the family that wished him gone by morning.

After Johnny had given his grandmother a kiss, he turned politely to Dave. "Goodnight."

Before Dave could reply, Johnny and Rachel went back into the kitchen.

Evidently aware that Rachel was standoffish and not her usual friendly self toward visitors in their home, Mrs. Harrod apologized for her. "Please excuse Rachel's rudeness. She's just a little surprised by your visit. She's not usually this way."

"You know from the time Johnny came to us when Jenny took sick, Rachel has been devoted to him as if he were her own child. She's not sure what it means now that you've come back. Be patient with her and give her time to get used to you," Mr. Harrod explained.

"Don't worry, I'm as uncomfortable with the situation as she is. I just ask that you folks be patient with me. It's been a while since I've been around people without worrying about my back." Dave ran his fingers through his hair.

"Well, take your time and stay with us a while. I can always use some help around the place. In the morning, Wayne will be over, and if you want, in a couple of days we can ride over to see Jesse. He's sure going to be glad to see you."

Mr. Harrod's voice had a soothing quality that gave Dave the feeling that everything would be all right. Dave felt comfortable with him and hoped they would have more opportunities to talk, just the two of them. But tonight he was weary to the bones and just wanted to go to bed.

As if sensing his mood, Mrs. Harrod stood up. "Where do you want to sleep? We've Mary's room upstairs, or we've the old bunkhouse where you used to sleep when you came visiting Jenny. We use it now for Jesse's family when they sleep over. The hands have a new bunkhouse that we built a couple of years ago between here and Wayne's place."

"The old bunkhouse will do fine." Dave was quick to say. The thought of trying to sleep upstairs in Mary's room after what he'd become accustomed to was more than he wanted to tackle. The old bunkhouse would be like returning to an old friend.

Mrs. Harrod gave him a kiss on the cheek and patted his arm. "I'm so glad you're here, Dave. Now don't you talk too long with this man of mine. You look tired out and need to get a good night's sleep. You all can talk tomorrow." She turned and went into the kitchen.

"She's right, you look like you could use some rest. Let's go get you settled." Mr. Harrod got a lantern from a hook on the porch, lit it, and led the way first over to the barn where Dave's horse was stabled so they could retrieve the saddlebags, haversack, and rifle. Then Mr. Harrod led the way to the old bunkhouse.

"We have too many hands now for this small bunkhouse. And the Missus wanted the bunkhouse for the hands further from the house because of the girls and Johnny. It has worked out fine to have this available for Jesse's family when they stay over."

Dave was surprised at the inside of the bunkhouse. It wasn't like a bunkhouse, but more a large bedroom. All the bunks that he remembered were gone. Now there was a double bed in one corner, with a nightstand and lamp, and a smaller single bed in the opposite end of the room. In between was a baby's crib. The room had curtains on the windows and a braided rug covered the floor. Besides a small table and chairs in the middle of the room, it had a couple of chests of drawers against the wall and by the doorway a row of hooks on which to hang things.

Mr. Harrod put the lantern down on the table. "I'll leave you now. If there's anything you need just let us know. And sleep in as late as you want. Ma will get you breakfast anytime you're ready in the morning." He took Dave's hand in both of his. "We're all happy you're home. Goodnight, son. I'll see you in the morning."

"Thanks, I'm glad to be here."

With a final shake of his hand, Mr. Harrod turned and left the bunkhouse.

For a reason he could not fathom, Dave felt tears welling up in his eyes and he was close to weeping. Shaking himself to get control of the strange feelings, he put the saddlebags and haversack on the small bed and surveyed the room. Feeling grimy and in need of washing up, he remembered the stock trough that had been out back of the bunkhouse where the boys had always washed in the summertime after a days work. Wondering if it was still there, Dave undressed, took a towel from the top of the chest, put out the lantern, and slipped out the back door.

In the moonlight, he spotted the old trough full of water. Putting his towel on the old tree stump that he remembered the boys had put there for just such a purpose, he lowered himself into the cold water. The trough was about six feet long and three feet wide. It more than accommodated his body. Dave allowed the cold water to soak into his skin and his body to relax as he tried to think through the day's happenings. It was too much for him. He couldn't seem to get his mind to settle on one thought long enough to think it through. Finally, he just let his mind drift with the quiet night sounds and watched the moonlight giving everything a ghostly shadow affect.

Realizing that he was falling asleep in the trough, he forced himself to get out and dry off. The towel felt strange to his skin, which wasn't used to something so soft. Silently laughing at himself, he gathered up the towel and returned to his room. He kept imagining Rachel's face if he'd fallen asleep in the water trough and been found there stark naked the next morning. He wasn't sure that Rachel would think it was funny. Johnny, on the other hand, would probably see the humor in it, but he was glad he'd not taken the chance.

With just enough help from the moonlight to prevent bumping into any of the furniture, Dave crawled between clean sheets for the first time in over a year. The feel of the sheets against his bare skin was soothing. Not being used to a pillow, especially one with a revolver under it, he had a little trouble getting his head positioned comfortably. He heard the words from Mr. Harrod that no one was hunting him anymore, but years of habit were hard to break. He felt more secure with the gun in reach.

The dip into the water trough had refreshed him, but Dave still felt a weariness that wasn't just from that day's activities, but from months of tension. However, feeling as safe as he had in a long time, he drifted into a deep dreamless sleep.

Chapter 8

Rachel lay in her bed thinking over the surprise events of the evening. She had gone about the normal mealtime preparations after seeing her father ride out. She couldn't imagine where he had gone without telling either her ma or herself where he was going.

Rachel had gone into Johnny's room to tell him that supper was ready. Her heart seemed to take an extra beat as it often did when she looked at the curly haired, brown-eyed little boy. Even after six years, Jenny looked out at her from his eyes. How she still missed her older sister.

"Hey, Aunt Rachel, is supper ready?" Johnny looked at her across the little wooden desk where he sat with a pencil in his hand.

"You finished with your homework?" Rachel walked over to the desk and tousled his hair.

Johnny grinned. "Yeah, all but this one question. I can't get it to come out right."

"Let me see...there you have a plus and it should be a minus." She pointed to the place where he needed to change the symbol.

"That's it! You're smart, Aunt Rachel." Johnny erased the plus symbol and put a minus, and then completed the math problem. "Now can I come downstairs?"

"Sure, just put your books away first." Rachel turned and heard her mother calling them to supper. She went down ahead of Johnny who put his books away.

When she had entered the kitchen, a stranger stood by the table with her father. A stranger yet someone with a familiar look.

She had heard Pa say, "Rachel, don't you remember Dave, Johnny's Pa? He's come back to us."

Shocked, she couldn't take in what she heard. Johnny's Pa! What did he want? Was he here to take Johnny away? She had responded with a nod of her head and was saved from further conversation with the tall bearded man in the worn, dusty clothes by Johnny thundering down the stairs. Rachel had watched Johnny as he was introduced to his father for the first time. Tears filled her eyes and she blinked to hold them back. Jenny should have been there. It wasn't right that Dave got to know his son when Jenny never had that chance.

Her memory of supper was a blur. Rachel couldn't take her eyes off the man who sat across from her. He was familiar to her, especially his voice. But eight years had made a difference. He had been a clean-shaven young man of twenty-four when he left. He returned a bearded, rough looking man. Rachel watched him as he answered a question from her father. Even his voice was deeper. She did admit he had a certain appeal but the same question kept going through her mind. Why was he here?

After supper she and Johnny had washed and put away the dishes. Dave had offered to help but she was glad when her folks had taken him out to the porch to visit. She helped Johnny get settled in bed, then went to her own room.

Turning over and pulling the sheet up closer to her chin, she wondered what it would mean for Dave to be back in his son's life. Rachel remembered the terrible time when she was twelve and Jenny had died so suddenly. And then she woke that terrible morning a few days later to learn that Dave had left her, too. She remembered that awful empty feeling as if by riding off he had taken her heart with him and she had thought the tears would never end. Her comfort had been taking care of the little toddler. And her anger at Dave leaving. Not only leaving his son, but leaving her. She was still angry.

She watched out the window at the moonlight and wondered where he had been. What kind of life he had lived? Even with the beard, he was ruggedly handsome. She shook herself. Why was she thinking about how handsome he was? What if he was there to take Johnny? No, she was not going to let that happen.

As if from the bottom of a deep well, Dave sensed that someone was in the cave. Without thinking of anything other than protecting himself, he reached for his gun, and tried to focus his eyes in the bright early morning sunlight.

The gasp that Rachel gave as he sat up in bed with the gun pointed at her brought Dave suddenly wide-awake. As scared as she was at how close he'd come to shooting her, he was even more frightened.

"I'm sorry, Rachel." He let the gun sag to the covers. "I'm really sorry. You startled me. I wouldn't hurt you for anything." He tried to reassure her.

She was white and shaken, as she stood in the doorway with a pot of coffee and a cup in her hands. He thought she probably had never seen a gun pointed at anyone, with the person holding it ready to use it, much less one pointed at her.

"Ma sent me over with some coffee. I knocked, but you didn't answer, so I came on in," she said, in a way of explanation. "Ma thought you might like some fresh coffee first thing in the morning like my Pa does."

Rachel stared at his bare chest.

As Dave had sat up, the covers had fallen down around his waist exposing his broad muscular shoulders, arms, and hairy chest. It also revealed the massive scars on his left side where the bullet had entered. The result was a series of ugly scars that he would carry to his grave as a reminder of the time on the mountain. He realized he sat there with only a sheet partially covering his body. He pulled it up closer to him.

Rachel's face turned from white from shock to red from embarrassment. Stiffly she placed the coffeepot on the table and retreated to the doorway.

"Ma said to say that she's got breakfast for you when you're ready." Then she was out the door, closing it behind her.

Dave sagged back on the bed. Of all people to come in on him, it had to be Rachel. He feared he'd really bungled any hope of friendship from that direction. Realizing that he'd slept way past his normal waking time, Dave got up, dressed quickly, sat down at the table, and enjoyed a cup of fresh coffee.

Guns, Dave knew, didn't play a part in the Harrod family's lives except for hunting rifles and the occasional need to shoot a ranch animal. They would probably be shocked to learn that he slept with a gun under his pillow. What a different turn his life had taken in the last few years compared to the normal civilized world in which the Harrod family lived. He would have to be careful not to bring the harsh, wild life of the desperado trail into their world. He didn't want that for his son, and he wanted to leave it behind for himself.

As he sipped on the second cup of coffee, and thought through what had happened, he decided he would adapt to their world as much as he could. If what Mr. Harrod had said was true, he had no reason to be fearful and the gun was not needed. He put the gun and holster into the haversack. Unless something happened to indicate differently, he would leave it there. He would just have to learn to sleep without it.

In some ways, he'd become undisciplined in his living habits. Living out on the trail didn't require much civilized behavior, but here he would try to match the Harrod's way of doing. Dave made the bed and put the coverlet back on it. If it had just been for himself he probably would have left the covers thrown back ready for him to crawl into that night. It seemed more logical to Dave, but he knew women-folk put great store in the beds being made-up every morning.

He unpacked the saddlebags and haversack and put his belongings in the chest of drawers. He then slid the saddlebags and haversack under the bed, out of sight. As he looked around the bunkhouse, he felt it would pass even Rachel's inspection.

For a reason he could not understand, Rachel's approval was important to him. Somehow, he knew that without Rachel on his side, he would never reach a close relationship with his son, but to win her over to his side, he would have to do better than he'd done this morning.

Taking a last look around, he picked up the coffeepot and cup and crossed the yard. Dave was almost to the house when he realized he'd forgotten to put on his boots and was still wearing the moccasins he'd slipped into when he got out of bed. Knowing that the rough-made moccasins might look strange to the Harrods, he was tempted to go back for his boots, but he was almost to the porch. He could change after he saw Mr. Harrod and found out what the day's work was. At least he could make himself useful the few days he was to be at the ranch.

As he stepped onto the back porch, he heard voices in the kitchen. Dave was about to make his presence known when he heard his name spoken.

A voice he recognized as Wayne's said, "Now, Rachel, don't be too hard on Dave. I'd be jumpy too if the first thing in the morning you walked in on me." There was a teasing tone to his voice.

"I didn't just walk in on him. I knocked first." Rachel's voice sounded firm and a little exasperated.

Dave decided that maybe eavesdropping would be all right for once and he needed to hear what was said about him. Glad now that he'd forgotten to put on his boots since the moccasins had made no sound as he'd crossed the porch.

Rachel's voice continued, "You don't know what it was like, Wayne, to have that gun pointed at you, and I can tell you, he was close to pulling the trigger without even knowing who was there."

Dave frowned and thought she was being a little unfair. After all, he had apologized.

Mr. Harrod's voice responded, "But Rachel, you've got to remember that Dave's been a man on the run for several years now. With every lawman in the country looking for him, how he managed to avoid capture, I'll never know. But he's had to live in a way that sleeping with his gun has probably become a habit."

"Well, Pa, that's another thing. He's not the Dave that left here six years ago, the one that I remember, or that Jenny cared about. Why, he doesn't even look the same. He's so thin and has that beard. He looks rough and mean."

"Now, Rachel, you know better than to judge a person by their appearance." Mrs. Harrod spoke up. "We just aren't used to Dave with a beard. It's cut neat and he has a recent haircut. You can tell that in spite of the rough way he has had to live he made an effort."

"If you just knew, Rachel, all that he's been through," Mr. Harrod broke in, "you would be more patient with him. I don't know near everything of course, but let me tell you his experiences this last winter." Mr. Harrod preceded to tell them what Dave had shared with him yesterday afternoon.

Dave didn't mind him telling, or, for the others knowing, but he did mind the reason Mr. Harrod felt he needed to tell the others. Dave didn't like the idea that he had to prove himself to Rachel. Why couldn't she just take him at face value and judge him on his behavior as she got to know him again? He received his answer as Mr. Harrod finished repeating what Dave had told of his experiences on the mountain.

"Pa, I admit that I don't really have a reason to be distrustful of Dave, nor to dislike him. But Pa, what is he doing here? What does he want? Is he after Johnny? Does he want to take him away from us, to go off and disappear again as he did after Jenny died? I couldn't stand to lose Johnny, too."

Dave could tell from the sound of Rachel's voice that she was close to tears.

"Why has he come back at all and why has he come back as if it were a normal thing for a man to abandon his son?"

Bowing his head, Dave had no argument with that accusation. He had abandoned his son.

Mr. Harrod's voice was kind and patient. "Baby, don't cry. You have to remember that Dave is, after all, Johnny's father and he has a right to see his son. I know how you care for Johnny, but I don't think Dave would just take him, or at least I hope not. We have to pray that the Lord will give us all wisdom to handle things in the best way for both Johnny and Dave."

"We care about Dave, too, and he needs our help to try to get his life going again. Maybe he needs Johnny more than we do." Mrs. Harrod spoke so softly and sadly, that Dave almost didn't hear what she said.

Dave felt shattered by what he'd heard. Rachel was afraid he was there to steal Johnny away from them! And Mr. Harrod had not really told her he was convinced that Dave wasn't there to do the very thing that Rachel feared.

His first thought was to saddle his horse and leave, but that was exactly what he had done after Jenny had died, and what Rachel thought he would do now, only she feared he would try to take Johnny with him. Dave didn't know what to do. He wanted to show them that he hadn't changed so much from the man that had married their daughter, but he didn't know how to convince them.

Spotting Mr. Harrod's razor and shaving mug on a shelf on the back porch next to a mirror, Dave decided that one thing he could do was to shave. To change his appearance might placate Rachel enough for her to give him time to win her approval. As much as he hated the idea of having to prove himself, he would try.

Moving quietly, he picked up the razor, shaving mug, and mirror and quickly carried them to the bunkhouse. Being as careful not to nick himself and as cleanly as he could, he shaved off the beard that he'd worn since the previous fall. Dave would have preferred hot water, but at least Mr. Harrod kept his razor sharp. He put on his boots and quickly crossed the yard to the back porch again. He replaced the razor, shaving mug, and mirror on the shelf.

He was about to pick up the coffeepot and cup and make his presence known to those who were still talking in the kitchen, when he spotted Johnny walking toward the house dragging a hoe. Dave quietly strolled out to meet him. Just to look at his son helped him understand a little about Rachel and her fears. He was such a handsome little boy. Dave felt a pain in his chest as he looked at him.

"Hey, Johnny, you been hoeing?" Dave asked the obvious because he couldn't think of anything else to say.

"Yes, sir, I guess I'll have to hoe all summer long," Johnny answered in the exasperated tone of a boy set to a chore that wasn't his favorite.

Dave remembered his own childhood and his dislike of anything that had to do with a hoe. It made him feel something in common with Jonathan.

"You headed to the house now?" Dave moved into to step with the little boy.

"Yes, sir. Grandma told me I only had to do five rows this morning because you come to visit. I got them done. Now maybe I can get some milk and something to eat," Johnny said, looking up at him with a serious look on his face. "My breakfast done left me."

As they approached the house, Johnny slowed down and finally came to a stop.

Dave stopped with him.

Looking up at him with a look that so reminded Dave of Jenny, Johnny seemed to have trouble deciding whether to speak. Finally, in a quiet, serious voice he asked, "Are you really and truly my father?"

Dave felt the boy deserved a serious answer. He squatted on his heels to be at eye level. "I'm really and truly your father. I've been gone a long time and couldn't come to visit you until now. But I'm here and I hope we can get acquainted. Is that all right with you?"

The boy didn't answer immediately. When he did answer, it caught Dave by surprise. "All my friend's fathers live with them. Are you going to live here with us now?"

The logic of the question was there, and Dave wanted to answer in the affirmative, but he didn't know what was going to happen in the future. He wasn't about to tell him something that might not be true.

"I don't think so, but I plan to come visit from now on."

In the simplicity of his child's mind Johnny seemed to see the simple solution. "Well, why don't I just come live with you?"

Hearing the boy say that made Dave want to take the boy with him and made a home for them somewhere. That he would take Johnny away from them was exactly the fear the Harrods had, especially Rachel. That would cause too much hurt and pain, and he'd no right to do it. It would even hurt Johnny to take him away from the only family he'd known all his life.

With a sigh Dave answered, "I can't take you with me now, but maybe some-day. What do you say we go in and ask your grandmother if we can get something to eat?"

"All right, Pa. Maybe if you ask, Grandma will give us some of the pound cake she baked this morning." It was the first time the boy had called him anything other than sir. Dave stood taller and felt a surge of energy. He wanted to be the pa that Johnny deserved.

Johnny leaned his hoe against the porch, and as if it were the most natural thing in the world, reached up and took Dave's hand as they climbed the steps, crossed the porch, and entered the kitchen.

As they walked in, hand in hand, the conversation that had evidently been on going came to an abrupt halt.

Wayne immediately jumped up from where he sat and enveloped Dave in a bear hug. "Dave, you old rascal, it's good to see you."

Even as he tried to respond to Wayne's greeting, Dave was aware of Rachel's reaction to his and Johnny's entrance into the kitchen.

She looked as scared as she had earlier when she'd stood in the bunkhouse.

Dave realized that Rachel would view any indication he and Johnny were getting close as a threat.

"Hey, Wayne, you haven't changed much. I hear that you have a wife and two kids now. Congratulations."

"Talk about not changing, you don't look much different than you did six years ago. Just a little thinner maybe." Turning to Rachel, Wayne said, "What do you mean he looks rough, he doesn't even have a beard."

Rachel blushed and didn't look at Dave.

He guessed she was aware that he knew she'd been talking about him. To help her out he said to Wayne, "I did have a beard. This is the first chance I have had to get rid of it in a long time."

"Well, you looked all right with the beard but I prefer you without one, son. You look more like your old self," Mrs. Harrod said. "You haven't had any breakfast. What would you like?"

Dave would have liked breakfast, but it was his own fault that he'd slept so late. He didn't want to ask for anything special. On the table amid the cups and saucers was a round pound cake with several slices already missing. He remembered what Johnny said about wanting some milk and pound cake.

"If it's all right, Johnny and I would like to have a glass of milk and a piece of cake."

He got an answering grin from Johnny.

"Dave, that's not a proper breakfast, but if that's what you want, that is the easiest thing to get. Both of you sit down at the table there with the others."

Rachel returned to her chair as if she didn't know what to do with herself. She didn't enter into the conversation as Wayne told Dave about his family and the work he and Mr. Harrod were doing around the ranch.

Dave didn't deliberately ignore her, but it was easier for him to talk with Wayne and Mr. Harrod. They had both interrupted their normal routine of work because of his arrival at the ranch. Soon Wayne asked him if he wanted to look at the new buildings and corrals.

Glad for an excuse to leave the kitchen and the constant pressure he felt from Rachel's presence, he accepted immediately. As he walked toward the new barn and corrals, Dave learned that they planned to move one of the herds to another part of the ranch the next day. Dave volunteered to help, glad for an opportunity to be useful.

Mr. Harrod and Wayne both seemed pleased with his offer.

Johnny, who tagged along behind throwing rocks at clumps of grass, asked if he could go along the next day.

Mr. Harrod quickly said, "No."

Dave understood that the boy wanted to be a part of the men's work, but nine was a little young for a boy to herd cattle.

Obviously, Mr. Harrod and Wayne did well with the ranch and had several hands working for them. They ran close to ten thousand head of cattle on fifty thousand acres. Through the thirty years Mr. Harrod had ranched in the area, he slowly bought the land to the west and south of the main ranch. He had been especially careful about obtaining deeds to land with water holes. By not over grazing, he managed to survive during the drought years with his cattle in good shape.

As they talked of the on-going work of such a large ranch, Dave concluded that Mr. Harrod really did need any help he could get. Dave decided that he would stay around for a couple of weeks and help them as much as possible. It was one way to repay a little of what the Harrod's had done by taking care of Johnny. Dave felt at ease talking with the men, and the hurt he'd experienced that morning as he'd stood on the porch and listened to Rachel's words receded.

Before he was ready for it, they heard a bell ringing from the direction of the main house.

"That's the dinner bell." Mr. Harrod climbed down from the railing of the corral where he'd sat as they talked.

"I'll head back to my place for dinner. Nancy will have it waiting," Wayne said. "This afternoon I'll take a wagon into town to pick up some supplies. What are your plans, Pa?" Wayne waited for his father to speak.

"I thought I would ride out and look over the herd before we start moving it tomorrow." Looking from Wayne to Dave, he continued. "You're free to do what you wish, Dave, either go to town with Wayne or ride out with me. For that matter, do nothing at all if you want."

Dave wasn't ready to face the town. Too many people knew him. "I'd like to ride out with you and look over the herd if that's all right."

Wayne nodded. "Fine. I'll see you at supper then. Ma asked us over so you can meet Nancy and the boys. We'll be over around six. I think Ma told me to tell Nancy to bring a pie." With a wave of his hand, Wayne walked toward his house that was about a quarter of a mile down the lane from the new barn.

Dave and Mr. Harrod walked toward the main house. This was the first opportunity Dave had had to be alone with Mr. Harrod since he used the razor without asking permission. It wasn't something he would have done under normal circumstances. Dave felt that a man's razor was a personal thing and wasn't to be shared.

Getting his courage up he said, "I got to confess something. I used your razor and shaving mug this morning. I thought I should let you know."

Mr. Harrod laughed. "I wondered if you would tell me. I didn't shave this morning yet I noticed the mug was wet when we left to walk out here." He stopped walking and looked intently at Dave. "You heard what Rachel said this morning, didn't you? You shaved off the beard because of what she said."

Dave saw no reason not to be truthful. "Yes, I heard and I want you to know I'm not here to take Johnny away from you. I do want to get to know him and be a part of his life from now on if I can. But I know he's better off here with you folks. He couldn't have a better home or be better cared for, so Rachel doesn't need to worry."

"I believe you, Dave, and I'll tell Ma, just to ease her mind. But you know, it might do Rachel good to have to stew a bit. She was rough on you this morning. It's not like her, but she was anyway." Pausing to think, he continued, "Let's not say anything to Rachel nor Johnny about this and just see what happens."

Dave didn't understand Mr. Harrod's reasoning. He would have thought it just as well to set Rachel's mind at ease too, but he would defer to the older man's judgment.

"Since you used my razor, then I guess that means you don't have one of your own."

"No, I lost it last fall when I got shot. And since I was used to the beard I didn't bother to buy one last week when I finally got to a store."

"Well, don't worry about it. I have another one someone gave me last Christmas that I haven't used. I'll look for it this evening. You might as well use it."

They climbed the back porch and Johnny ran up from the opposite direction. Johnny soon had them both laughing at his tale about trying to catch a lizard by the tail, as they washed up in the basin on the porch.

Upon entering the kitchen, Dave didn't feel like laughing. The feeling of distrust coming at him from Rachel, where she stood by the stove, seemed to lower the temperature in the room considerably. There was no welcome smile from her as there was from Mrs. Harrod.

Dave wasn't going to let Rachel ruin his enjoyment of Johnny's company. He had already missed so much of Johnny's life and had no reassurance that he would get to spend much time with him in the future. This time, as they sat down at the table loaded with food, Dave was prepared to have his hands taken for the blessing.

Just as Mr. Harrod had predicted, Johnny was over his shyness at meeting his father and kept up a running commentary on anything that came to his mind.

Throughout the meal, Dave was aware of Rachel's silence, but he didn't try to talk to her. Instead, he enjoyed the talk with the Harrods and the questions from his son who never seemed to run out of words.

When Mr. Harrod announced what he and Dave planned for the afternoon, Johnny immediately wanted to come along. After talking it over with Mrs. Harrod and checking if he had done all of his chores, he was given permission to tag along. Dave was glad Johnny was allowed to come, but he noticed the look of disapproval on Rachel's face. The only way he could satisfy her would be to go away.

After the meal, the men went to the barn to saddle up. As they rode out, Dave was pleased to see that Johnny was a good rider for his age. He'd half-expected Johnny to ride in all directions but evidently, Johnny seemed to know that one of the rules of riding with the men was to stick close to his grandpa and do what he was told.

Dave could see the ranch was well cared for and prosperous. The main ranch buildings were in good repair as were the corrals. He'd only seen a couple of hands that morning, but as they rode out toward the herd, he saw a wagon and several hands busy repairing fences. As they neared the herd, he saw several other riders working in various directions. Evidently, they were bunching the herd in preparation for the move. One of the riders broke away from chasing some stubborn steers back toward the herd and rode to meet them.

"Howdy, Mr. Harrod, the herd looks good. We should be ready to move tomorrow."

"Cody, this here is my son-in-law, Dave Kimbrough, Johnny's Pa." Mr. Harrod said in a way of introduction. "Dave, this is Cody Brown, he's in charge of this herd. He's a good hand."

Dave reached across and shook hands with the young rider who didn't look any older than twenty.

Broad shouldered and lean of hip like many riders, Cody had an open, good-natured face. Dave liked him at first sight.

"Hey, Johnny, you here to help rope some calves?" Cody grinned and winked.

"Sure, Cody, where do you want me to start?" Johnny leaned forward in the saddle.

"Maybe next time." Mr. Harrod voice was also teasing.

Dave suspected that this was a running tease with Johnny. He liked the easy way Johnny interacted with the young rider. He remembered when he was Johnny's age and knew he hadn't had as much self-confidence. His own childhood had been so much more isolated than Johnny's. His mother had drawn his father out of his shell and provided the family with interaction with others. After her death, his father had not really changed, but instead returned to his former behavior.

In the last years since Jenny's death, he'd chosen to behave much like his father, even in ways he didn't like. As he watched his son talk with the young cowhand and his grandfather, Dave felt he'd done a good thing for Jonathan by leaving him with his grandparents. He could have done worse.

As he listened to Mr. Harrod and Cody make plans for the next day, Dave looked forward to working with them and the other riders. He just hoped he hadn't forgotten the skills necessary to work well with the cattle.

The afternoon faded as they headed back to the house. It had been a relaxed afternoon and Dave wished it could go on. He didn't look forward to suppertime, and Rachel's cold reception. He hoped that Wayne and his family being there would relieve some of the tension for him.

After taking care of his horse, Dave went to the bunkhouse to change his shirt. His other shirt wasn't too clean either, but at least it wasn't sweaty from the afternoon ride. While changing, he heard a wagon roll into the yard, and Johnny yelling. Children's voices answered. Wayne had arrived with his family. To give them time to get into the house, he went out to the trough and rinsed out his shirt. He hung it on a chair to dry.

Dave walked across the yard and into the kitchen.

Wayne said, "Come on in, Dave, and meet Nancy."

A pleasant looking redheaded woman in her middle twenties put the dish she carried on the table and turned to him with her hand out. She shook Dave's hand with a strong firm grip. "It's good to meet you and finally be able to put a face to a name. Wayne has talked about you since before we married."

Dave liked her straightforward way and felt a positive acceptance coming from her. "I'm glad to meet you too, Nancy."

"These are our boys, Matt is three." Nancy pointed to a chubby redheaded three-year-old who giggled as he bounced up and down on his father's foot. "And our David is five." Nancy indicated a blond-haired, serious looking boy who sat next to Johnny at the table ready for supper. "Boys, this is your Uncle Dave who's come to visit. This is Johnny's Pa."

Dave looked at Wayne who grinned back at him. "That's right, Dave, we named David after you. And he's carrying the name well." Wayne reached over and tousled his son's blond curls. "David's got his mother's smarts and his uncle's good looks."

Dave didn't know what to say. He'd known that he, Jesse, and Wayne had developed a good friendship in the years he and Jenny had been married. He'd no idea that Wayne felt it so strongly as to name his first born after him.

Before his silence could become awkward, Mrs. Harrod told everyone to find a seat, as supper was ready.

Dave found himself seated as usual by Johnny, with David on the other side of Johnny, and Mr. Harrod at the end of the table on his left. He found himself facing Rachel again. Wayne and Nancy were seated next to Rachel with Mrs. Harrod at the other end of the table and three-year-old Matt in the baby's chair next to her.

Dave recognized it as the same baby chair he'd made when Johnny was born.

The family took each other's hands and bowed for the blessing, that Mr. Harrod had asked Wayne to offer, Dave felt that too much had happened too quickly. Only the day before he'd been at the springs worried about whether the Harrod's would even let him see Johnny.

He looked around the table at the bowed heads and felt overwhelmed at the welcome they had given him, all except Rachel. He was still looking at her bowed head when amen was said.

She raised her head and caught him staring at her. Their eyes held for a moment before she turned away. Dave felt a tingling through his body as if struck by a bolt of lightning. Something about Rachel drew his eyes and left him wanting... something.

Dave was saved from having to make much conversation during the meal and even later as they sat out on the back porch in the cool of the evening. The Harrod's were a talkative family and the talk centered on family doings and the work of the ranch. Wayne and Mr. Harrod made plans for moving the herd and getting some fences repaired.

Mrs. Harrod, Nancy, and Rachel talked of the gardening, recipes, and the children.

The three boys wandered in and out, as they played together.

Dave felt carried along with them as if he'd never left. He was included in the talk, but left alone when he didn't have anything to say. Except for the talk he'd had with Mr. Harrod at the springs, no one had asked any questions about his life of the last six years.

When Wayne and his family headed home, Dave said his goodnights and returned to the old bunkhouse. He planned to be up early the next morning to ride out with Mr. Harrod and the cowhands. Exhausted in spite of having slept in that morning, he was ready for some silence and be by himself. The day had been the first time in six years that he'd been around so many people who were constantly in conversation and it was going to take some getting used to. Images of the beautiful upper valley in the mountains filled his mind as he drifted off to sleep. It had been so peaceful there.

Chapter 9

When Dave woke the next morning it was still dark, but he sensed that daybreak wasn't far away. He got up and opened the door. Lights were on in the kitchen of the house, and as he looked toward the barn and corrals, he could see other lights. The men were up getting ready for the day's work.

Dave started to close the door and noticed a small bundle on the step of the bunkhouse. He picked it up, closed the door, and lit the lantern. Opening the box, he found a shaving mug, straight razor that folded into the handle, and a small mirror.

Mr. Harrod had remembered their conversation and had kept his word.

Wishing for hot water, Dave grasped the pitcher, quickly poured some cold water into the basin, and hurriedly shaved. It was much easier this morning because he wasn't shaving off a beard. After he'd cleaned up the shaving gear and thrown the dirty water out the back door, he finished dressing for the day. He wished for a jacket. The early morning air was cool, but by midday, it would be hot. His long coat was too much, so he went in his shirtsleeves. He also wished for the chaps that he'd cut into strips to make the snowshoes. Chaps helped protect a man's pants from the wear and tear of riding through the brush on the range.

Others on the drive would have their rifles as well as handguns. When handling cattle they never knew what might happen, and Dave felt better having his own weapon handy. Picking up his rifle, canteen, and gloves, Dave blew out the lantern and walked across to the house. He was surprised to see Rachel in the kitchen dressed in a shirt, divided skirt, and boots.

"Morning, Dave." Mrs. Harrod walked over to him from the stove where she had bacon frying. Before he had time to put the rifle in the corner, she gave him a hug and kiss on the cheek. "You look better this morning, son. You must have slept well. Now sit at the table and eat a big breakfast. You'll need it working the cattle."

"Morning," he responded.

Mrs. Harrod took his canteen, gloves and hat. She put the hat and gloves on a shelf by the door and took the canteen to the pump at the kitchen sink to fill it.

Dave put the rifle in the corner and then he sat at what was now his usual place at the table. Rachel placed a steaming cup of fresh coffee in front of him.

"Thank you, Rachel." He looked up at her.

Rachel accepted the thanks with a nod and turned back to the stove where Mrs. Harrod dished up plates of fried eggs, bacon, and fried potatoes. Rachel placed the food in front of the men, and Mrs. Harrod added a pan of hot biscuits and a bowl of gravy on the table.

Mr. Harrod said a prayer for the food.

Dave grinned at Mrs. Harrod. "Sure am glad I made it for this breakfast."

Mr. Harrod took three biscuits. "Well, eat up. We'll have the noon meal out on the range at the chuckwagon. I promise it won't be as good as Ma's cooking."

They didn't waste time talking but quickly ate and were soon ready to leave the house.

Rachel left the kitchen first. When he and Mr. Harrod walked out to the corral, she was already mounted. She wore a felt hat that shaded her face, and her hair hanging down her back in a thick braid. She was so pretty sitting on her horse that Dave had to work to keep from staring.

He was surprised that she rode out with them. The others seemed to accept it as a matter of course. It brought up the memory of Jenny riding out beside him to herd cattle before Jonathan was born.

Dave rode his mare at the beginning of the day, but suspected that before the day was over, he would exchange mounts from the remuda several times as the horses tired from the rough riding.

Cody Brown was in charge. "Dave, you can start out at drag."

Being at the back of the herd was the dustiest place to work. Dave knew that Cody didn't know of his abilities and had placed him at the spot for the least experienced hand. He pulled his bandana up over his nose and mouth to keep some of the dust out of his mouth and lungs and worked hard keeping the stragglers bunched up with the slow moving herd.

After a couple of hours, Cody rode up. "How's it going?"

Dave pulled down the bandana. "Fine. There are the usual cows that don't want to get moving but no big problem. I do need to go catch another horse. My mare needs a break."

Cody nodded. "You do that and then start as swing rider over there on the left flank. I'll have Randy take up drag."

Dave nodded and headed toward the remuda driven by Manuel. A big black gelding was soon roped and his saddle moved from his mare to the fresh mount. With a wave at Manuel, Dave headed over to the new position. He had to ride harder to keep the herd bunched up and moving but there was considerably less dust. Using his coiled rope as an encouragement for the cattle to keep with the herd and while adjusting to the new mount Dave drove himself to show Cody that he could handle the new position. The day was one of hard riding, but Dave enjoyed it.

It was the first time in a long time that he had worked with men in such an open way without fear of the law.

Throughout the morning, he kept track of Rachel's activities. He was impressed to see that she was a superb rider and not only kept up with the men, but out rode several of them.

At noon, the men ate in shifts and kept the herd moving slowly. Mr. Harrod saw no reason to hurry the herd as that would only work off fat. The first day of a drive was always the hardest as the cattle were not inclined to keep moving.

Mr. Harrod rode up in the middle of the afternoon, and Dave stopped for a few minutes to give his horse a breather.

"How's it going?" Mr. Harrod handed him a full canteen and took the one Dave had emptied.

"I'm doing okay." Dave grinned at him. "My backside is getting more of a workout than usual. I haven't herded cattle for a couple of years."

"Doesn't look like you've forgotten any of your ranching skills." Mr. Harrod looked out over the herd. Dave could tell when he caught sight of Rachel on the far side because his face softened.

Dave took a swig of water from the canteen. "She rides well and evidently has helped you with cattle before."

"Yes, she likes to help but it always makes me uneasy. You know cattle can be unpredictable. I would appreciate your help keeping an eye on her." Mr. Harrod removed his hat and wiped his face and neck with his bandana. "The new pasture is about fifteen miles. We'll stop early today and take two more days. Tonight I'll leave a few riders to keep the cattle bunched. We'll return to the ranch house for supper and sleep in our own beds."

By the time they rode into the ranch yard, Dave was exhausted. He'd worked hard all day, partly because that was the only way he knew to work, and partly because he knew Wayne and Mr. Harrod were watching him. They were all tired and after a supper of fried chicken and little talk, Dave excused himself and headed for bed. Johnny tried to liven things up with his chatter, but Mrs. Harrod was the only one doing much responding to him.

When Dave got to his room, he found his few clothes washed and ironed. He appreciated Mrs. Harrod's thoughtfulness. The clothes he'd worked in that day were filthy from the dust and sweat. After stripping, he wrapped a towel around his waist, turned out the lantern, and went out back to the trough. Bathing in the cold water was a relief from the dust and heat of the day. He didn't linger but headed back into the bunkhouse and was soon asleep.

The next morning they all packed bedrolls for they would sleep out under the stars that night. The dawn was softly shedding light over the land as they headed out.

Mr. Harrod wouldn't let Rachel sleep out with the men, so she didn't ride with them. Dave was acutely aware all day that she wasn't there. The day seemed longer and less bright.

Even with the dust and heat, Dave enjoyed the next two days of hard riding. The cattle were fat from the spring grass and were not inclined to move on to the new grazing, but the afternoon of the third day they reached the new range. He gazed out over the tall grass where the herd would spend the summer fattening up even more. In the fall, Mr. Harrod and Wayne would sell this particular herd. Dave was relieved that he didn't have to stay at the line shack that was close to several different water sources. Mr. Harrod left two cowhands to ride herd on the cattle. Another pair of cowhands would relieve the cowpunchers every month.

Since they were closer to Rock Corner than the ranch, Wayne and Mr. Harrod decided they would all ride into town that evening and spend the night at the boarding house.

❖   ❖   ❖

Rachel had enjoyed the day out on the range. It was hot, sweaty work, and she was exhausted by the end of the day. She knew she was really a help and could herd cattle as well as any of the men. She did admit to herself that she showed off a little with her riding. She could tell that Dave had kept his eye on her. Why it mattered to her what he thought she didn't know, but it did.

The next morning she watched the men ride back to the herd with their bedrolls attached to their saddles. She had mixed feelings about staying behind. In a way, she wanted to show Dave she was as tough as the riders were, but she didn't really want to sleep on the hard ground and appreciated her bed.

Rachel kept busy helping her mother bake and clean. She also tried to help keep Johnny busy because he also missed the men. On the second day, she went to the bunkhouse and swept it out. Two shirts and a pair of pant hung on the hooks and were in worse shape than the dust cloth she was using. He must have taken the other clothes with him. Looking around at how neatly Dave kept his things, she was puzzled at how little he had.

She gathered some flowers from the garden, took them into the kitchen, and placed half of the flowers in a vase on the table. On impulse, she put the other half in a jar and then left it on the table in the bunkhouse.

Her thoughts kept returning to the tall, thin man with the ruggedly handsome face. She did like that he had shaved his beard off. She shook her head to clear it of such thoughts.

"What's wrong, Aunt Rachel? Why are you shaking your head?" Johnny had come into the kitchen.

"There's nothing wrong, honey. I just have cobwebs in my brain and need to shake them out." She smiled at Johnny.

"How do you know if you got cobwebs and how did you get them?" Johnny sat at the table.

Rachel wanted to laugh and couldn't think how to explain the expression so a nine year old would understand. "Have you washed your hands for supper?" She hoped that would get her past his question.

"No ma'am. I'll do it now. Are we going to eat soon?" Johnny walked to the back porch and poured some water into the basin.

Rachel followed him and looked toward the south where the men were herding the cattle. "Yes, as soon as the biscuits are done. It'll just be your grandma, you, and me this evening."

"I wish Grandpa and Pa would get back. I miss them." Johnny dried his hands and went into the kitchen.

As he passed her, Rachel pushed his hair back from his eyes. "I know you do. But remember that we're going into town tomorrow and they'll probably be there. Pa said they would spend tonight at the boarding house."

Johnny's eyes lit up and a big grin spread across his face. "I forgot we're going in the morning. Going to town is fun."

Rachel took the pan of biscuits out of the oven and set them on the table. They were having a light supper of biscuits and warmed up gravy.

Mrs. Harrod came into the kitchen. "Oh, you've rescued the biscuits. I could smell them clear upstairs and knew they were done. Have you washed your hands, Johnny?" Mrs. Harrod sat at the table.

"Yes ma'am. I'm ready to eat." He sat at his usual place.

"Would you say the blessing for us?" Rachel took Ma and Johnny's hands.

"Sure." Johnny bowed his head and gave a short, but appropriate prayer. He had a way of keeping his prayers short at the beginning of a meal. He already had two biscuits open on his plate and spooned a generous serving of gravy on top of them.

Mrs. Harrod only took one biscuit. "I'm glad tomorrow is Saturday. I worry about the men out on the cattle drive. I like them all back at home."

"Are you worried about anything particular or just because it's a cattle drive." Rachel wasn't sure what was bothering her mother.

"Oh, nothing specific. But you know men do get hurt when working around those cattle."

Mrs. Harrod took a drink from her glass of tea.

Johnny looked up from his plate that was almost empty. "You think Grandpa or Pa will get hurt?"

Rachel was reminded again how children took what was said so literal. "No, Ma didn't mean that. She just knows that sometimes it happens. But nothing is going to happen to Grandpa, nor your pa." She found it strange to be referring to

Johnny's pa. It had been so many years that they hardly referred to Dave and usually, not in Johnny's hearing. She was still getting used to it.

Daylight was just filtering through the window of the room at the boarding house. Dave dressed and went down to the dining room, leaving the other three cowhands he'd shared the room with all snoring in their bunks. Dave had forgotten how cowhands could snore, and he hadn't slept well. He planned to buy another set of clothes, and then head back to the ranch. He figured Mr. Harrod would ride back with the Mrs. Harrod, Rachel, and Johnny.

Wayne and Mr. Harrod came in to the dining room as Dave attacked his second stack of flapjacks.

Mr. Harrod sat at the table. "Morning, Dave, you're up early. Did you get any sleep sharing that room with those noisy fellows?"

Wayne sat and reached for the coffeepot. "It couldn't have been any noisier than your snoring, Pa. I don't know how Ma puts up with you."

"She does it out of love, son, out of pure love." Mr. Harrod and Wayne both laughed.

Dave sat and grinned at them, envying the easy relationship that the father and son had. Dave wondered if his father had lived would they have ever reached a point that they treated each other as equal adults. He somehow doubted it.

"What are your plans for the day, Dave?" Mr. Harrod helped himself to the food that was on the table.

"I want to go to the general store for some things, and then I thought I would ride back to the ranch," Dave responded. "Does Mr. Smithy still run the store?"

"Sure, he's still here and he's got his boy working with him now," Wayne said. "Well, I'm riding out as soon as I eat. Nancy and the boys have been at her folk's place since Thursday. I need to go get her before the grandparents finish spoiling the boys rotten." Turning to his father he asked, "Pa, you going to check on that fencing? Smithy said it ought to be in by now. We need it for the holding pens and I don't want to leave it too late."

"You're right, we want to get that job started. I'll go over with Dave and ask about it. You know Smithy, if we don't stay on top of it, he'll let it slide. Ma and the girls should be there at the store sometime this morning."

It took Dave a moment to think who he meant by girls. He'd forgotten that Mary lived in town and would be meeting with her sister and mother.

As soon as Wayne had eaten, he left them to ride out to his in-law's place.

Mr. Harrod and Dave lingered over a last cup of coffee. As they spoke of the week's happenings and plans for the ranch, Mr. Harrod talked as if Dave planned to stay around. It made him feel uneasy, as if things were decided that he had no control over. But since he'd no real plans of his owns he didn't know what to tell Mr. Harrod.

Dave could see how he could settle at the ranch and work for Mr. Harrod. Compared to the last few years, it would be an easy life. There was no real future for him at the ranch, but he wanted more time with his son. As he and Mr. Harrod walked over to the general store, he made the decision that he would remain through the summer, then after the fall work was done, move on. He would leave his decision for a few weeks, see how things were going, and then talk to Mr. Harrod of his plans.

They arrived early to the mercantile, but the street was already busy with families and riders coming to town for their Saturday shopping. Rock Corner was the biggest town within a hundred miles.

Dave saw several faces that he remembered from the past. He noticed that people watched as he and Mr. Harrod entered the store, but no one came up to talk to them. Dave grew nervous as people recognized him.

He still had difficulty believing he was a free man and had no worries about walking the streets. Not wearing a gun made him feel even more insecure, for there was always a chance of someone not knowing of the dropped charges. But the town had a no-weapons policy. Dave wanted to get his shopping done and ride back to the ranch as soon as possible.

While Mr. Harrod talked with Smithy about the ranch supplies, Dave wandered. He still had twenty-two dollars from the sale of the furs, but that had to last a while, how long he didn't know. He looked longingly at a pair of chaps, but decided to do without them. He chose two shirts, a pair of pants, and drawers. At the last moment, he added a denim jacket to the stack. He walked up to the counter to pay for his purchases.

Mr. Harrod looked from Dave to Smithy. "You remember my son-in-law, Dave Kimbrough, don't you? This is Johnny's Pa."

Smithy reached across the counter to shake Dave's hand. "Sure I remember you Dave. Welcome back."

Noticing Dave about to get his money out, Mr. Harrod waved his hand. "Put your money away, Dave. This goes on the ranch bill. Smithy, anything Dave needs you put it down to the ranch."

"I appreciate that, but you all are already feeding me." Dave didn't know whether to insist or not.

Since Smithy had already written the items in a ledger, Dave decided not to object.

"No problem, Jake, we'll just add Dave to the ledger," Smithy replied.

Dave had almost forgotten Mr. Harrod's name was Jake. He'd always called them Mr. and Mrs. Harrod. Years ago, they had told him to call them whatever he chose. He'd not felt free enough to call them Ma and Pa as Jenny had and felt it disrespectful to call them Jake and Minnie.

Rachel drove into the wagon yard and turned the team and wagon over to the man in charge. Mr. Harrod would get it later to be loaded with supplies to take back to the ranch.

"Can I go find my friends?" Johnny jumped up and down in anticipation.

His grandma took her big basket out of the wagon. "Yes, but keep an eye out for your grandpa. He'll want to see you."

"Yes, ma'am." Johnny took off in a run.

"Ma, you know we may not see him for hours now." Rachel put her arm through the curve of her mother's arm as they slowly walked toward the main part of town. Rachel looked at each man she saw, expecting to see Dave.

"I know but I didn't give Johnny any money for candy so I think he'll check back with us." Her mother chuckled and patted her arm.

"I should have known. That's what you used to do to us kids." Rachel saw her sister just ahead on the boardwalk in front of the general store. "Mary!"

She turned and waved. "Ma, Rachel. I hoped I would find you all here."

Mrs. Harrod gave her older daughter a kiss on the cheek. "We're looking for your pa. The men stayed at the boarding house last night if they got the herd situated."

"I thought I would come home with you and visit a few days." Mary shaded her eyes against the sun.

"By the way, Mary, Dave came home. He should be with your father," Mrs. Harrod said quietly.

Mary looked from her mother to Rachel. "You mean Dave Kimbrough, Johnny's father?"

Rachel nodded. "Yes, and it seems that he may stay awhile." Rachel hadn't meant for her tone to be so dry.

Mrs. Harrod shifted her basket from one hand to the other. "We are so thankful. It is an answer to prayer."

"Hello." Mrs. Jones spoke as she walked up to the group on the boardwalk followed by Mrs. Yeager.

Stepping back, Rachel gave the two ladies from church space, as she knew they wanted to speak to her mother.

Rachel stood and let the conversation roll around her. She watched people going in and out of the general store when she saw her father and Dave come out. For some reason her stomach gave a twist and her breathing seemed to slow as she watched the tall cowhand walk toward her. She couldn't help noticing how masculine and ruggedly handsome he was.

Dave and Mr. Harrod had just left the store carrying their purchases when Johnny ran up to them at in at full speed.

"Hey, slow down there partner," admonished Mr. Harrod.

"Hey, Grandpa, Pa." Johnny grinned up at them.

"Where's your Grandma?" Mr. Harrod gave Johnny a hug.

As if it were the normal thing, Johnny gave Dave a hug as he answered his grandfather.

"They're talking to some ladies up the street."

As Dave returned the greeting from his son, he felt a twist in his being. He was surprised at how strongly he felt seeing Johnny after only a two day's absent. Just being with the boy did something to him that he hadn't felt in a long time, as if a part of him that had been hidden was discovered again.

Dave followed Mr. Harrod up the boardwalk and spotted Mrs. Harrod, Rachel, and a very stylish young lady talking to a couple of older ladies.

Mary had always been the quiet, studious one of the family. She hadn't changed as much as Rachel over the last six years. Dave would have recognized her anywhere. She excused herself from the others and walked up to Dave.

"Dave Kimbrough, I don't know whether to be mad or glad to see you. I'm so pleased you're back for Johnny's sake, but what in the world took you so long?" She gave him an intent look.

Dave removed his hat and stood looking down at her serious face. "Hello, Mary, it's good to see you too, and I don't know what took me so long."

Mr. Harrod cleared his throat. "At least he's here now, and for that we are all thankful."

Johnny looked up from Mary to Dave. "Aren't you happy to see Pa, Aunt Mary?" His voice was anxious.

Reaching over to tug his hat down, Mary gave him a smile. "Yes, Johnny, I'm happy to see your pa, but I had to fuss at him for being so long coming back just as I fuss at you when you're late for school."

Mary's response to Johnny broke the tension of their meeting. They were laughing when Mrs. Harrod and Rachel waved goodbye to their friends and joined them.

Mrs. Harrod gave her husband a kiss on the cheek and then turned to hug Dave. "I'm glad to see you're in one piece. Did Wayne ride on to Frank's place?"

"Yes, he rode out right after breakfast," Mr. Harrod gave Rachel and Mary both hugs. "They should be back at the ranch by the time we get there."

Dave had been acutely aware of Rachel's presence. In the hubbub of Mrs. Harrod and Mary's greetings, she'd acknowledged Dave with a nod. For some reason he felt let down that she didn't give him a hug as she had her father. He wanted the tension eased and the barrier removed from between them.

Mrs. Harrod told Mr. Harrod that Mary would come home with them for the night and attend church the next morning.

Dave noticed that people on the street watched as the family chatted. His uneasiness returned in full force, it was time for him to return to the ranch.

He waited for a break in the conversation. "It's good to see you again Mary, and I'll see you this evening at the ranch. Mr. Harrod, I'm going to ride back to the ranch."

"I understand, Dave, all these women talking gets me down too. You go on and take your time getting back. After the work you've put in these last three days you deserve a rest," Mr. Harrod said with a grin.

Mrs. Harrod spoke up. "There's plenty of food at the house. You go on in and help yourself. I declare but you've gotten thinner in just the last two days."

Dave sensed that Mrs. Harrod would not rest until she'd gotten enough food into him to replace some of the weight he'd lost over the winter. He was down about thirty pounds compared to when he'd left six years earlier.

"Can I ride back with you, Pa?" Johnny asked. "Can I, Grandpa?"

His son wanting to ride back to the ranch with him surprised Dave but also pleased him. He held his breath as he waited for Mr. Harrod's reply.

"That'll be fine, if your pa doesn't mind putting up with you. What do you think, Mother?" Mr. Harrod turned to his wife for her approval.

"Why that would be all right with me, if it's all right with Dave. Would you mind Johnny tagging along with you?" questioned Mrs. Harrod.

"I'd be pleased to have him ride with me." Dave grinned at Johnny who grinned back.

Dave noticed that Rachel wasn't smiling with the rest of the family. She wasn't actually frowning, but near enough.

Dave wanted to say something to her, but didn't know what. He couldn't think of anything to reassure her that he wasn't taking Johnny away from her.

Chapter 10

Dave walked across the street to the boarding house to get his bedroll and rifle with Johnny trailing behind. Then they headed to the livery where Dave saddled the horses.

Dave hadn't realized how tense he'd been until they rode out of town. Only then did he start to feel a sense of relief. He was surprised by how easily he could talk with Johnny.

"Where do you live, Pa, when you're not here?"

"I don't really live anywhere. I've been moving from place to place."

That seemed to puzzle the boy. "Everyone I know lives somewhere."

"Well, this past winter I did live in one place. I lived in a cave up in the mountains."

"No kidding, that's great. Was it a big cave?"

Dave almost laughed at how impressed Johnny was with the idea of living in a cave.

"Not too big, but it had a fair sized room and a stream flowing through it," Dave told the boy. He didn't tell him the reason he was in the cave, nor of the pain and hunger he had suffered through the winter. He didn't want his son to experience it even in the telling. Johnny had a safe protected childhood and that was the way Dave wanted to keep it.

"Are you going back to the cave to live?" The boy rode easy in the saddle as he turned toward his father.

"I don't think so. I might visit it some day, but I don't think I want to live there again." Dave did tell him of the mountains and the upper valley where he hoped to have a ranch someday.

"Will you take me with you when you go to start your ranch?"

The look Johnny gave him told Dave much more than the words. His son was having fears of his going also, as Rachel had, except his fear was of again being left behind.

Dave didn't know what to say to the nine-year-old. He wouldn't lie and promise something he didn't know if he could keep. On the other hand, his son needed some sort of reassurance from him.

"Johnny, I'll tell you the truth, I don't know what I'll be able to do. I want you with me, but I'm not going to promise something I might not be able to do. I didn't take you with me when you were a baby because I couldn't. It wasn't because I didn't want you or love you. I just couldn't take you with me. And I couldn't stay with you either. Do you understand at all what I'm trying to say?" Dave heard a pleading in his voice.

Johnny didn't respond at first, but rode along in silence for a while. Then he looked at his father. "I didn't know you wanted me when I was a baby. I'm glad."

Dave didn't know what to say. He'd never imagined what the boy had thought about his going.

"I just got one thing to ask, Pa."

"Sure, son, what's that?" Dave hoped he could answer whatever it was.

"If you have to go away again and leave me behind, will you tell me before you go?"

Dave reined up on his horse, reached over and pulled back on the reins of the other horse. He bent down to be at eye level with his son. "I promise before I leave I'll tell you and what's more I promise to come back. Let's shake on it."

Very solemnly, they shook hands before riding on down the road. Dave's words seemed to satisfy the boy.

Johnny wiped his brow. "I'm getting hot, Pa. There's a creek not far ahead with some good-sized cottonwoods and with a nice place to swim. You want to go see it?"

"Sure, lead the way." The idea of going swimming was especially appealing considering the day getting hotter. Dave let Johnny guide him off the road down to the creek. He remembered the creek, but not the swimming hole. After letting the horses drink, they tied them near by in the shade of the cottonwoods. They stripped and plunged into the cold water. Dave was pleased to see that Johnny was a strong swimmer. The water felt good after two days of dust and sweat of the cattle drive. Dave enjoyed the sensation of floating in the water.

Johnny was more energetic and soon splashed water at his father.

Laughing, Dave swam to the bottom and picked up some small pebbles. Resurfacing, he threw the pebbles in Johnny's direction, yelling at him to dodge the bullets.

The boy picked up on the game and dove down to get some pebbles of his own. His first throw caught Dave on the shoulder.

Laughing and yelling they both enjoyed the game that Dave had learned from the Indian, Charlie, until Dave cried for mercy and declared Johnny the victor. After they got out of the water, they lay on the grassy bank letting the sun dry them.

Dave lay with his eyes closed about to doze off when he realized how quiet Johnny was. Opening his eyes, he found Johnny staring at him with a serious look. "What's the matter?" He sat up.

"You sure been hurt bad lots of times." He pointed to Dave's chest and the scars left from the gunshot wound of the previous fall.

The wolf had left one hand with several jagged scars and claw marks on his leg. The bear had left his marks on Dave's neck. His body carried other marks from old injuries. Because most of the wounds had happened within the last year, those scars were still prominent against the white flesh.

He couldn't decide if Johnny was more impressed or concerned. He hadn't thought much about his different injuries. They had all just been something that happened, and he'd dealt with. These were not a normal part of Johnny's world, and he was intrigued with his father's life.

Dave decided to make light of it, "Yeah, I've just been at the wrong place at the wrong time. I'm hungry. Let's head in and see what we can find to eat at the house."

He quickly put on his clothes, but Johnny still sat on the grass as if thinking through something.

"Come on, get dressed, and let's go," Dave urged.

"All right, Pa. Can we come swimming again soon and play dodges the bullets?"

Dave wished he'd called it something else now, but that was what old Indian Charlie had called the game. "Sure, if I don't die of hunger first. Get dressed." Dave put his boots on and got the horses while Johnny dressed.

After they arrived at the ranch and took care of the horses, they headed for the kitchen where they found Maria, Manuel's wife, baking for Mrs. Harrod.

"Hey, Mrs. Maria. Grandma said there might be something to eat?" Johnny gave a grin.

"For you and your papa, there is food." She quickly set out fried chicken and biscuits for them and even let them have a big wedge of fresh baked apple pie.

Dave ate the last crumb of the piece of pie and leaned back in his chair content. "I heard your grandma talking about some things she wanted repaired here in the house. What do you say to you and me doing some carpentry work?"

Johnny's eyes got big. "Can I help? Like maybe do some nailing?"

"Sure, if you will tell me where to get the tools and stuff." Dave had to grin at the boy's obvious pleasure at being allowed to help. "What do we need to work on?"

"Well, Grandma told Grandpa that the banister is loose on the stairs. There's a shelf that came down in my room. Aunt Rachel has been trying to get a window unstuck in her room."

"And Señor Dave, this cabinet door is loose." Maria chimed in.

"Let's get started then."

They spent the afternoon repairing things around the house. Dave knew how it was on a ranch. With the work never ending with the cattle, and ranch buildings and corrals to repair, the house was usually the last place attended to unless the women insisted. Dave was glad to find something he could do to please Mrs. Harrod, and maybe even Rachel, but he didn't have much hope in that direction.

Dave had always excelled in working with wood and tools. His father had started teaching him and Indian Charlie had continued. By the time Dave had a place of his own, he could do whatever was needed in terms of repairs or building.

Dave enjoyed working with his hands. He let Johnny help as much as he could and still get the job done. The pleased look on his son's face was all the reward Dave needed for the patience it took to work with a nine-year-old.

The afternoon was almost gone when the Harrod's came into the kitchen. Dave and Johnny sat on the floor re-hanging the cabinet door that Maria had pointed out. They had been so engrossed in their work they hadn't heard the wagon pull up to the house.

"What's going on in here?" Mr. Harrod put the box of groceries he carried on the table.

Mrs. Harrod, who came in behind him, laughed. "It looks like they're doing your work, Jake. It's about time someone fixed that cabinet door."

Johnny jumped up from the floor and began to tell them of the other repairs they had done. His pride in helping was evident. Dave could only gaze fondly a his son.

Mr. Harrod walked over and inspected the job Dave was finishing. "I can't thank you enough, son, for getting the little lady off my back. She's been after me for six months to do that and I just never got around to it."

"Glad to be of help to you, sir. Any thing else I can do to help out just let me know." Dave gathered up the tools.

Mary and Rachel came into the kitchen carrying packages.

"Come on, Johnny, help your Grandpa unload the wagon," Mr. Harrod said.

"Sure Grandpa. Did you get me anything from town?" he asked hopefully.

"Of course we did, a new hoe to help you keep down those weeds in the garden," he said, with a chuckle in his voice and a wink at Dave.

"Oh, Grandpa, you know what I mean. Did you get any hard candy?" Johnny asked in exasperation as he followed his grandfather out the back door.

Mary carried a valise. "Let's go change clothes and then help Ma with supper."

Rachel gathered up several packages and followed Mary up the stairs.

Dave wanted to be out of the kitchen before they returned. Four women scurrying about the kitchen was too much for him. He gave the cabinet door one more check, then taking the tools, followed Mr. Harrod and Johnny out the back door.

He could see that the wagon was packed, and they could use help unloading it. Manuel had come up to help and set boxes of groceries on the porch for Johnny to take into the house.

Mr. Harrod instructed Manuel. "The rest of this stuff either goes to the storeroom in the barn, or to the bunkhouse kitchen. Johnny and I will get these groceries into the house here."

Dave spoke up, "I'll get these tools put away and help Manuel unload the wagon."

"Thanks, Dave. I know he'll appreciate the help." He seemed pleased at Dave's offer. "Jesse and Edna sent word they're coming to spend the night. We'll have supper when they get here."

Dave had his things in the old bunkhouse where Jesse's family usually stayed. "Do you want me to clear out of the old bunkhouse and go down to the hand's bunkhouse to sleep?"

"My goodness, no, that old bunkhouse is now your place. Jesse and Edna will stay here in the house in Mary's room. The kids can sleep in Johnny's. Mary will sleep in Rachel's." Mr. Harrod explained with a chuckle. "And to tell you the truth Ma really prefers for everyone to sleep in the main house together. Why, she would rather that you slept upstairs, where she could keep an eye on you, than out at the old bunkhouse."

Dave was relieved that he wasn't loosing his place. He would have gladly bunked with the cowhands if needed, but he preferred having a place where he could retreat and get away from all these people. He didn't know if he would ever get used to so many people in one household. Yet the more he was around them, the more he became attached to them.

After he and Manuel unloaded the wagon, he went to change his shirt before going to the house for supper. Although earlier he'd dropped off his purchases from town onto his bed, he hadn't noticed that the baby's crib was no longer there. Someone had also swept the place and left a small vase of flowers on the table. Dave assumed it was Maria at Mrs. Harrod's instructions. It had been many years since anyone had done anything to show concern for his comfort. The touch of a woman's influence had been missing from his life since Jenny's death.

When he heard the horses and buggy pull into the yard, he knew that Jesse and his family had arrived. He waited until they settled in the house before he went across for supper. Wayne, Nancy, and the boys drove up from their place at the same time so he went into the house with them.

Jesse greeted Dave with a firm handshake and a look that told Dave he was truly glad to see him. Dave had always thought of Jesse as more quiet than Wayne, and he still seemed the same.

Dave remembered Edna because she and Jesse had married two years before Jenny died. She greeted him with a hug and a kiss on the cheek. "I'm awfully glad to see you. You look good, but too thin."

Dave decided he would have to put on some weight just to satisfy all these women.

Supper, with fourteen people around the large table, was a noisy affair. The grown-ups ate at the big table and the children, including Johnny, ate at a smaller table brought into the kitchen for that purpose.

Dave found himself seated next to Rachel. She engaged the others in animated talk, but it was evident to Dave that she deliberately avoided him. Except for polite greetings, she had yet to say anything to him since that awkward moment the first morning. Dave didn't try to force a conversation with her and really didn't enter much into the back and forth around the table unless spoken to directly. With so many others there, it wasn't necessary and he just listened to the happy, banter of the family. The things they talked about were of such a normal life compared to the one he'd lived the last few years that he felt distanced from them.

After the meal the men went out to sit on the back porch. The women cleared the dishes and started more food to cooking for the next day. Dave was impressed that planning the food for so many was such a major job for the women. As the men talked, and as Dave could hear some of the talk of the women from the kitchen, he concluded that the Harrod's still had the custom of attending church services every Sunday morning, only now they didn't go into town on Saturday and stay over night at the boarding house.

Mr. Harrod had told him that a couple of years after Dave left, the people in the community got together and built a church building at the community cemetery where Jenny was buried. It was located at the crossroads between the Harrod's Lazy H Ranch and Rock Corner. Now the distance was shorter to church services from the ranch. In telling Dave about the building of the church, Mr. Harrod had also casually mentioned that it was easier to tend the cemetery and Jenny's grave.

As Dave sat on the porch listening to the others, he decided he didn't want to attend services with the family the next morning. It had been too long and there would be too many people from the past. He felt a need to visit Jenny's grave, but not with people around. The Harrod's would assume he would go with them the next morning unless he said something.

Edna came to the door and asked Wayne and Jesse to get the children who played in the yard. It was time to start the baths for the little ones and tuck them in bed.

As Jesse and Wayne went in search of the children, Mr. Harrod asked Dave to walk with him to the barn where he had a sick horse he wanted to check on. Dave was glad for the chance to speak with Mr. Harrod without the others around.

As they walked toward the barn Dave said, "Mr. Harrod, about church in the morning. If you don't mind, I don't think I'll go with you. I need to take some time to ride out by myself."

"Is everything all right, Dave?"

"Sure, it's just that I haven't been around so many folks in a long time. I get to feeling hemmed in and to needing some time alone to think things through."

Mr. Harrod was quiet for a few minutes. "You know we're so used to the whole family being around that we tend to forget to look at things from a different point of view. We're just so glad to have you back and maybe forget that for you a lot of memories are being stirred up."

Dave felt relieved by the older man's understanding.

Standing outside the stall looking at the sick horse, Mr. Harrod turned to him. "Is Rachel's behavior bothering you? She hasn't been very friendly toward you. We can all see that. If you want, I'll talk to her."

Dave was quick to say, "No sir, don't worry about Rachel. I understand what she's feeling and it's no big problem." He couldn't say it didn't bother him because it did, more than he wanted to admit.

"Well, I'll do whatever I can to help you, Dave. I want you to feel a part of this family and free to let us know what you need. Ma will be disappointed you're not going to church with us, but she'll understand when I talk to her. She'll want you here for Sunday dinner tomorrow. On Sundays we usually just have one big meal in the middle of the afternoon."

Taking down the lantern to light their way back to the house, Mr. Harrod hesitated. "Dave, you got to do what's best for you. Even about dinner tomorrow, Ma wants you here but don't you worry about it. If you want to take off the whole day, that's fine. But I'll ask you, if you decide to leave again like before let me know, so I can be ready to help Johnny understand."

"Don't worry, Mr. Harrod, I'm not going to do that to Johnny. I've already promised him that before I leave I'll tell him."

As they approached the house, Dave decided he'd had enough for one day. "I'm going to turn in. Tell the others goodnight for me, will you?"

"I'm ready to turn in myself. You get some rest and we'll see you whenever you decide to show up tomorrow." Mr. Harrod turned and with a wave headed toward the back porch.

Dave cut across the backyard to the old bunkhouse. Not long after he'd gone in and closed the door, he heard a wagon leave taking Wayne and Nancy home with their children.

He laid awake for a long time, thinking of the week's events. He was surprised that the family was aware of Rachel's behavior. He hadn't realized the others paid that much attention to him. He wanted to talk to Rachel about it, but they were never alone. And he really didn't know what he could say to her.

Johnny's developing feelings for him was something he hadn't thought about either.

He grew fonder of the boy every day. The time spent with his son on the ride back to the ranch and the play at the swimming hole was like a gift. But that Johnny might be feeling the same fondness for his father was a new idea. It made him feel uneasy for some reason he didn't understand. Dave just knew he didn't want to do anything to turn his son away from him.

Chapter 11

Just after daylight, Dave rode the brown mare down the lane to the road and toward his old ranch. What did he hope to accomplish by seeing it? He rode the mare hard as if he needed to get there as soon as possible.

He came up over the hill and saw the ranch that he'd started before he'd met Jenny. He looked for a sense of her being there. But the ranch was changed. New barns and corrals had been added. The house was almost twice its original size. Jesse and Edna had added to it as their children were born. It wasn't his place anymore and the image he'd held on to of Jenny at the ranch seemed to drift further away.

He felt a sense of loss, not the acute grief like when she'd died, but a distant sense of past happiness that had gotten lost in his grief. For the first time he could really think of it as Jesse and Edna's place and be content with that. He couldn't think of anyone he would rather be living at his former ranch than Jesse and Edna and their children. He felt that Jenny was also pleased. As he sat on the mare looking down at his past, he tried to sense whether Jenny was still there but she was no longer a presence.

Dave rode away from his old ranch and knew there was somewhere else he needed to visit. He'd ridden the mare hard as if the ride would help him deal with the emotions that had rushed to come to the surface.

As he kicked the startled mare into a gallop, he sensed that something was just beneath the surface of his control, and was about to overwhelm him. For so many years, he'd held himself in tight control and hadn't let himself feel the weight of all the pain from his past.

He covered the miles between Jesse's place and the next place he felt compelled to visit in a fast half hour of riding. The mare tired as they approached the little cemetery.

Dave circled around the white church building and rode up to the cemetery from the back. The services were still going on. Horses, wagons, and buggies were staggered around the building. No one stood outside to see him and he was in such a mood he didn't care if he was seen.

He had picked a small bunch of wildflowers on the bank of a stream where he'd stopped to let the mare drink. After tying the horse to the picket fence, he went into the cemetery. Even with the new graves since the last time he'd been there, Dave had no trouble spotting Jenny's. He'd never seen the headstone. The Harrod's had taken care of that after he'd left.

JENNY HARROD KIMBROUGH
BELOVED WIFE OF DAVID AND
MOTHER OF JONATHAN
GONE BEFORE US TO HEAVEN
RESTING FOREVER IN OUR HEARTS

Dave knelt by the grave and thought back to that cold January day, almost seven years earlier, when he'd thought he would die from the agony of leaving her here. Pain and sorrow of the loss, of what might have been, still lingered but he didn't sense Jenny's presence as much as he sensed her memory woven into a part of his being. He laid the wildflowers by the headstone of the well-tended grave. Looking up at the blue sky with white clouds drifting over, he felt released from a weight he'd carried far too long. Maybe he could start to rebuild his life, as if he'd finally let go of something without needing to lose a part of himself.

Dave didn't know how long he knelt by the grave when he became aware of singing. The sweet sound of the hymn, *Amazing Grace,* floated out across the land. As he listened to the sound of faith and forgiveness, he knew he'd finally forgiven himself for letting Jenny die. Maybe some day he could forgive himself for abandoning his son.

The last sounds of the song drifted across to him. Dave mounted his horse and rode away. He had accomplished what he needed to at the cemetery. But because he wasn't ready yet to face all the people, he put distance between himself and the need to talk with anyone.

He rode aimlessly until he found himself at the swimming hole. It was now almost noon on a clear hot summer day. Both Dave and his horse were soaked with sweat. He let the mare drink slowly from the stream and then tied her up in the shade of the cottonwoods to rest, and munch on the grass. Dave stripped and dived into the pool. He felt as if he'd been on a long journey that morning. Instead of feeling weary, he felt more rested in his mind than he had in years. After swimming in the cold water, he was almost eager to go back to the Harrod's and have Sunday dinner with the family.

Just as he had when he was here with Johnny, he relaxed on the grassy bank and let the sun dry his body. A week of eating Mrs. Harrod's cooking was starting to have an effect he realized as he looked at his ribs. He was still thin, but not as gaunt as he'd been. Thinking of eating made him realize how hungry he was. He'd left the ranch before daylight and missed breakfast.

When he rode up on the tired mare, Johnny and little David were out by the barn. They helped him strip the horse, rub her down, feed her some oats, and give her a half bucket of water. After the ride he'd put the mare through that morning, she would need a day to rest before he took her out again.

The two boys were full of chatter, but neither asked Dave where he'd been. It was obvious that Johnny took his position as the oldest cousin seriously as he told little David what to do.

Dave grinned at them. "Do you fellas know how long until dinner will be ready."

Johnny stuffed his fists into his coverall pockets. "I suspect any minute now and I'm hungry as a weasel in a hen house."

"Then I better go put on a fresh shirt." Dave headed to his room. He changed into some fresh clothes and ran a comb through his hair.

Stepping out of the bunkhouse, he heard the bell and saw six-year-old Hattie ringing it on the back porch. Grabbing each of the boys by the hand, he ran across the yard and up the porch steps with the boys laughing and squealing in delight. Holding the door open, he herded the three children into the kitchen, which was filled with the aroma of roast beef and fresh baked rolls.

The leisurely meal and the talk afterwards was the first Dave had truly enjoyed since his return. Although the Harrod's treatment of him had not changed, something had changed within him. He felt a part of the family for the first time, as if he had a right to be there. He entered into the general conversation around the table, even telling some of his experiences of the last six years.

Dave found himself being more natural. He noticed that all the Harrods were more relaxed around him, all except Rachel. Dave had to give her credit; she was at least consistent in the coolness and standoffishness she showed toward him. With everyone else warming up to him, Rachel seemed the outsider. Dave wanted to reach out to her and tell her it was all right, but he didn't know how.

A couple of hours before dark, Jesse and Edna gathered up their children and headed for home. Wayne and Nancy stayed a while longer before going to their house with their two boys. Little three-year-old Matt was already asleep on his father's shoulder. The children had played together all afternoon, and as children will do, they hadn't been willing to slow down until exhaustion had taken over.

Later that evening, Dave sat on the top step of the back porch, leaning against a post, and watching the stars come out.

Mr. Harrod talked about the ranch and the work for the next week.

Dave thought Johnny had gone to bed when he came out and sat down next to his father on the step. The night air started to get cool and the boy gave a shiver. Dave put his arm around his son and drew him close without a word. Johnny settled his head on his father's shoulder with a sigh of contentment, and after a while was asleep.

Mr. Harrod, rocking slowly back and forth in the rocking chair on the porch, grinned at Dave. "You'll never get him awake now. Once he goes to sleep, he doesn't stir until morning. Here, give him to me and I'll take him to bed." Mr. Harrod started to stand.

"No, don't get up. I'll take him." Dave gathered the sleeping boy in his arms and took him into the kitchen where Rachel and Mrs. Harrod had just finished their work.

"Poor little fellow has played himself out." Mrs. Harrod smoothed the hair back from her grandson's brow. "Rachel, go with Dave and help him get Johnny bedded down, will you."

"Sure, Ma." Rachel led the way up the stairs. Dave followed her, sensing she was softer when she dealt with Johnny. What would it take to get her to think more kindly of him?

Johnny was heavy in Dave's arms by the time he got him to the top of the stairs. His son would not be a child for many more years. He was growing up fast and his father had already missed too much time with him. Dave savored the feel of his son in his arms, and it was almost with reluctance that he placed him on his bed in his room.

Rachel got a nightshirt from the peg on the back of the door as Dave removed his boots, pants, and shirt. He and Rachel put the nightshirt over Johnny's head and arms and he didn't stir until they pulled the sheet up over his shoulders. Johnny then turned over to his side, and with a sigh of contentment, drifted into the deep sleep of a child with no worries.

On impulse, Dave leaned down, kissed his son on the forehead, and stroked his hair. How pure and innocent his boy looked in the soft glow of the lamp. Glancing up he saw Rachel watching him with an expression that might have been puzzlement. As he started to say something, she turned and left the room. Dave felt that he had missed a moment some way that could have bridged the distance between them.

Rachel went into her bedroom and closed the door. She leaned against it and listened as Dave went down the stairs. She had been in such a state of confusion since he had shown up after a six-year absence. Only a man who didn't care about his child could stay away for that length of time. Then why had she sensed such love from him for Johnny as Dave tenderly kissed the little boy after putting him to bed?

Her anger at Dave didn't make sense. He was Johnny's father and had a right to come back. Rachel put her nightgown on and sat in her bed with her Bible on her lap. Usually it was so easy to decide what to read and to say her prayers. But she felt guilty about her treatment of Dave. As a Christian, she was supposed to give everyone a second chance. All of that forgiveness the scriptures spoke of, where was that in her relationship with Dave?

Thoughts of the last few days were crowded out as she remembered the terrible time when Jenny died and they had buried her. Rachel had been twelve and had not known how to talk about her grief. It had taken her several years to begin to trust Dave in the first place. After Johnny was born, she had let go of her resentment of Dave's taking Jenny. Then she had lost both Jenny and Dave. He had not only left Johnny, but he had also left her. Was that what she really couldn't forgive him for, leaving her? And if she let herself get close to him again, how would she go through that pain again?

No, she wasn't going to let it happen again. Not to her, or to Johnny.

Chapter 12

The next two months went by so quickly that Dave had trouble realizing he'd been at the ranch for so long. He quickly fell into a routine of work with Wayne and Mr. Harrod. The wide range of experience and abilities that Dave had accumulated over the years soon led them to assign him the jobs that needed someone who could work alone and not need guidance. He also worked when needed with the other cowhands. He did all the carpentry jobs on the ranch. Dave didn't mind what task he did as work was work to him.

He heard the cowhands talking about payday. No mention was made of pay and Dave didn't mention it. He could work for ten years for the Harrods and still not repay what they had done for Johnny. The only times he needed money were the few visits he had made to town and that was only for meals at the boarding house. Anything he'd tried to buy at the general store Mr. Smithy added to the ranch bill.

Gear and tools that he needed for work were available at the ranch. Not long after he had arrived, a pair of chaps and work gloves appeared on a peg in the bunkhouse. He assumed that Mr. Harrod noticed his looking longingly at the chaps at the store.

Mrs. Harrod had gotten her wish. Dave had put on fifteen pounds, mostly through his chest and shoulders. It seemed as if during the summer he couldn't get enough to eat and was always more than ready for mealtime. His shirts strained at the buttons. They wouldn't last much longer.

Dave tried to spend the evenings, Saturday and Sunday afternoons with his son. They had managed to make it to the swimming hole several times a week, especially as the heat of July and August settled in on the land.

Rachel had not warmed up to him and if anything seemed more hostile. He knew it had to do with the closeness that he and Johnny developed. Many times he wanted to invite her to come along and be a part of their activities, but the barrier that had risen between them when he first arrived was still there. Dave didn't know if it would ever come down.

He went into the kitchen for supper and found Rachel helping her mother as usual.

Mrs. Harrod waved toward the table. "Go ahead and sit down, Dave. Supper will be ready in about fifteen minutes."

Dave was acutely aware of Rachel. He listened to the swish of her skirt as she moved about the kitchen. Her hair was made into a crown as she had worked it into two braids and wrapped them around her head gave her a regal look. Although he preferred her hair loose and flowing down almost to her waist. It was all he could do not to reach out and touch it.

Johnny came running into the kitchen.

Mrs. Harrod turned toward him and waved the big spoon she had been using to stir the gravy in the huge skillet. "Young man, go back and enter this room in a proper way. You know you're not to run in the house."

"Yes, ma'am." He turned and went back to the hall and then more sedately entered the kitchen.

Dave grinned and winked at him.

Johnny was a typical nine-year-old and at times needed a firm hand to help him stay within the limits of what was acceptable behavior to his grandparents. Dave believed it was too confusing to have too many bosses and left the discipline up to them. Johnny appealed to Dave a few times to take his side or come to his rescue. Dave refused to be involved in a conflict. Fortunately, Johnny wasn't a boy to try the limits too often.

Dave was more and more at home on the Lazy H. His relationship with Wayne had grown until they were good, easy friends as they had been years before.

The friendship with Jesse still existed, but not as close as with Wayne. Jesse wasn't around as much. They only saw Jesse once each week at the most.

Dave couldn't completely shake his feeling of uneasiness, because of too many years spent watching his back trail. He was still uncomfortable about going into town or being in any gathering where there were too many people he didn't know. His return to the ranch had been so easy, maybe too easy.

August was fast coming to an end and Johnny would soon be going back to school. He would ride a pony back and forth from the ranch to school. Jesse's little girl, Hattie, would start school. Wayne and Nancy were trying to decide whether to start David at five or wait a year. David seemed to want to start school more to be able to ride a pony with Johnny than actually going to school.

The ranch work centered on keeping the cattle near water sources and grass to feed them in the hot dry August heat. Dave didn't mind the heat, but the dryness worried him. Even with that, Dave couldn't remember a more enjoyable, lazy summer.

Chapter 13

One morning the last week of August, Dave and Mr. Harrod sat over break-fast discussing the day's work.

Mr. Harrod took a swig of coffee. "You want to help me carry a load of salt to the north herd?"

Dave looked out the kitchen door to the morning that was all ready too warm. "Might as well. It needs doing. I'll start by getting the wagon hitched up." He finished his coffee, left the cup in the dry sink, and headed to the barn. When he got the harnesses down he noticed a frayed patch and took time to repair it.

Johnny came in and watched him. "What you doing, Pa?"

"Your grandpa and I are taking a load of salt to the north herd."

"Can I come? I can help?" Johnny's high-pitched boy voice was bright with anticipation.

"Go ask your grandpa. If he says it's all right, you can come." Dave smiled as Johnny without another word ran to the house.

Within minutes he was back. "Grandpa said I can come with you if I promise to help."

Dave tousled his son's hair. "I'm glad. You can start by getting a couple of canteens of water and put them in the wagon. Ask your grandma to pack us some sandwiches and tell your grandpa I'll have the wagon hitched up in about fifteen minutes. Then we can load the salt."

"Sure Pa. And I'm going to ask Grandma to pack some cookies with those sandwiches."

Again, the boy took off running. Dave grinned as he watched the boy run cross the yard. Didn't he do anything at a walking speed? Johnny disappeared into the house. Dave turned his attention to getting the horses harnessed and hitched to the wagon.

Hearing a noise outside the barn door, he thought it must be Johnny return-ing. He'd forgotten to tell Johnny to bring a jug of water for them to take along for the horses. Dave started past the wagon to go to the water trough and get it himself.

He sensed someone's presence beyond the door, as he stepped out of the barn. A blow to the side of his head knocked him to his hands and knees. With his head spinning, he barely hung onto consciousness. Dave was aware of rough hands grabbing his arms, pulling them behind his back and jerking him to his feet.

He heard Mr. Harrod shout at the top of his voice. "Hey, what do you think you're doing there?"

Shaking his head to clear it, Dave saw through a mist of pain, Mr. Harrod, Manuel, and Cody running toward them. Not far behind them were Rachel, Mrs. Harrod, and Johnny.

Dave tried to stop the swaying and only managed to stay on his feet because of the two men holding onto his arms. Squinting through the pain, Dave glared at the third man who pointed a rifle at Mr. Harrod with a determined look on his face. Roughly dressed, the men looked as if they had been on the trail for a while.

The man with the rifle took a firmer hold on it. "Hold it right there, mister. We got papers that say this fellow is wanted in New Mexico for killing a rancher and his wife. We aim to claim the bounty, so back off!"

Dave saw that Cody had his rifle and Manuel wore his revolver. He didn't want this to turn into a shootout with Johnny and the women there. "Hold it, Mr. Harrod. Let's see if we can't figure this out. Take a look at his papers." Since the shock of the blow to his head, he couldn't seem to see properly and had to squint to bring the man into focus.

Mr. Harrod seemed barely able to keep his temper under control. "Mister, let's see the paper that you say gives you the right to beat up on an unarmed man."

The man handed a paper over to Mr. Harrod who read it through quickly. "It says here that you're wanted for killing some people in New Mexico, in July, two years ago. There's a five hundred dollar bounty on you dead or alive. What do you know about this, Dave?"

"I don't know anything about it except I wasn't in New Mexico two summers ago. I spent July of that summer in a jail in Brownsville, Texas. You can wire the sheriff there."

"All I know, mister, is what that paper says." The man's face seemed to harden. "Now, we're going to take Kimbrough into Rock Corner and turn him over to the sheriff. We'll let the law take care of him. We just want the reward."

Dave felt a trickle of blood running down the side of his face. He wanted to lift his hand to his head, but as they were tied behind his back, he couldn't. He didn't remember his hands being tied.

He tried to clear his head and spotted Johnny standing by his grandmother. The boy had a hurt, frightened look on his face. Dave wanted to tell him it was all right, but he couldn't find the words. And he really didn't know if it would be all right or not. Mrs. Harrod and Rachel looked shocked at what they saw, as if they couldn't believe it.

Mr. Harrod's brow furrowed into deep lines of concern. "They have a reward poster and we can't stop them without shooting. Let them take you to Rock Corner and the sheriff there. We'll ride in right behind you."

Dave just nodded his head. It was all he could do to stay on his feet.

"Ernie, go bring the horses and be quick about it." The man with the rifle told one of the men holding Dave.

The man on his left quickly went around behind the barn and quickly rode up leading three other horses. They had come prepared to take Dave back with them.

Mr. Harrod turned to Manuel. "Run saddle mounts for me and Cody."

"Si, Señor."

Wayne came riding down from his house. "Pa, what's going on?"

Mr. Harrod nodded at his son. "I'll fill you in as we ride into town with these fellows."

The man still holding on to Dave shoved him against one of the mounts, forced his left foot in the stirrup, and swung Dave up into the saddle. The sudden movement sent his head swimming worse than ever.

Dave couldn't look at Johnny again.

"Don't let them take Pa! Grandpa, stop them." Dave vaguely heard him yelling.

Mrs. Harrod's voice held a quiver. "It will be all right, Johnny. Your grandpa will ride in with them and get it straightened out."

Rachel's voice was steady and low. Dave could barely hear her. "Hush now and calm down, Johnny. We will get this figured out."

He wondered how they could say that when he could see no assurance that it would work out all right at all.

They rode up to the small jail facing the main street of Rock Corner and a crowd gathered. It was none too soon for Dave as his heading was pounding. The sheriff whom Dave remembered came out to meet them.

The man that seemed to be the leader of the three men waved the reward poster. "We've brought in a prisoner and claim the reward. You need to get him into a jail cell."

Mr. Harrod dismounted. "Sheriff, you remember Dave, my son-in-law. He says he was in jail in Brownsville when these murders happened. You need to wire the sheriff there and verify it. I'll vouch for Dave until then."

Sheriff Grant scratched his head and carefully read the reward poster. He didn't seem real sure of what to do. "Let's put him in a cell for right now and I'll send the wire. Why is his head bleeding?"

Mr. Harrod hooked his thumb toward one of the men. "He hit him with the stock of a rifle. Took him by surprise. We need to get Doc to come take a look at him."

Two of the men dragged Dave off the horse and took him into the jail. The sheriff indicated a cell, and after the men had released his hands from the rope, they threw him into the cell. The sheriff clanged the door shut and locked it with a key.

Sheriff Grant turned to the three men. "You men go on and leave. I'll find you at the hotel when I get word back from Brownsville."

The spokesman for the three men said, "We're going to wait in town until you do. We earned that reward money and we mean to have it. Come on, boys. Let's go get a drink to celebrate." The three men tromped out.

Mr. Harrod, Wayne, and Sheriff Grant stood in front of the small cell.

The sheriff spoke first, "Sorry about this, Dave, but those fellows have a proper reward poster. I don't know of it being withdrawn so I have to assume it's still good."

"Sheriff, I didn't do it. Just wire the sheriff in Brownsville. He'll tell you I couldn't have been in New Mexico when they said I was."

"Don't worry, Dave, we'll send a wire," Wayne said.

"But until I get an answer from both Brownsville and New Mexico I can't let you out of here. I'll have Doc come look at your head. That's all I can do until I hear back from these wires," the sheriff explained.

Dave lifted his hand to his head and when he took it away, it was bloody. He hadn't realized until then that it was bleeding so much.

Mr. Harrod spoke up, "Cliff, if I guaranteed that Dave would be available to you, couldn't you release him to me. I give you my word on it."

The sheriff shook his head. "No, Jake, I can't do it. Not even for you, as much as I trust you. Until I get it straightened out, he has to stay in jail. Besides, he may be safer here than out at your place. The reward poster says dead or alive. Those three bounty hunters might just take a notion to shoot him and take his body back to New Mexico. You should be glad they only knocked him on the head."

Wayne spoke up, "I think the sheriff is right, Pa. But one of us should stay here with Dave just to make sure he's all right."

"Can you stay awhile? I need to get back to the ranch and let the women know what is happening. There probably won't be an answer to the telegram until tomorrow anyway." Turning to Dave, Mr. Harrod patted him on the shoulder through the bars. "Don't worry, son, it will work out; it just may take couple of days."

Dave looked up at his father-in-law's concerned face and all he could think to say was, "I'm sorry. I didn't mean to bring anything like this down on you."

Mr. Harrod shook his head. "You've nothing to be sorry about. You just take it easy and you'll be back out to the ranch in no time."

"Johnny, is he all right?" Dave couldn't keep his voice steady. He didn't know if it was concern for Johnny or the effect of the blow to his head.

"Now, don't worry, son. Johnny's fine. I'll bring him in to see you tomorrow."

"No, don't do that!" Dave took hold of the bars.

Wayne stepped up. "Why not?"

"I don't want him to see me in here. Not in jail, you understand?" Dave pleaded. The last thing he wanted was for his son to have a memory of his father behind bars. It was bad enough that Johnny had seen him tied up and taken away like a common criminal. It didn't matter that Dave knew he was innocent.

"All right, don't worry about anything. Wayne and I'll take care of everything."

The sheriff and Mr. Harrod returned to the jail office. Wayne pulled up a chair and sat down next to the cell.

It wasn't long until Doc came. "What did this?" He gingerly examined the gash on the side of Dave's head.

Wayne responded, "The butt of a rifle with some force behind it."

Dave didn't say anything and just concentrated on keeping from moaning at the pain of Doc putting a bandage around his head.

"There, that should do it. It's not too serious although you probably have a slight concussion. You want something for the pain?"

Dave had a headache but nothing the he couldn't deal with. "No thanks, Doc. If I hold still, it's not too bad."

Doc gathered up his things and closed his black bag. "I'll stop in this evening to make sure you're all right." He left the cell.

"Wayne, I'm all right. You heard Doc. You don't have to stay."

"Well, if you think you'll be okay. I do have work to do and Nancy and the boys will start to worry." His steps were slow and reluctant as he left.

Dave felt awfully lonesome after Wayne left as there wasn't anything to do but pace the small cell, wait, and think. What Johnny must be thinking of his father? And Rachel? What must she be thinking about him? He paused in his pacing. When had he come to care so much what Rachel thought of him?

Chapter 14

Rachel couldn't believe what they had witnessed that morning. She kept seeing the look of pain and the blood trickling down the side of Dave's face. She put her arm around Johnny's shoulder and guided him to the house, as the men rode away.

She thought of their conversation. "Come on Johnny. There's nothing we can do but wait for them to come back and let us know what is going on."

Johnny had looked up at her with eyes full of tears. "We can pray, Aunt Rachel."

Rachel squeezed his shoulder. "You're right, we can pray for your pa."

Her mother sat in one of the chairs at the kitchen table. "Come here Johnny." She held out her arms to her grandson and pulled him onto her lap. His legs dangled so that his feet touched the floor. She held him close and rocked him.

Rachel knew she was too old for such comforting but she almost felt like she needed it.

The afternoon was almost gone when Pa rode back into the ranch yard. Johnny was the first one out the door.

"Grandpa, where's Pa?" He pulled on his grandpa's arm.

"Now, hold on, Johnny. Let me get into the house and find something to drink." Mr. Harrod handed the reins of his horse off to Manuel, slowly climbed the stairs to the porch, and entered the kitchen. He sat at the table with Johnny leaning against him.

After getting him a glass of water, Rachel waited for her father to tell them what had happened.

"The sheriff said the wanted poster was real and that he would have to telegraph the people in Brownville. Until he got an answer, he thinks Dave is safer in the jail. Wayne is going to wait until Doc looks at Dave's head and then he'll be on in." Mr. Harrod swallowed half the water in the glass.

"You think Pa is hurt bad, Grandpa?" Johnny laid his head on his grandpa's shoulder.

"No, I think he may have a headache for a day or two. But he can lie on the cot there in the jail cell and rest." Mr. Harrod hugged his grandson. "Don't worry. We have to be patient and pray."

Rachel excused herself and went up to her room. She sat on her bed and remembered the fear she felt when she had seen the rough looking men tying Dave's hands. The sight of the blood running down the side of his head was the worst. She couldn't stop thinking about it. As angry as she was at his coming back, she didn't want to see him hurt. Putting her face into her hands, she began to cry. She couldn't understand her feelings. When Dave was away from the house working, it was as if she was on hold until his return. Then when he did return, she felt fearful and angry at him. What was wrong with her?

Straightening her hair and smoothing her dress Rachel looked in her mirror. Her eyes seemed unusually large and her brow furrowed . Going downstairs to help her mother start supper she lifted her eyebrows to clear her worry lines, as she didn't want to add to her mother's concern. She enjoyed the work on the ranch and had no desire to go into town much. Her parents had given her the chance to continue in school as Mary had done. But she preferred to be at home learning to cook and manage the house. Since she was sixteen the young men in the area had been coming round, but none had quickened her interest nor had her thinking about them. Not like she was thinking about Dave.

Her mother had a pot of beans simmering on the back of the stove. The heat from the fire left it hot in the kitchen. Her mother was on the back porch shelling peas with Johnny helping.

Rachel stood at the open back door. "Ma, you mind if I make some cookies for Pa to take in to Dave?"

Her mother looked up at her and smiled. "No, honey, you make what you want."

Rachel didn't know why she felt the need to bake something for Dave. Of course, it was a Christian thing to do. She spent the next hour making a double batch of sugar cookies. Her pa and Johnny would also want some. She had just taken the last pan out of the oven when Wayne rode in from town.

She carried a tray with glasses of water knowing that in the day's heat both Wayne and Pa would be thirsty. Wiping the sweat from her face, she waited to hear about Dave.

"What did the doctor say, Wayne?" Mrs. Harrod asked after giving her son time to quench his thirst.

Wayne poured some water on his bandana and wiped his face. "He said that Dave should take it easy for a few days and that he would have a headache for sure. But that Dave isn't bad hurt."

Mr. Harrod refilled his glass of water. "Well, if he has to stay in jail a few days that will keep him quiet."

"Do you think he will have to stay in jail very long?" Rachel didn't know why she cared but she did. Was Dave beginning to be of more importance to her than she wanted? She sighed as she didn't like having uncertainty in her feelings.

"It depends on the answers from the telegrams. We need to pray that it will come out all right." Mr. Harrod pulled Johnny close. "Now, don't you be worrying about your pa. He's going to be back in a few days."

As she looked at the little boy with his eyes all wide with concern and fear, Rachel felt her heart catch.

"Can I go see Pa? Can I, Grandpa?" Johnny's voice entreated and his chin trembled.

"No, you need to be patient and wait. As soon as we know what the outcome will be, then we'll decide."

Johnny pulled away from his grandpa and ran across the yard to disappear in the old bunkhouse.

Rachel wanted to go after him but knew the boy needed a place to cry alone.

"Pa, do you think it might be better for Johnny to go in and see Dave?" She laid her hand on her father's arm.

He placed his work-roughened hand over her small one. "In some ways it might be better. But Dave asked me not to bring him. He doesn't want his son seeing him in jail. I understand and respect that."

"I'm not sure I do." Rachel responded.

Wayne stood and put on his hat. "I understand sis. I wouldn't want my boys to see me in jail. Maybe it's something to do with being a father. Well, I'm going home." He strolled up the lane toward his house.

"Pa, do you think it would help if I go see Dave? Then I could tell Johnny that he's all right." Rachel wasn't real sure she wanted to see Dave in a jail cell either.

"Sure, if you want to. That might help Johnny and Dave. I'd better go to the barn and make sure the chores are done. Call me for supper." He kissed his wife and hugged his daughter, then ambled toward the barn.

The next day in the late morning, Mr. Harrod came to the jail and brought a basket of food from Mrs. Harrod.

Dave was glad to see him. The cell was starting to seem mighty lonesome.

Just before noon, the sheriff came back to stand next to Mr. Harrod holding a telegram. "Not much help from Brownsville." He gave the telegram to Mr. Harrod to read. "It says the sheriff from Brownsville is out of town and won't be back for three days. I have to keep you here until I get an answer."

Dave and Mr. Harrod sighed at the same time.

"I had hoped this could be settled quickly," Mr. Harrod said. "I understand, Cliff. What about those three bounty hunters? Are they still around?"

"Yeah, they're over at the boarding house. I'm sure they won't leave town until they know if they're getting their money."

Mr. Harrod stayed a little while longer and then left to head back to the ranch.

Toward the middle of the afternoon, the sheriff came in carrying two telegrams that had just come through. "Good news, the sheriff in Brownsville got back early and says here that you were in his jail the month of July two years ago. He says charges were dropped for lack of evidence. He doesn't say what charges."

Dave realized how worried he'd been by the intense feeling of relief at the news. "Does that mean you are going to release me?" Dave asked eagerly.

"Well, we've got a problem from New Mexico. This telegram says they have to hear direct from Brownsville before they can drop the charges. It may take another day or so."

"Do what you can to speed it up, Sheriff. I want to get out of here."

"I know how you feel, Dave, and believe me, I want you out of here as soon as possible. I already wired the sheriff in Brownsville to contact New Mexico. We should have an answer tomorrow."

The rest of the day dragged on as the heat of the afternoon built up in the cell. Dave lay on the cot trying to be patient, but his thoughts were anything but patient. Just as the late afternoon shadows were starting to fill the cell, Dave heard some one come in from the front office. Glancing up he saw that it was Rachel. Quickly he got to his feet.

Without thinking he said, "What are you doing here?"

"Wayne was coming in to get some feed and check on you. I rode along with him." She slowly looked over the small cell and finally at Dave. "How are you doing?" Her look was one of concern but her voice was calm and matter of fact.

"I'm fine. Just bored waiting for the sheriff to get an answer from New Mexico." Dave was puzzled. He hadn't expected Rachel to visit him. Although he did admit to himself she brightened up the jail. She was dressed in a light blue dress and a straw hat with a matching blue ribbon. She was a pretty sight after the drabness of the jail ceil.

He pointed to a chair by the far wall. "There's a chair. Pull it up and let's talk if you got time." It seemed rude to tell a lady to pull up her own chair but he didn't have much choice being locked in the jail cell.

Rachel sat in the chair after moving it beside the cell. "What do you want to talk about?"

Dave wanted to talk about her feelings toward him and the tension that had been between them all summer, but he wasn't ready for what she might say, instead he responded, "Just talk about anything. What's been going on while I been gone?"

"What's been going on is everyone is worried and upset. Johnny has missed you something awful. He just stays around the house all day moping and waiting for Pa to let him come to town to see you. This afternoon I thought he would defy Pa and come. I wish they had let him. It would ease his mind. He thinks you must be dying or they would let him see you." Rachel had started out in a calm voice, but as she talked, Dave could hear an undertone of anger.

He wasn't ready to deal with it, but they might as well get it out in the open. "You blame me for upsetting the family."

"Well, who else can I blame? If you hadn't gone off after Jenny died and had stayed to be the father to Johnny you should have been, none of this would have happened. And, once you went away, why didn't you just stay away? Johnny was doing fine without you. The longer you stay the harder it will be for him when you go away again."

Even though he had known how she felt, it still hurt to hear her say the words. It hurt more than he had thought it would.

"I'm sorry, Rachel. You're right, I shouldn't have left, but I can't go back and undo it. I'll just have to live with it."

"And the rest of us, including Johnny, we have to live with it too. And, whatever else you will bring down on us like those bounty hunters. How do you think Johnny felt? Seeing those men hurt you and take you away like that? It isn't fair, you know."

"You're right, others also have to pay for my mistakes." Dave was afraid to ask, but knew he needed to get their disagreement in the open now that they had started talking. "What do you want me to do now, Rachel? How can I make up for what I did in the past?"

Rachel didn't seem to need to think. "You can't make up for it, it's already done. The only thing you can do is not make things worse now. I think you should go away and leave Johnny to grow up in peace. You could at least try to think about him for a change instead of yourself."

Dave looked at her angry face and saw no give there. He wanted to say, but what about me? Didn't she care about his life? But he saw no flicker of concern that he could appeal to for himself. He felt he could not fight her, not in his present condition.

"All right, Rachel. I won't stay around and bother you any longer. You all have done wonders with Johnny, and I want what's best for him. I'll leave as soon as roundup is over. I owe it to your pa. I give you my word." Dave could not keep the sadness out of his voice, nor the overwhelming sense of sadness that pressed on his heart.

A startled look flirted across Rachel's face, as if she'd said, and gotten more than she'd planned. Before she could respond, Wayne and the sheriff came in from the front office.

Wayne grinned and gave his sister a hug as he pointed to a telegram in the sheriff's hand. "It says that New Mexico has dropped the charges against you and calling in the reward posters. You're a free man, Dave."

Dave sighed with relief. He just wanted to get out of jail and go somewhere to come to terms with what he had promised Rachel.

The sheriff unlocked the cell door and motioned Dave toward the front office. "I stopped over at the store where those three fellows have been hanging out since they brought you in and showed them the telegram. I told them to leave town by morning. You can go back to the ranch anytime you get ready." Sheriff Grant held out his hand to Dave. "No hard feelings I hope. I was just doing my job."

Dave shook hands with the sheriff. "No hard feelings, it's just one of those things from my past I have to deal with."

"Sheriff, what about the way those fellows came to the ranch and almost killed Dave without even giving him a chance?" Wayne asked.

"The reward poster was still out, Wayne, he was still wanted. They may have been a little rough, but they didn't break any laws. There's nothing to hold them on, and I just want them out of town," the sheriff explained.

Wayne nodded. "It doesn't seem fair, but you're probably right. Can I take Dave home now?"

"Any time, you're not wanted for anything in Rock Corner, Dave. I don't know about other places, if there are any other wanted posters out on you. I would hate for something like this to happen again. You realize those fellows could have shot you and taken you back dead. I couldn't have done anything about that. If there are other places you're wanted, you need to get it cleared up." The sheriff seemed genuinely concerned.

"Thanks, Sheriff. I'll see what I need to do to clear up any other charges."

Wayne talked all the way back to the ranch as the three of them rode in the wagon filled with feed. It was a good thing because neither Dave nor Rachel had much to say.

Dave dropped off the wagon at the old bunkhouse, telling Wayne that he would be up to the house later for supper. When he entered, he found Mrs. Harrod sweeping the floor. She immediately put down the broom and gave him a long hug.

"Oh, Dave, are you all right?" She brushed the hair back from his brow.

Dave held her in his arms. "I'm fine. I'm real sorry about all the bother I've been."

"What do you mean, bother? You're no bother to us, Dave Kimbrough. I'm just glad you're all right." She hugged him again.

"How is Johnny? What does he think about all this?" Dave was afraid of the answer and had not had the courage to ask Wayne or Rachel earlier.

"Well, I'll tell you the truth, Dave. He'd been one upset little boy. He hasn't said a whole lot except to ask why we let the men take you, and why we wouldn't let him come to town to see you. He'll be all right now that you're home safe."

As she stepped back to look up at him, she caught a tear from the corner of her eye with her apron. "I better get back up to the house and get supper on the table. I'll send Johnny down and you two can talk until supper is ready."

"Thanks, Mrs. Harrod. I'm eager to see him."

Mrs. Harrod patted his arm as she left.

Dave stood in the doorway watching her as his thoughts turned back to the talk with Rachel. Only moments after Mrs. Harrod entered the house, the back door flew open and Johnny ran across the yard to him.

Dave caught him up in a big bear hug that was fiercely returned.

"Hey, partner, how you doing?" Dave smiled at the boy although he felt an overwhelming sadness at the thought of what he'd promised Rachel.

Grinning back Johnny asked, "Hey, Pa, you doing all right? Did you get those men that put you in jail? Are they going to come back?"

"Whoa, Johnny, slow down. One question at a time. I'm fine and I'm glad to see you. And those men won't be back." He sat down on the door stoop with Johnny by his side.

Johnny leaned over and wrapped his arms around his pa's waist as if he were afraid to let him go. Dave held him close.

"I was scared, Pa. If I had a gun those men wouldn't have taken you to jail. I would have shot them."

Dave realized with horror that Johnny would have done what he said. It made him see it from Rachel's point of view. What his coming back had brought into Johnny's life. He didn't want to expose his son to the type of world in which he'd spent the last six years. Dave felt his heart breaking as he held his small son close to him. But Rachel was right, and he needed to leave them for Johnny's sake.

The fall roundup would start in a few weeks. He owed it to the Harrods to help with the fall work and then he would leave. As Dave smoothed the hair down on his son's head, he hid his feelings. He would wait until later to tell Johnny that he was leaving again. Dave felt a sense of sadness that was like a cloud of gloom hanging over an otherwise sunny day.

As Dave sat on the stoop with his arm about his son's shoulder, the implications of what he'd promised Rachel began to push at his thoughts. He'd not realized until now how he'd let his mind drift into thinking there would be a way to stay with his son. There was no way.

Johnny started playing with a piece of string tied in a circle that he'd pulled from his pocket. He played at making Jacob's Ladders as he sat contently with his father.

Dave needed some time to think. He needed to get used to the idea that he was really leaving in a few weeks. As he tried to imagine where he would go, the only place that came to mind was the upper valley in the mountains. But he didn't have enough money to get properly outfitted. Other than the cave, there was no shelter there for the winter. It would take him most of a summer to build a cabin.

Right after the roundup and with winter coming on wasn't the best time to start looking for a job on a ranch. But that's what he would have to do. The thought of the lonely life of a grub-line rider through the winter filled him with misery. It would have been easier if he hadn't spent the last few months surrounded by such warmth of family. But he would keep his word to Rachel. More than anything, he wanted what was best for Johnny. He wished with all his heart that Rachel was wrong. As he looked at his son and remembered the man with the rifle ready to shoot, he knew she was right. He had to leave.

Dave thought about Rachel and how scared she must be about his being there. Johnny interrupted his gloomy thoughts.

"Pa, have you been fighting with Aunt Rachel?" He twisted the string into various patterns.

"What makes you ask that?" Dave thought it would be better to find out where the question came from before answering.

"She's usually real friendly and polite to folks, but she's not to you. The kids at school usually act that way when they're fighting."

Dave needed to answer carefully. He didn't want to get Johnny caught up in the tension between him and Rachel.

"Don't worry about it. She's just worried about my being here. She's not really mad at me and I'm for sure not mad at her."

"Well, I hope she stops being worried. I want you two to be friends."

"One day we'll be friends, but it may take us a little time. Tell me what you did today." Dave wanted to divert Johnny's mind to something else and he spent the next hour listening to the goings on at the ranch from his son's perspective.

After supper, Johnny begged to sleep in the old bunkhouse with his father.

Mrs. Harrod asked Dave what he thought about the idea.

Dave grinned. "Sure, as long as you don't snore too loud."

"I don't snore. Do I snore, Grandpa?" Johnny looked up at his grandpa, evidently not too sure.

"I don't think so, but I snore so loud myself that I probably wouldn't hear even if you did." His grandpa reached over and ruffled his grandson's hair.

Sitting in the jail cell doing nothing but wait for two days had left Dave exhausted. He soon told Johnny that he was ready to head to bed.

They walked from the house to the old bunkhouse where the boy put on his nightshirt and climbed into the small bed in the corner. "Goodnight, Pa. I'm glad you're back home."

"Goodnight son. I'm glad I can be here." Dave reached over to the bedside stand and turned out the lamp. Johnny fell asleep immediately. Dave lay awake a long time listening to his son's slow breathing. Off and on during the night Dave woke as several storms passed through the area with thunder, lightening, and hard rain. As far as he could tell, none of it woke Johnny. Dave envied the sound sleep of a child who had no worries.

Morning broke dull and cloudy with a steady rain falling on the dry land. The gloominess of the day matched Dave's thoughts as he lay watching the rain through the open door.

Johnny still slept soundly.

Dave got out of bed and dressed. Walking over to the small bed, he shook Johnny by the shoulder. "Time to get up, sleepy head."

"Morning, Pa." The boy stretched and began to pull on his pants, shirt, and boots. "Wow, look at it raining."

"Well, your grandma will be waiting breakfast for us. Put on my slicker and run to the house in between the raindrops." Dave put the slicker over Johnny's head. It was too big for him and he walked holding it up like a skirt.

He put his son's hat on him and sent him off to the house running behind him. They were both laughing at the sight of Johnny in Dave's yellow slicker by the time they got to the house and stomped into the kitchen.

Mr. Harrod and Wayne sat at the table drinking coffee. Mrs. Harrod was by the stove stirring something in a big pot. Rachel wasn't in the kitchen and Dave assumed she was upstairs.

Mr. Harrod chuckled. "It's good to hear you laugh, Dave. Come eat your breakfast you two sleepy heads. Wayne and I have already eaten, but we'll stay and talk awhile. I need to ride out to the south herd, but I'm going to wait a bit and hope the rain will let up. I hate riding in the rain although I've sure done my share of it through the years."

Dave ate his breakfast and listened to the men speak of the work that needed done before they could begin the fall roundup.

Mr. Harrod leaned back in his chair. "I'm thinking to combine all the herds for the roundup."

Wayne nodded. "That might be the best way but we might also think about leaving the herds where they are and moving the crew."

Rubbing his chin Mr. Harrod nodded. "We could do that but it seems like extra work. What do you think, Dave?"

He liked how it felt that they genuinely seemed to care about his opinion and wanted his input concerning the work of the ranch. If it were just a question of working on the ranch and with the Harrod men, he wouldn't think of leaving. But he wanted to do what was best for Johnny.

Responding to their question, he offered his opinion. "I would probably have just one roundup. It will be less work and time."

After they had looked at it from several perspectives, Mr. Harrod declared that was what they would do. The roundup itself would take three weeks if everything went all right. Mr. Harrod and Wayne decided to start the first week in October.

Dave calculated that would put his leaving about the first week of November. Johnny's birthday was the second of November, so he would wait until after that. He listened to Mr. Harrod and Wayne make final plans. Dave wanted to tell his two friends what he was thinking and feeling, but that had never been something he did easily.

It stopped raining by the middle of the morning, but the sky loomed heavy with clouds, which promised more rain later in the day. The men decided they had better get on with the day's work before the rain started again. With a heart as gloomy as the weather, Dave followed them out of the house to start the workday.

Chapter 15

Johnny slept at the old bunkhouse with his father for the next several nights.

Dave liked having him there, but in a way, was afraid of too much closeness with his son. It would only make the pain of leaving that much more difficult to bear.

The week before Johnny started back to school, his grandmother decided it was better for him to sleep in his own bed.

For the next month, the ranch work fell into its normal pattern as everything was prepared for the fall roundup. Dave tried to keep as busy as possible. A heavy cloud of gloom was forever over his head. When he awoke in the mornings, his first thoughts saddened him and he was tired as if he'd not slept during the night. The nights filled with dreams of Johnny, Rachel, and Jenny until he found himself not wanting to go to sleep.

He rarely smiled now, except at Johnny, and would go for long periods without speaking unless spoken to. The family, not understanding what the problem was, went out of their way to be even more kind and helpful. For Dave the result was that he felt even worse and more depressed.

Dave walked to the house for breakfast. The day was clear and promised to be a hot one.

Johnny sat at the table ready to eat. "Morning, Pa. Can we go swimming today?"

"Don't you have school?" Dave sat next to his son.

"This is Saturday, Pa. I don't go to school on Saturday." Johnny looked up at Dave with a frown.

Dave rubbed the back of his son's head. "I know you don't go to school on Saturdays. I forgot that this is Saturday and sure, we can go to the swimming hole. But ask your grandma." Dave hoped that a swim with his son would help him feel better.

"Can I go Grandma?" Johnny nodded and grinned in expectation.

Ruffling his hair, Mrs. Harrod said, "That sounds like a good idea and I'll fix a picnic for you."

Mr. Harrod said, "Jesse and the family will be here for supper so get back early."

Later as they left the kitchen heading out to the barn, Dave noticed that Mrs. Harrod winked at Johnny as she handed him a package with some sandwiches and cookies for their lunch.

Dave enjoyed the ride and the swimming. Johnny wanted to play dodge the bullets.

Earlier in the summer, Dave had tied knots in a rope and fastened it to a tree limb that hung out over the water. He taught Johnny how to take a running swing on the rope and let go when he was out over the middle of the pool of water. Johnny loved to swing out, drop into the water, and then swim back to the bank for as long as Dave would let him.

Dave lay on the bank letting the sun soak into his body and trying to recover some mental energy. He watched Johnny, who yelled and squealed, swinging out on the rope to drop into the water. Dave realized that Johnny would never be a nine-year-old again and that he would not have many more times like this with him. If he felt this much pain while he was still with his son, he wondered what it would be like after he had to leave him.

Toward the middle of the afternoon, he called Johnny out of the water to get dressed, wanting to keep his word to Mrs. Harrod to be back early. Dave had thought ahead and had brought clean clothes to change into before catching the horses for the ride back to the ranch.

On the ride back, Johnny was as talkative as ever, and if anything, he seemed more excited than usual.

Dave just assumed that he felt good after the swim.

When they rode into the yard, he saw that Jesse's buggy was already at the barn with the horses in the corral.

Hattie and little Dave stood on the back porch, as if waiting for them. They took care of the horses and then walked up to the house. Hattie went over to the bell on the back porch and rang it.

Dave guessed that Mrs. Harrod had called to her from the kitchen to alert everyone to supper. He stopped on the back porch to wash before entering the kitchen. and Johnny and his two cousins stood there grinning and giggling but not saying anything.

Dave was puzzled by their behavior, but the children often puzzled him. As he walked behind the three children into the kitchen, he was unprepared for the surprise they had planned for him. The whole family stood around the big kitchen with a large sign hanging over the table that read, HAPPY BIRTHDAY, DAVE! Beside his usual place at the table was a stack of packages wrapped in brown paper.

"Don't just stand there, Dave, come on in and sit down so we can eat." Wayne came over, took him by the arm, and led him to his place at the laden table. Everyone talked at once and found their places.

"My goodness, Dave, don't tell me you forgot that today is your birthday," Mrs. Harrod asked in wonder at his look of astonishment.

"I never even thought about it, Mrs. Harrod." He could not believe the trouble they had gone to for him. It had been six years since anyone had remembered his birthday.

"How old are you, Uncle Dave?" Hattie asked.

Dave had to stop and think. Everyone laughed and teased him that he didn't know how old he was.

Mrs. Harrod came to his rescue, "Well, you're two years younger than Jesse and the same age as Wayne, so that makes you thirty-one-years-old today."

"Go ahead and open your presents so we can eat." Wayne encouraged.

Nancy punched him on the arm. "Now, Wayne, give him time. You won't starve to death if you have to wait a few more minutes. But hurry up, Dave, we want to see what you got."

When Dave sat down at his place and picked up the first gift on the stack, he found that his hands were trembling slightly, and he didn't know why.

Wayne and Nancy gave him a pair of winter gloves. Jesse and Edna, a fancy shirt; he was sure Edna had picked it out. The package with a couple of bandanas had Rachel's name on it. Johnny's gift was a small pocketknife with three blades. Mary and her finance, Tim Winters, gifted him with a leather belt.

Mr. and Mrs. Harrod's gift was the last one he unwrapped. At first he thought it was a billfold but when he opened it, the face of his son looked back at him and he almost lost the tight control he was keeping on his emotions. The folded picture holder contained two pictures, one of Johnny in his Sunday suit looking solemn, and the other in his ordinary shirt and pants, showing his usual grin.

"Thank you all. I can't believe this. And Johnny never gave a hint about it all afternoon," he said in wonderment.

"That's the amazing thing," Mr. Harrod agreed. "Now that the presents are opened, Jesse, why don't you say the blessing so we can eat."

Dave didn't hear the blessing for the food. His thoughts and emotions were in an uproar. The last time anyone had remembered his birthday had been at this same table the year before Jenny's death.

After the amen when everyone started talking and passing the food, Dave saw that all his favorites had been prepared. As he took an extra piece of fried chicken, he looked down the table at Mrs. Harrod and winked at her.

After the meal was eaten, the women cleared the table and Mrs. Harrod poured coffee for those who wanted some. Johnny and Mary went into the hall off the kitchen. Soon they were back with Johnny carrying a large cake covered with white icing. It only had a few candles on it, but there were enough to cause the little ones to start laughing and clapping their hands. Johnny set the cake down in front of his father.

"Make a wish, Pa, and then blow out the candles," he urged.

Dave quickly blew the candles out with one breath as everyone clapped. He glanced over at Rachel. Could she guess his wish?

"Now let's have some cake." Wayne passed his plate to Mrs. Harrod, who stood over the cake with a big knife ready to serve it.

"Wayne, I declare, you're worse than the children. It's Dave's birthday cake and he will get the first piece." Mrs. Harrod cut a big wedge for Dave. It was a fresh apple cake, Dave's favorite.

Everyone stayed late talking around the table since they were in a festive mood. It was late by the time Dave got back to the bunkhouse and put away his gifts. He stood the pictures of Johnny on top of the chest of drawers. He could tell they were recent, but didn't know when they had gone to town to have them made. He wasn't even aware that Rock Corner had a photographer.

The family usually didn't make such a fuss over birthdays. Mrs. Harrod would bake a cake and there would be one gift from the whole family. Dave couldn't get over the special effort they had made for his birthday. It left him with mixed feelings—of gladness that they cared enough to do it, but also of regret that he would soon have to leave them. As he looked at Johnny's pictures before turning out the lamp, he was thankful he would have at least that much of his son to take with him.

Chapter 16

Rachel made sure Johnny said his prayers and turned down his lamp. She hoped he could go to sleep after the excitement of Dave's birthday surprise. After putting on her nightgown, she sat and brushed her long hair and thought about Dave. The look of love that had shown from his eyes as he gazed at Johnny's picture had left her breathless. What would it be like to have someone regard her picture with such a look? Dave had been so quiet and withdrawn since the bounty hunters had taken him to jail. She didn't know if it was what had happened or if he was still having a headache from his head wound. But she missed his smile which only came out now for Johnny. The pictures of Johnny had been her idea and she was glad she had insisted that her nephew go to town with her to the photographer. The gift had obviously meant a great deal to Dave.

"Good morning, Ma." Rachel gave her mother a kiss on the cheek and then turned to put her apron on.

"Morning, honey. Let's get breakfast on the table so we can get ready for church." Mrs. Harrod put the biscuits in the oven to bake.

Rachel got out the big skillet and put ham slices to fry. "Ma, I thought about making a Star of David quilt. I know we don't usually set the quilting frame up this early in the fall but I'm anxious to get going on it. What do you think?"

Ma looked at her quietly for a moment and then nodded her head. "I don't mind you starting a quilt. I'll work it with you. We might get it made before Christmas." Her mother smiled at her.

Rachel smiled back. "That's what I was hoping." Ma seemed to know what she was thinking.

After she had the breakfast dishes cleared away, Rachel carried a box of fabric pieces into the kitchen and placed it by the table. She began to choose colors and when she had a fair sized stack of fabric remnants set aside, she used some brown paper to cut out her pattern.

After putting a stew on to simmer, her mother sat at the table. "Tell me what to cut out and which colors to use."

Rachel looked at the remnants of cloth. "Do you know Dave's favorite color?"

"I would say it's blue. Any shirt that he picks out almost always has blue in it." Her mother's voice held a hint of laughter.

Ducking her head, Rachel tried to hide her grin. "Then let's make the quilt different shades of blue with a black border. We have a lot of blues and black." Yes, her mother knew what she was thinking.

During the following days, every spare minute Rachel was busying cutting out fabric pieces until she had enough to form the number of one-foot squares she would need for the quilt.

Chapter 17

They started the fall roundup the week following Dave's birthday. It was hard, backbreaking work. The cowhands rode from dawn until dark, and then often rode the night herd. They branded any calves they found that had dropped after the spring roundup. They tallied the cattle. They then divided the herd among the cattle that would go to market that fall and the cattle kept for breeding and to fatten for the next year's market.

The cattle had grazed freely for months. Although the cowhands knew where the cattle were within a ten to twenty mile area, it was tough work to trail them in the canyons and breaks and force them where the cowhands wanted them to go.

Dave had worked around cattle all his life. Rounding up cattle was some of the hardest work a cowhand could do. Dave enjoyed the challenge of showing the cattle who was boss. He always felt good at the end of the day to see a bunch of steers that had made every effort to elude him, peacefully gathered with other cattle to make up the herd.

The branding was his least favorite part of ranching, but he was good at roping the calves and throwing them quickly. The smell of the hot branding iron burning the calf's hide always made him feel slightly sick to his stomach, and he would avoid it if possible.

For the next two weeks, he chased steers, and by night he was so exhausted he slept without dreaming. The other riders asked him what was driving him so hard. He told them he was just doing a job.

The Lazy H had a large remuda of horses with an older hand, Herb Stillers. He had been a top hand in his day and had done a good job with the horses. Although no one knew his age for sure, Dave suspected he was close to sixty.

Dave soon had five of the mounts including his favorite, the brown mare that he rode consistently. Herb tried to keep them ready for him. The brown mare was an excellent cow horse. Once a calf was roped, she stood with tension in the rope until released by Dave. Someone in her past had trained her well. She responded to just the pressure from his knees which left his hands free to work the rope.

It wasn't unusual for Dave to ride back to the remuda four or five times a day to exchange horses. He rode them hard, but he refused to be abusive. When he sensed a horse reach its limit, he was quick to turn it back to the remuda and mount a fresh one. Usually, he rode the brown mare at some time during the day.

Mr. Harrod insisted that the men work in pairs so that if one got into trouble, someone else was there to help. Dave found himself riding most of the time with a shy young rider named Randy Good. Randy didn't talk much, which suited Dave just fine, but he was an excellent cowhand. From the first day they rode out, they discovered they worked well together.

Randy had worked at the Lazy H four years, ever since he'd ridden in on a scrawny pony and asked for a job. He'd been fourteen at the time. As far as anyone knew, he had no family and settled on the Lazy H as his family. Dave had no doubt that Randy's devotion was to the extent of giving his life for the brand. As they worked together, Dave realized that part of that devotion transferred to him.

The other hands teased the freckle-faced cowhand, the youngest rider at the ranch. The men didn't mean anything by the joshing, but Dave remembered his own years of being the youngest drover on a ranch. It would have helped to have one of the older riders befriend him. Quietly, he put himself between Randy and the teasing. None of the men wanted to tangle with Dave. He never said anything threatening, but the cowhands seemed to consider Dave dangerous and walked carefully around him. It had nothing to do with the fact that he was the owner's son-in-law, but everything to do with something about Dave himself.

Dave missed seeing Johnny, but Mrs. Harrod would not let the boy come out to the roundup. Dave agreed that it was too dangerous. Some of the cattle were not at all happy about being rounded up and there had already been some minor injuries among the riders.

Nancy and Rachel came out each day by wagon bringing bread they had baked that morning and other goodies. They helped Wally, the cook, prepare, and serve the noon meal for the hands. Mrs. Harrod stayed at the ranch and took care of little David and Matt. She did the baking with Maria's help. The women worked just as hard at roundup time as the men.

Dave rode to the chuck wagon area where several riders were already sitting on the ground. He walked over to the worktable and took a plate of food. "Thanks Nancy. It looks good." Rachel placed a couple of pieces of bread on top of the ham and beans. "Thanks Rachel."

She nodded but refused to look at him while Nancy gave him a big smile.

Dave walked around the chuck wagon so he didn't have to see Rachel. Off to the side were a few of the riders watching and he heard someone ask, "Miss Rachel don't seem to like that Dave Kimbrough. Wonder what he did to deserve it?"

"Don't know but he done somethin' or else she be friendly to him like she is to us."

Dave did his best to ignore the whole thing and concentrate on his work. He would have skipped the noon meal and avoided her all together; but he worked so hard that by noon he was famished. He always ate as quickly as possible and then would grab another horse and head on back out to chase down some more cattle.

The cattle, like horses, had different personalities. Some were meek and easy to handle, but others were stubborn or even downright mean. Dave noticed one big steer who was both stubborn and mean that he'd chased back to the herd on several occasions. The steer had charged at a couple of riders. Dave pointed the animal out to Randy and warned him to watch himself.

As the herd grew in size in some ways it became easier to handle. Mr. Harrod and Wayne made the decision about which cattle to send to market and were ready to divide the herd. The cattle they didn't plan to sell this year would be moved to the winter range. They would drive the rest of the herd to the railroad a hundred miles north of Rock Corner.

The day they started to divide the herd, Dave went to the remuda and saddled the brown mare. He'd grown fond of the animal and her easy gait. He always felt more relaxed riding her than other horses. When he returned to the herd, he spotted Mr. Harrod trying to coax the big brindle steer back toward the main herd. Dave started over to help.

The steer got past Mr. Harrod. As he turned to head off the animal, his horse stepped into a hole and went down in a heap. Thrown clear of his horse, Mr. Harrod landed hard on his leg.

Dave could hear the bone break above the other noises.

Instead of continuing to run, the big steer stopped and turned to face his pursuer, who now lay on the ground. Digging one hoof into the dirt, it lowered its head and charged at the prone figure.

Dave kicked the mare with his spurs and got his rifle out. He couldn't shoot the steer before it reached Mr. Harrod, so he put the galloping mare between the steer and the man on the ground. The fifteen-hundred pounds of charging steer hit the mare with the force of a locomotive. Dave felt a piercing blow to his leg, and then he flew through the air. He hit the ground and rolled, trying to find the steer at the same time.

The steer stood by the downed mare and looked confused, swinging its head back and forth. Its horns dripped blood. The steer turned toward Mr. Harrod and started at him.

Dave had managed to hang onto the rifle. Kneeling on the ground, he brought the rifle up to his shoulder, and fired at the steer until it was empty. He watched the steer collapse to the ground.

Randy was the first one to ride up. Dave knew that several others would not be far behind. As Dave rose to his feet, he could barely put his weight on his left leg. Randy dismounted and ran to Dave.

"Your leg is all bloody. Are you hurt bad?" The young rider asked.

Dave looked down at his leg in surprise. He hadn't realized the steer had gored his leg so bad. Suddenly, he could feel the rugged hole the steer's horn had dug in his leg. The wound was throbbing and he could feel the warm blood flowing down his leg. The dampened fabric of his pants stuck to his thigh.

"Don't move, Dave. Let me tie the leg with my bandana to stop the blood."

"Tie it real tight, Randy. We got to see to Mr. Harrod," Dave told him.

After Randy tied the bandana around the wound, Dave used the rifle as a cane to move over to the prone man. He saw at a glance that Mr. Harrod's leg was badly broken. The leg was bloody and the pants leg ripped. Dave could see the bone through the skin just above the knee.

Mr. Harrod was unconscious, which was a blessing considering the pain from the broken leg. He felt around Mr. Harrod's head and found a lump but no blood. Maybe the older man had just been temporarily knocked out.

Wayne rode up at a gallop and when he saw his father's condition concern was plain on his face. "We've got to get Pa back to the house. How should we do it?" He waited for Dave to say something.

Dave sighed and straightened his shoulders. He had to take charge if Mr. Harrod was to survive. "Randy, go get the supply wagon that's down by the chuck wagon." Randy didn't wait for more instructions but mounted his horse and raced off.

Cody had ridden up to the group. Dave yelled at him. "Send Jim Hanks to town and have Doc meet us at the ranch. Wayne, you stay and help me get your pa ready to be moved."

Dave tried to think what was best for Mr. Harrod. They must stop the bleeding and keep the leg as still as possible. He took his belt off and strapped it around Mr. Harrod's upper thigh above the break. He then used a stick to twist it tightly in place. He hoped it would stop the bleeding.

"Wayne, you, Cody, and I need to drive your Pa home in the wagon. You tell the others to go on with their work. They know what to do. Go put Ed in charge and then come right back."

"All right, Dave." Wayne caught up his horse and rode toward the herd.

Randy arrived with the supply wagon. The cook had piled the bedrolls into the bed of the wagon to make a soft place for them to put Mr. Harrod.

"Take the tail gate off and bring it over here." Dave called to them. "Bring a couple of bedrolls."

Cody and Wayne rode back at the same time.

"Let's put a bedroll spread out on the tail gate and then all of us together carefully slide Mr. Harrod onto it. If you can help it, don't move the broken bones. Once he's on the tailgate, we can lift him into the wagon and cover him with blankets. Any questions?"

When Dave finished speaking, they all turned and carried out his instructions. Within five minutes, they had Mr. Harrod in the wagon, ready to start the trip to the ranch house.

Randy rode to warn the women so they would be ready when the wagon arrived with the injured man.

Dave sat in the wagon bed steadying Mr. Harrod's leg. He watched Wayne gently place his father's head in his lap. Dave nodded to Cody who was driving the wagon that they were ready to start the slow ride back to the house.

Mr. Harrod didn't regain consciousness during the trip, for which Dave was thankful. It would have been difficult to keep him still. Dave shifted his leg trying to relieve some of the throbbing pain. The ride seemed to be taking hours.

Dave didn't try to make Wayne feel any better about the situation. They both knew it was a serious injury and there was no way to be reassuring about the outcome.

The ranch building had just come into his sight when Dave saw Rachel riding toward them. Evidently, as soon as Randy had given the women the word, she'd ridden out to meet them. She rode along side of the wagon and looked at her father.

"What happened, Wayne? How did Pa get hurt?" she asked.

"I didn't see it but I heard Dave firing his rifle and when I got there, Pa was lying on the ground out cold."

Rachel's eyes widened with shock. "You mean Dave shot him?"

Chapter 18

"Of course not, Rachel, would you make sense. There was a dead steer, Dave's horse was dead, Dave was bleeding, and Pa was hurt. My guess is that steer charged at Pa and Dave put himself in between." Wayne told her in exasperation.

Dave thought she was going to ask him directly what had happened, but they had reached the ranch yard. Mrs. Harrod, Nancy, and Maria waited for them.

Moving cautiously because of his own injury Dave climbed down from the wagon.

"It's bad, Mrs. Harrod. Wayne sent a man for the doctor."

Mrs. Harrod reached out, touched Mr. Harrod's arm, and then drew back. "Let's get him into the house."

Dave spoke to the men, "Grab a corner of the tailgate, and carry Mr. Harrod up to his bedroom as gently as possible. Maria, go ahead to have the bedcovers pulled back." Dave was no help himself because he had trouble walking on his leg.

Mrs. Harrod was wringing her hands. "Maria, go ahead to the bedroom and have the covers pulled back and then go get some water to boiling."

Dave slowly climbed the stairs behind Mrs. Harrod.

The large bedroom was filled with the men carrying the injured man.

Dave cautioned, "Place him in the bed on the tailgate and leave him until the doctor gets here."

After the men had carefully lowered Mr. Harrod onto the bed, Dave turned to Randy. "Go care for the horses and Cody, you get a fresh horse and go tell Jesse and Edna they need to come."

Dave leaned against the doorframe of the bedroom to steady himself. "Maria, go on down and get some water to boiling. And Nancy, why don't you go and reassure little David and Matt that their grandpa will be all right."

Mrs. Harrod nodded. "Yes, you all go on. We will take care of things until the doctor comes."

Softly so as not to alarm her more that she already was, Dave said, "Mrs. Harrod, check to see how bad the leg is bleeding. You may need to loosen that belt."

After she saw the break and the still bleeding wound, she drew in her breath and turned even paler. Dave hoped she wouldn't faint.

Mrs. Harrod straightened up and took a deep breath. "Rachel, go to the closet and get me two clean sheets and get my medicine bag."

"What do you want me to do, Ma?" Wayne asked.

"Hold your pa's leg still while I cut your pa's pants off and clean the blood off his leg."

Dave stepped back so Maria could carry in a pan of hot water. Rachel followed behind with two clean sheets.

Mrs. Harrod soon had her husband's leg exposed. She pressed a bandage on the wound and washed all the blood from his leg.

She turned to Rachel and Wayne. "You two stay right here with your pa. If he moves or starts to come to, you call me."

"Where are you going, Ma? Don't you want to stay with Pa?" Rachel asked in bewilderment.

"I'm going to see about Dave's leg. He's leaving blood all over the house. I think we need to look after him too. We can't do much for your pa until Doc gets here and sets the bone."

Startled, Dave looked at the floor and saw the drops of blood. He'd not been aware that he was bleeding so much.

Mrs. Harrod took him by the arm. "Let's go into Johnny's room and see to your leg."

He ripped the pants leg for her to examine a nasty puncture wound on his upper thigh that was bleeding slowly and steadily. The bandana that Randy had tied onto his leg had slipped down.

Wadding up the bandana, Mrs. Harrod pressed it tightly against the wound.

Dave sucked in his breath through his clenched teeth against the pain.

"Hold this against the wound while I get some bandages and hot water." She was back in a moment with what she needed to tend to the wound. After cutting the rest of the pants leg off, she washed the wound and wrapped a bandage tightly around it.

"That should hold it until Doc can look at it." She put the remaining bandages in her medicine bag.

"It's fine. Doc doesn't need to bother. In a couple of days I won't even remember that big old steer."

"What happened, Dave?" she asked quietly.

"An ornery steer didn't want to be rounded up and Mr. Harrod tried to get him going toward the herd. His horse went down and threw him. The steer was about to charge so I had to empty my rifle at him."

Dave looked up to see Wayne at the door of the bedroom. "That doesn't explain your leg, or your mare being dead. How did the steer get a horn in you?"

"I didn't have time to fire my rifle before the steer would get to your pa, so I put my horse between them. As the mare went down, I was able to roll clear and get the rifle going. It all happened in only a few of seconds."

Mrs. Harrod's voice filled with emotion. "Thank the Lord you were there, Dave, or the steer might have gotten to Jake. Thank you, son."

Dave thought she was holding up well given the condition of her husband.

"Yes, Dave, thanks for everything, including getting Pa back here." Wayne seemed more his old self now that he was getting over the shock of the accident.

"Why don't you lie down here on Johnny's bed until Doc can look at your leg," Mrs. Harrod told him.

"I'm all right. You go back to Mr. Harrod. You need to be there if he comes to. Don't let him move at all." Dave encouraged her.

"Ma, come quick!" Rachel called from the next room as they heard a moan from Mr. Harrod.

Wayne and Mrs. Harrod immediately went to Mr. Harrod's side.

Dave heard a buggy in the yard and voices downstairs. He went into the hallway and waited at the top of the stairs.

Doc mounted the stairs carrying his bag and saw Dave at the top of the stairs with one pants leg gone and a big bandage on his thigh.

"I thought they said it was Jake that was hurt," Doc questioned in puzzlement.

"It is. He's in there." Dave pointed to the bedroom. "It's pretty bad, Doc. If you need any help setting the bone I'll be out here."

Doc gave Dave a sharp look and hurried into the bedroom. Dave waited in the hallway for what seemed like hours, but in reality was only a few minutes.

Rachel hurried past Dave as she went downstairs to bring up more hot water at Doc's request. As she passed Dave, she had a look of such concern that he wanted to reach out to her and tell her it would be all right. But the barrier between them was such that he simply made sure he was out of her way.

Mrs. Harrod came out into the hallway followed by Doc, leaving Wayne to watch Mr. Harrod.

"Dave, you're right, it's a bad break. I'm not sure how to get the bones back together and then hold them so the leg will heal without leaving him a cripple." Doc wiped his hand over his face.

"I was at a place a couple of years ago when a boy had a bad break like this. Maybe what they did would work for Mr. Harrod," Dave offered.

"What did they do?" Doc asked.

"They had to pull the leg hard and let the ends of the bone slide back together. They kept a pull on the leg to keep the ends of the bone from slipping past one another for about three months to allow the bone to heal."

"How in the world did they do that? I never heard of such a thing."

"Come in here and I'll show you." He led them into Johnny's room. Taking a tablet he found on the small desk, he drew an outline as best he could remember of what he and the father of the boy had rigged. He didn't tell them that the father had heard of that way of setting a bad break from a traveling medicine man. They never had a doctor available. It had worked and the boy had survived with no crippling effect.

Dave described what they had done. When he told about driving a big nail through the leg bone below the break to hook the cords onto to keep the leg pulled straight, Mrs. Harrod let out a small gasp.

"You're talking like you helped do this. You actually saw someone do it?" Doc questioned, trying to take in what Dave described.

"Yes, I helped the father. There was just the two of us there with the boy. Someone had to do it."

"I can see how it would work, but it's awfully chancy. We've already got a big potential for infection and this would add to it. But if we don't do something Jake will never use that leg again, even if he lives."

Doc turned to Mrs. Harrod and patted her on the shoulder. "Minnie, I don't know what else to do but try what Dave has described. I can't make that decision. You and the children have to decide. But it needs to be quick, or we won't ever be able to get the ends of the bone together."

"You mean right away?" Mrs. Harrod fought for control.

Dave could tell that the tears were just below the surface.

"Just as soon as we can. It would be easier on Jake if he would remain unconscious." The doctor waited giving her a chance to absorb what he was asking.

She sat down abruptly on the edge of Johnny's bed, as if her legs would not hold her any longer. "I wish Jesse and Mary were here. If it needs to be soon then Wayne and Rachel will have to help me decide."

Dave got up slowly. "I'll go watch Mr. Harrod, Doc. I'll send Wayne and Rachel in here for you to tell them."

Rachel was standing by one side of the bed with Wayne across from her. Dave cleared his throat. "Doc wants to talk with you all in Johnny's room. I'll watch your pa and come get you if he wakes up."

Wayne gave him a concerned look. "Thanks, Dave. We appreciate your help."

After they left, Dave noticed that Rachel had brought up a pot of coffee with some cups. He poured himself a cup and wished he had some food. It was after noon and breakfast had been many hours ago. As he sat by the bed, through the window, he noticed Randy seated on the steps of the old bunkhouse, waiting in case they needed him again. Dave thought about what it would take, if Doc decided to rig up a pulley. Randy could get what they would need quicker than he or Wayne.

Mrs. Harrod, Wayne, and Rachel followed Doc into the room. He couldn't tell which of them looked more scared.

"Dave, Minnie here and Wayne and Rachel have decided we have to give what you described a try. Will you help us do it?" Doc asked.

It was the last thing Dave wanted to do, but he saw no way out. "I'll do what I can. Where do you want to start?"

"First thing is for you to tell us what we need and just tell us what to do. I may be Doc here, but you've seen it done."

"Please, Dave, tell us what to do," Wayne's eyes begged Dave to help him save his father.

With a sigh, Dave took over. He sent Wayne to get Randy, and to send Maria with the children over to Wayne's house. Wayne didn't understand why, and Dave didn't take the time to explain to him that he didn't want them there in case Mr. Harrod came to in the middle of the operation. Dave remembered how the boy had screamed as they had driven the nail through his leg. He wished he could send the rest of them away and he and Doc could take care of it, but he knew they wouldn't go.

Mrs. Harrod began to finish undressing her husband while Doc readied bandages.

Dave waited on the landing for Randy.

Randy came into the house as far as the foot of the stairs and looked up at Dave. "You want me for something?"

"Yeah. Go to the barn and get some cord, a hammer, a twelve-inch nail, and a small pulley. I think I saw one in the tack room. Also, get a fifty-pound sack of feed and bring all that stuff up here to the bedroom. Do it quick."

"Yes, sir." Randy turned and left the house.

Johnny would soon be coming in from school. Dave stepped back into the bedroom and touched Rachel on the shoulder. "I know you want to stay and help with your pa, but I don't want Johnny coming in. Would you go meet him and send him to Wayne's? Tell him to stay there until he is told differently. Will you do that for Johnny?"

Mrs. Harrod looked up startled, "My goodness, I clean forgot about Johnny. He mustn't come here. Go on, Rachel, do as Dave says, and send someone to town for Mary."

"All right, Ma, I'll get back as quick as I can." Rachel left with obvious reluctance, taking a long look at her Pa as she left the room, as if fearful it might be the last time she would see him alive.

Dave wanted to get the leg set as fast as possible, it would be best for all of them. He was glad to have Rachel gone so that she would not see the procedure.

Randy, carrying a sack filled with the gear they needed to rig a pulley, followed Wayne into the bedroom.

Dave instructed Wayne and Randy to rig the pulley from the ceiling. He went downstairs to file the long nail to a sharp point and then dropped it into a pan of boiling water along with the knife and needle that Doc would need to use. Not really knowing why he thought as he did about the need to keep things clean around a wound, he still insisted that everyone wash their hands with the strong lye soap.

Putting the nail, knife, and needle on a clean cloth, he went back upstairs.

With Wayne, Randy and Mrs. Harrod holding the injured man down, Dave and Doc quickly positioned the nail against the leg. Dave drove it through the thighbone just below the break with one hard sharp blow of the hammer. He and Doc tied the cords onto the two ends of the nail where it was now protruding on either side of the leg.

Mr. Harrod began to scream and Wayne and Randy had difficulty holding him as he tried to jerk out of their grip.

Dave yelled above the screaming for Mrs. Harrod to help hold down her husband because he knew the worst part was still to come. With Doc holding the leg at the upper thigh, Dave put his full weight on the rope attached to the nail in the leg.

Suddenly there was a grating sound and Doc yelled, "The bone just slipped back in place. The two ends are together I think." Startled, Doc stopped yelling. The room had gone suddenly silent as Mr. Harrod fainted.

Dave treaded the cord through the pulley hanging from the ceiling and tied the end around the bag of feed. He gradually released the weight of the bag of feed.

Doc nodded. "The weight holding the bones straight."

Dave watched as the Doc stitched and bandaged the wound.

Mrs. Harrod wiped the sweat off her husband's face.

It had only taken fifteen minutes from start to finish. Dave was thankful that part was over.

Doc pulled a sheet up over Mr. Harrod legs. "Now we must keep the weight on the pulley. You can't take it off for several weeks. He's going to hurt bad for several days, but then the pain will ease somewhat. He may develop a fever and be really sick for the next few days but he'll be all right."

Dave wasn't so sure of the outcome, but Mrs. Harrod and Wayne needed some assurances.

Doc helped Mrs. Harrod straighten the covers around her husband and then gave her some packets of white powder for the pain.

"As soon as he comes to, give him this powder mixed in a tablespoon of water. Then try to get him to drink as much water as possible and maybe take some soup. I want someone sitting right here by the bed day and night. Make him stay as still as possible." Turning to Dave, he said, "Now we need to look at your leg."

Dave had forgotten his leg in the need to help Mr. Harrod. The bandage had a little blood seeping through, but not much. He was so tired and hungry that he just wanted to be left alone.

"It's all right. Mrs. Harrod took care of it. I do need to get some different pants though."

"Well, if you're sure your leg is all right, I can check it later. Minnie, why don't you take these boys downstairs and you all get something to eat. I'll sit here by Jake awhile. It's going to take months for him to heal and you must keep up your strength." Doc shooed them all out of the room.

Now that the urgency to keep going was over, Dave felt the need to lie down and let his own body heal.

Chapter 19

Rachel and Nancy rushed up on the porch and into the kitchen just as they came downstairs.

Seeing their faces, Dave realized they thought Mr. Harrod had died. "Mr. Harrod is asleep and Doc is with him," he told them quickly. "The leg is set and rigged in a pulley. He just has to heal now."

Their relief at hearing that he was still alive was evident. Rachel broke into tears with her arms around her mother. Wayne took Nancy into his arms. Dave and Randy were the only ones in the kitchen not crying.

"Randy, help me see what food we can get together for everyone. I'm starving." He told the young cowhand.

Wiping her eyes on her apron, Mrs. Harrod patted Rachel on the shoulder. "You'll do no such thing, Dave Kimbrough. You men sit down at the table and we'll have you something to eat in a minute. Rachel, go get the butter and milk out of the cold storage. Nancy, you get the table set and cut that fresh loaf of bread." Dave noticed it seemed to revive Mrs. Harrod to have something to do that was within her domain.

Dave gladly turned the cooking chore over and sat wearily at his place at the table. It had been two weeks since he'd been back to the house...two weeks of not seeing Johnny.

He was about to ask about him when Jesse rode up, quickly dismounted, and ran into the kitchen.

His mother gave him a kiss and a hug. "I'm glad you're here, Jesse. Your pa's broke his leg bad. Go on up to him. Doc is with him."

Jesse didn't say a word, but headed up the stairs two at a time.

As Dave looked out the kitchen door he saw that the afternoon was gone. It was supper they were about to eat and not the noon meal as he'd thought.

The meal was ready and on the table by the time Jesse came slowly back down the stairs. He walked over to Dave and held out his hand. As Dave took it, Jesse said, "Doc told me what happened. I can't tell you how much it means to me, what you did for Pa. Thanks, Dave."

"I just happened to be closest, Jesse. You would have done the same thing," Dave protested.

"You say what you want, Dave, but we know what you did," Jesse answered, while the others nodded agreement.

Dave felt embarrassed by their gratitude.

"Sit down, Jesse, and say a blessing," Mrs. Harrod told her oldest son.

"Be glad to, Ma."

Dave ate his fill and then excused himself. He felt half-naked with one pants leg gone. He looked silly, but no one laughed. The day had been too hard on everyone.

Randy left the kitchen with him. Usually the hands didn't eat with the family, but Mrs. Harrod had insisted that Randy stay and eat.

As Dave walked toward the old bunkhouse, he asked Randy to saddle a horse for him. After changing his pants, he intended to ride over to Wayne's house to see Johnny. Ordinarily he would have walked that short distance, but his leg bothered him. By the time he had changed, Randy had a horse saddled for him and was waiting outside the bunkhouse.

"Thanks, Randy, for saddling the horse, and for all your help today, you did a good job."

Randy hung his head at the praise and thanks. "I'll put the horse away when you get back, just tie him up here."

"The way I'm feeling, partner, I'm going to do just that. I shouldn't be over at Wayne's but about half an hour. I want to let Johnny know that his grandpa is all right."

It was a short ride to Wayne's house.

Johnny sat on the front porch steps with his head in his hands and Dave was glad he'd made the effort to come see him. He dismounted and walked up the path. Johnny lifted his head and realized he was there.

"Pa!" He bounded down the steps as fast as his legs would carry him. He wrapped his arms around Dave as if he intended never to let go again.

"Hey, Johnny, how you doing?" Dave hugged his son tightly. "Come on, let's sit on the steps." Dave almost had to drag Johnny back to the steps. It was as if Johnny were afraid to let go, afraid Dave would disappear again.

"Is Grandpa dead?" Johnny looked up with dark eyes so like his mother's.

"No, Johnny, he's not dead. I won't lie to you, he's bad hurt. The bone in his leg broke clean in two."

Dave realized how scared Johnny was and that he was old enough to imagine all kinds of things. He felt Johnny would do best with the simple truth.

"Could he still die, like tonight or tomorrow?" Johnny looked up at Dave with his brows drawn together in worry.

"I don't think so, but he might. I'm not planning on it. But he will be in bed for weeks and we're all going to have to help out."

"Sure, Pa, I'll help, but what can I do?"

"You can bring him things, like a glass of water. You can be quiet for the next several days so he can heal in peace. Then after he's feeling better, you can go in and talk to him, and tell him what's going on around the ranch. There's a lot for you to do to help out."

As they talked, Johnny leaned his head on his father's shoulder and Dave wrapped his arms around the boy. Johnny's birthday was only two weeks away, and Dave had planned to leave immediately afterwards. But with Mr. Harrod hurt, Wayne would need him to stay. Dave almost felt Mr. Harrod's accident was a blessing to him because he could delay leaving Johnny for a few more weeks. As he thought about it, he felt his spirits lift. He was shocked at himself for being thankful for the accident. He truly didn't want Mr. Harrod suffering, but he could not prevent it. He would accept the gift of more time with his son.

He and Johnny were so deep in conversation they didn't hear Wayne and Nancy as they walked up.

"What a good idea, for you to come and tell Johnny about his grandpa," Nancy said, with her eyes shining.

"Dave has been full of good ideas today. I don't know what I would have done without you. You saved Pa's life." Wayne's voice had a quiver to it.

"I'm glad I was there and able to do something."

"Uncle Wayne, will you tell me what happened when Grandpa got hurt?" Johnny asked.

"Your pa can tell you better than me." Wayne put his arm around Nancy's waist.

"Your pa is worn out and ready to find his bed. I'll tell you some other time." Dave promised as he started to stand up. He barely made it because Johnny was still hanging on. "I'll tell you what, Johnny, why don't you sleep in the old bunkhouse with me. I don't think your grandma will mind for tonight."

"What another good idea," Nancy exclaimed. "Mary got to the house a little while ago. She's not planning to have school tomorrow. So you don't go back to school until Monday."

"Good, I can start taking care of Grandpa tomorrow then." Johnny was pleased with the idea.

"I'm going back to the roundup tomorrow if Pa's all right," Wayne said. "But I want you to stay off that leg for a day or so. I don't want it to get infected. Besides that, with me at the roundup, I would like for you to be here for a few days."

"You're the boss, Wayne. Whatever will help you out," Dave replied.

Nancy glanced from Dave to her husband. "Pa Harrod will probably have too many people around for the next few days, but I can understand Mary and Jesse wanting to be here. I encouraged Wayne to go on out and get the roundup finished. I think that's what Pa would want."

"I think you're right, Nancy. Well, come on, Johnny, let's go put me to bed." Dave and Johnny said goodnight and mounted the horse. Riding double, they were soon at the old bunkhouse where Randy waited on the steps.

"I see you picked up another stray. What you going to do with that one?" Randy grinned as he got up and took the reins from Dave.

"Ah, Randy, I'm not a stray," Johnny protested.

"Come on, Johnny, it's time to hit the hay. Thanks, Randy. I'll not be riding out tomorrow, but Wayne will head back to the roundup." Dave told the rider who nodded in understanding.

"I plan on riding out early if there's nothing else wanted done around here," Randy said.

"Not that I know of. Go get a good night's sleep, you deserve it."

Randy led the horse off.

Dave and Johnny went into the old bunkhouse. It had gotten dark while they talked on the porch steps. Dave was so tired he suggested they go straight to bed without lighting the lamp and Johnny didn't seem to mind. He'd had an emotionally tiring day as well.

Chapter 20

Dave woke to a leg that was swollen and stiff. It was as if the muscles had frozen and any attempt to move them brought spasms of pain. With care he swung his leg over the side of the bed and slowly put his weight on it. The shot of pain that seared up his leg almost caused it to buckle. With difficulty, he walked over to the hook where his clean pair of pants hung. He needed to let the leg heal some before he rode back to the roundup. There was no way he could ride a horse today.

As he grabbed his pants and started to pull them on be noticed that Johnny was watching him. "Morning, son. You ready for another day?"

"Pa, I didn't know that you got hurt bad yesterday too."

"It's not bad. The old steer just got a horn too close is all. It'll be all right in a day or so and then I'll head back to the roundup. Don't worry about it." Dave tried to reassure the boy. "Get dressed and let's go get something to eat. I'm hungry."

After Johnny dressed, they walked to the house, moving slowly for Dave to adjust to the weakness and pain in his leg. Dave told Johnny how he and Mr. Harrod had gotten hurt and what had happened to the brown mare. As they walked up onto the porch, Dave told Johnny to be as quiet as possible and not to go upstairs, even to his own room, unless his grandmother said it was all right.

When Dave and Johnny entered the kitchen, he found Mrs. Harrod and Rachel preparing breakfast. Wayne and Jesse were at the table drinking coffee.

"Morning, Dave. Why, Johnny, where did you come from?" Mrs. Harrod gave them both a hug.

"I slept in the old bunkhouse with Pa. Was that all right, Grandma?"

"I think it was a good idea. In fact, I think you should sleep there for the next few nights if your pa doesn't mind putting up with you." She brushed back the hair from Johnny's forehead and gave him a kiss.

Dave sat stiffly at the table and poured himself a cup of coffee. "Putting up with Johnny isn't so hard, so maybe I'll let him stay," Dave said with a grin. "How's Mr. Harrod this morning?"

Jesse leaned back in his chair and stretched. "I sat with him until daylight when Mary took over. He's hurting bad, but the powders Doc left seem to help. From time to time he woke enough to know where he was."

Mrs. Harrod spoke up from the stove as Dave watched her stir the gravy. "He's started a fever and is awfully weak, but considering everything I think he's doing all right."

Jesse seemed weary. "Doc said to keep him still, which is hard since he moves in his sleep like he's dreaming. We're going to have to sit with him for several days, I'm thinking."

Mrs. Harrod set the bowl of gravy and plate of hot biscuits on the table. "I don't want you boys to worry about it. We have Mary, Rachel, and me to sit with your Pa. Nancy and Maria will help. Dave doesn't need to use that leg for a few days. You mind sitting with Jake, Dave?"

Dave grabbed a couple of biscuits as the plate went by. "You know I don't, just tell me when."

Jesse took a couple of biscuits, broke them open, and covered them with gravy. "Wayne, you take care of the ranch. Get the roundup finished. I need to go get Edna and the children, but we'll be back tonight. If you don't think Nancy will mind, we'll stay down at your place to keep the kids out of Ma's hair."

"Then Edna and Nancy can take turns helping out." Wayne turned to Dave. "I'm going to need you to help me out while Pa is down. Do you mind picking up the slack of Pa's work?"

"You just tell me what you want done." Looking up Dave saw Rachel watching him with an expression that he couldn't read. He wondered if she thought he was breaking his word about leaving. But Wayne really did need his help.

"Well, it eases my mind to know that Dave is here." Jesse took another biscuit.

"Wayne, would you mind asking Randy to pick up my saddle. As far as I know, it's still on the mare. Just have him put it with my bedroll in the wrangler wagon." Dave felt the loss of the mare more this morning than he had the day before.

Wayne passed the platter of eggs and bacon on to Dave."My guess would be that some of the hands have already gotten it for you, but I'll have Randy check. I'm going to miss seeing you on the mare, you two made a good team."

"Yeah, well, I'm going to miss her too." Dave knew if he had to make the choice again, he would sacrifice the mare, but he felt a major loss. He no longer owned a horse.

Mrs. Harrod took a swallow of coffee. "Johnny, I want you to finish digging the potatoes this morning. And then after lunch I want you to go down to your Uncle Wayne's and play with little David and Matt, so their mother can get some work done."

"Ah, Grandma, you don't mean all the potatoes by myself?" Johnny turned and looked up at his grandma in protest.

"I know it's a big job, but you just do what you can." His grandmother had raised five children. She knew that the chore wasn't too big for him.

Jesse grinned at Wayne. "Remember when we were kids and tried to skip out on a chore? Johnny, I'll tell you from experience, it cannot be done." Jesse reached over, ruffled Johnny's hair, and got a return grin.

"Before Ma can think of any chores for me, I'm heading back to the round-up." Wayne said, then he and Jesse left the kitchen together.

Mrs. Harrod got Johnny started toward the garden.

Dave watched his son through the kitchen door and noticed how Johnny dragged the shovel and tow sack. Johnny wasn't happy about his chore, but Dave knew it was better than letting him sit about the house all day.

Mrs. Harrod started clearing the dishes from the table. "Dave, how's your leg? We need to change the bandage some time today."

"It's all right, just a little stiff. Why don't we wait until this evening to change the bandage. It'll be fine until then."

"If you're sure it's all right, would you mind relieving Mary and sit with Jake awhile. I want you to check the pulley."

Rachel turned to her mother. "I planned to relieve Mary, Ma."

"No, Rachel, I want you to get some sleep. You were up most of the night and probably will be again tonight. We can't afford to get too worn down." Mrs. Harrod was definitely in charge of her husband's care.

"I'll be glad to sit with Mr. Harrod most of the day. I can't do much else with this leg." Dave told them.

"You came in as if your leg pains you." Mrs. Harrod walked over and put her hand on his brow, then brushed his hair back just like his mother used to do.

Dave liked the feel of her hand and the look of concern she gave him. "It's hurting but not too bad, not when I think of how bad Mr. Harrod feels."

"Well, you don't appear to have any fever. We will definitely change that bandage tonight." She patted his shoulder.

Dave finished his coffee and went slowly up the stairs to the bedroom where Mary sat next to her father's bed. She looked tired and glad to be relieved of her shift. After she left, he checked the pulley rigging and the cords tied to the nail. He'd worried about the cords coming loose but everything held fast.

His leg hurt more than he wanted to let on. He went into Johnny's room and got the chair and a pillow from the bed. Taking it back to Mr. Harrod's bedside, Dave sat down in one chair and propped his leg up on the pillow on the other.

After about an hour, Mr. Harrod seemed to wake. He was obviously in great pain. Dave wasn't sure he could handle him if he started thrashing about, so he called for Mrs. Harrod to come.

She immediately mixed some of the white powder with water and got Mr. Harrod to drink it.

He seemed to be awake but Dave wasn't sure if he knew what was happening. Mrs. Harrod had brought a small bowl of soup, and she was able to get Mr. Harrod to take a few spoonfuls. He soon relaxed and went back to sleep.

Dave was glad because the terrible look of pain on Mr. Harrod's face was hard to take.

"How often is he waking up and taking the medicine?" Dave helped straighten the covers.

"I've kept track for the doctor and it has been about every four hours. I'm hoping by tomorrow he can go longer between times. But for right now I don't see any point in letting him suffer needlessly." She smoothed her husband's brow. "He's hot with fever."

"The pulley is fine and he's keeping still enough. He should be all right in a few weeks." Dave wanted to reassure her.

"Dave, I've been around ranch work all my life. This kind of break will take at least four months, maybe even six months to heal properly. I'm making up my mind that Jake will be right here in this bed most of the winter. I haven't said anything to the others, because they've got to get used to him just being hurt."

Going over to Dave, she put her arms around him. "I'm so glad you're here. You can't imagine what a help you are to me."

He hugged her back. "I'm glad to be here, too." It gave him a warm feeling that he could be of help to the family and relief that he could put off leaving for even longer.

"Rachel and Mary are both asleep and I'm finishing dinner. If you don't mind sitting with Jake until noon, Rachel will take over then. I hope to sleep some myself this afternoon. I'm worn out."

Giving her husband another glance, she went back downstairs.

Dave sat back down with his leg propped and picked up Mr. Harrod's Bible that was on the table by the bed. He'd been reading about an hour when Doc surprised him as he walked into the room, followed by Mrs. Harrod who carried a pan of hot water.

"How's our patient?" Doc put his hand on Mr. Harrod's brow.

"He's sleeping soundly and seems to be all right for now." Dave got up stiffly from the hard chair.

Doc set his bag down and took off his coat. "I'm going to check his leg and change the bandage. Will you help me?"

Dave held the leg steady lifting it a couple of inches above the bed. He also kept an eye on the pulley.

Working carefully but swiftly to remove the bandage, Doc said, "This is looking good. The area around the wound is pink and still seeping some blood, but it isn't red with infection."

"That's good news." Dave was relieved and more confident of Mr. Harrod's recovery.

Doc felt Mr. Harrod's forehead. "He has a fever but I think it is just a natural reaction to the seriousness of the wound. Let me finish with this and then I'll work on your leg."

"Thanks, Doc. It could use some attention."

After putting a fresh bandage on Dave's leg, Doc and Mrs. Harrod went back downstairs again, leaving Dave to sit by the bedside with his leg up on the opposite chair.

Changing the bandage hadn't helped with his pain as Doc wasn't too gentle when he pulled the old bandage away from the wound. It appeared to be healing well and Dave was hopeful it would only take a couple of more days to heal to the point he could be back at work. Looking at the sleeping man, Dave was glad he could be of some help, but he had gotten used to riding out every day.

Just before noon, Rachel, who looked more refreshed than she had at breakfast, relieved Dave. She seemed surprised to see him reading.

He didn't tell her it was his third time to read the Bible. Books had always been good friends to him, and he took every opportunity to read.

For the next two days, Dave fell into a routine of sitting with Mr. Harrod most of the morning and resting his leg in the afternoon. In the evenings, he played either chess or checkers with Johnny. The boy seemed a little lost with his grandpa needing so much attention. Dave guessed he was still a little doubtful about his grandpa's recovery.

By Monday morning, Mary made the decision to reopen the school. She decided to travel back and forth from the ranch with Johnny for a while to help as much as she could in the evenings.

Mr. Harrod seemed to be doing as well as could be expected. With all the women looking after his every wish, Dave stayed out of the way as much as possible.

Rubbing his thigh, which still had a bandage, Dave looked at his son as he ate his breakfast. "Johnny, I won't be here when you get home from school. I'm heading out to help with the roundup."

Johnny's face fell with disappointment. "Do you have to go?"

Dave didn't want to miss any time with his son either. He felt a warming in his chest at the thought that Johnny didn't want him to go. "It will just be a few weeks and then I'll be back."

"Okay, Pa, I'll miss you." Johnny got up and gave his pa a hug.

Chapter 21

Dave put in long hard days of work for the next two weeks. He sorely missed his mare. None of the other horses could compare. Dave and the other hands finished the branding and divided the herds.

Dave sat on his horse watching the final dividing of the herd when Wayne rode up.

"Dave, I'm putting you in charge of moving the herd to the winter range. It shouldn't take more than a few days. Then I want you to be in charge of the ranch until I return. Once you have the herd settled keep Randy and a couple of other riders and send all the others over to Jesse's place to start his round up."

Dave straightened up in the saddle in response to being given so much responsibility. "Sure, Wayne. I can do that."

Wayne nodded. "I'm taking Cody as my foreman and all the other riders to drive the herd to the railway to sell. It's only a hundred miles but we will go slowly to not run any fat off the beef. I figure it will take about two weeks to get the herd there and shipped. Then I plan to take the riders with me to Jesse's ranch and help with his roundup. It may be a month before I will be back at the ranch. Until then you're in charge."

"I'll do my best and watch out for your family." Dave was torn between wishing he could go in Wayne's place so he didn't have to be away from his family, and relief that Dave didn't have to leave Johnny. But Wayne needed to go to be able to sell the cattle and help Jesse with his roundup. Jesse brought his crew over to the ranch to help with the family roundup and it was his turn now.

Dave had a lot of time to think during the next few days as he helped move the herd to the winter pasture.

Regardless of what Rachel thought, or the danger of more problems coming to the Harrod's because of Dave's presence, he couldn't run out on the family when he could be of real help to them. He had developed somewhat of a reputation as a gunfighter during his years on the run. It wasn't something he had chased after but after several times of having to defend himself and being successful, people began to talk. There was always the chance that some young gun hand would challenge him. Staying away from town was the best way to avoid it. Wayne really did need his help and it allowed him to stay at the ranch for the time being.

There still had been no opportunity to talk to Rachel. Between her caring for her father and Dave working with the cattle, they had hardly been in the same room together. Dave didn't make much effort to talk with her even if they had an opportunity. It puzzled him why she was in his thoughts so often. She'd made her attitude toward him so clear and there was no indication that she was going to change her mind about wanting him to leave.

Johnny's birthday was coming up and Dave wanted to give him something special. He had five dollars left and he tried to think of what a boy would want on his tenth birthday, but everything he thought of cost more than he had to spend. The decision weighted heavily on his mind. It might be the only birthday of Johnny's that he would be there to help celebrate.

Between his sadness at leaving soon, worrying what to get Johnny, and concern for Mr. Harrod, Dave was even quieter than ever around the family. At meals he would eat, listen, and respond only if spoken to directly. He didn't think about how he might seem to the others, he just had things on his mind.

Dave sat with Mr. Harrod in the evening. The first several weeks after the injury had been very painful for Mr. Harrod. Dave could see it in his eyes and on his face. The pain had finally leveled off until Mr. Harrod seemed only to hurt if he wasn't careful about how he moved. His movements were limited with his leg attached to the pulley rig. Dave grinned as Mr. Harrod grumped and complained about being confined to his bed but otherwise he seemed to be mending fine.

Dave tried to visit him often to talk about the ranch work to relieve him from all the women who constantly fussed over him. The sheriff and other friends in the area had also been out to see him. He didn't have to deal with being lonely, for he was hardly ever alone.

Dave stayed with him on Sunday mornings while the rest of the family went to church services. He hadn't gone to services with the family since his return, so he was the logical one to stay.

On Sunday morning a week before Johnny's birthday, Dave hadn't had much to say as he sat by Mr. Harrod's bed.

"Dave, I asked you a question." Mr. Harrod looked at him intently.

It brought Dave back from where his mind had wandered. "I'm sorry, Mr. Harrod, what did you ask?"

"What's on your mind, son? You have been so quiet and acting as if you're real worried about something. What is it?" Mr. Harrod shifted his good leg.

"Oh, I've just got my mind on something and trying to figure things out."

"Anything I can help you with?" Mr. Harrod furrowed his brow in concern.

Dave always found it easy to talk to the older man. "Well, for one I'm trying to figure out what to get Johnny for his birthday. I want it to be special. I've never given him a gift before and I want it to be one he will remember." Dave didn't feel free to share that he wanted it to be something that would remind Johnny of his father after he left.

Mr. Harrod chuckled. "I know what you mean. Womenfolk seem to find it so easy to give gifts. They almost know by instinct what to buy. Me, I just do the best I can to come up with something that won't make the person mad at me." Looking thoughtful he asked, "What have you thought of as possible gifts?"

"I thought of a rifle, but he's too young yet. And I thought of a new pony. Jud Sawyer over east of here has the prettiest little paint pony that Johnny would love to have."

"That's a good idea as he needs his own pony to ride back and forth to school. I've been meaning to get him a pony of his own but never got around to it. What's the problem with that for Johnny's birthday?" Mr. Harrod looked puzzled.

Dave was almost embarrassed to tell him, but now that they were talking about it, he decided to go ahead. "The main problem is that Jud wants seventy-five dollars for the pony and I've only got five dollars to my name. Since the mare got killed, I don't even have a horse of my own and no money to buy myself one, much less get one for Johnny." Dave had not intended to say so much, but once he got started, it all seemed to come out.

Mr. Harrod, lying propped up on pillows, just looked at him. "What do you mean you only have five dollars?"

"Well, I have five dollars left from selling the furs last spring." Dave couldn't figure out Mr. Harrod's reaction.

"My goodness, son, the things we take for granted around here. I guess I assumed you knew or someone had told you. Although who I thought should tell you other than me, I don't know."

Dave was puzzled now. "What should I know, sir?"

"I don't know exactly where to start. I guess back to six years ago when you left. You remember meeting Jesse and me in town when you turned the ranch over to Jesse?"

Dave nodded. That cold dark day was burned in his memory. The sense of aloneness and hopelessness had been a physical pain as he had ridden away.

"After you rode out, Jesse and I talked about it. He didn't feel right about the way you had just handed him the ranch without any payment for yourself. I told him I wouldn't take anything for the care of Johnny. You had been so grim that day. He hadn't known how to argue with you. So we figured out a payment schedule that was more than fair to Jesse and a price that was fair to you. Jesse made yearly payments to the bank for almost five years. Last year he finally made the last payment. All that money is in the bank at Rock Corner in your name.

"And every time you sent money, Minnie and I added it to your account. She would have had my hide if we had kept any of that money. The Lord had blessed us so much, and Johnny has brought so much love and joy to our lives that to accept money for his care would have taken something away. I don't know if you understand. I hardly know how to explain how we feel about it."

Dave didn't know what to say. He could hardly take it in.

Mr. Harrod ran his hand through his hair. "The last time I was at the bank, Tim told me you had about twelve thousand dollars in your account, so I think you could draw out some for a pony for Johnny."

"But Mr. Harrod, I don't feel like that should be my money, but Johnny's. I sent it for him." Dave wanted his son to have whatever was there.

"I know that you did, son, but it's not his. It belongs to you. You need to think about what you want to do to get established for yourself." Mr. Harrod gingerly shifted his position slightly. "We love you and Johnny being here with us, and if you want to stay on, then we will be delighted. But if you want to get a place of your own again and build it up with Johnny, then that's what you need to do."

Dave had to look away and stare out the window to keep control of himself. The dream that he'd not even allowed himself to dream offered to him, and the money available simply for the taking.

As if sensing the turmoil that Dave felt, Mr. Harrod continued to talk as if to give Dave time to think through his thoughts. "Now about a horse for you, don't you worry. I'll talk to Wayne. We just hadn't thought about it, what with me being laid up and all. As far as I'm concerned, you need to pick out at least three of the best horses on the place. You just let me know which ones, and I'll see that you get a bill of sale. Also, I'll see that Wayne adds you to the payroll. I don't know what we were thinking by not doing it before."

Dave waved his hand and said, "You don't need to do that, Mr. Harrod. I'm more than glad to help you out. Besides you're putting me up and feeding me."

"We pay our top hands forty a month and found and that's the least we can do for you, our own son-in-law."

"I don't know if you should think of me as a top hand. I sure have caused you trouble through the years." Dave spoke quietly with his head hanging down.

"Dave, how can you say that? From the beginning, you made our Jenny so happy. She loved being married to you. I know you had some spats, but you always got whatever it was settled between the two of you. And, when you all had Johnny, she told me how thankful she was to have you there as his father." Mr. Harrod reached out and placed his hand on Dave's arm. "And, what about what you did for me? You only saved my life is all. As far as a cowhand, you are a far better one than Wayne or me. Why do you think Wayne left you in charge if he didn't think you were a good cowhand? He wouldn't take that kind of chance on someone he didn't think was capable of doing the job."

Mr. Harrod seemed concerned that Dave realize how he saw him. Mr. Harrod was about to say more when they heard the buggy coming up the drive. "I guess the family is back and the womenfolk will be getting dinner ready. You go into town tomorrow and get some money out of the bank. Buy that pony for Johnny, if that's what you want to give him for his birthday. Like I said, we put the money in an account in your name. We can't take any of it out even if we wanted, only you can."

As Mr. Harrod finished explaining about the money, Johnny came running in, still wearing his Sunday suit. "Hey, Grandpa, Pa. I got to change quick so I can go play some before dinner. No one else is coming for dinner. They're all coming next Saturday for my birthday." He turned and went to his own room without waiting for a response.

Dave and Mr. Harrod looked at each other and started laughing.

Mrs. Harrod came in taking off her hat and jacket and looked at the two men with a pleased expression. "Well, what's so funny? Have you two had a good time visiting?"

"I'm not sure what's so funny, Ma, except the way Johnny came running in and out like a whirlwind," Mr. Harrod explained.

Knowing Mrs. Harrod wanted to change her good Sunday dress for an everyday one, Dave excused himself and went out to the back porch. Sitting on the steps, he tried to think through what Mr. Harrod had told him. Twelve thousand dollars was a lot of money. It was enough to get started with a small herd in the mountains. That's what he wanted to do and he wanted to do it with Johnny.

For some reason it wasn't Johnny's face he saw in his mind but Rachel's. He'd given his word to her, and he could see where she was right. He didn't know what else might come down on them. But the thought of riding away from Johnny was almost too painful to think about and he felt a strange ache in his chest when he thought about leaving Rachel behind. Mr. Harrod had indicated they assumed he would either stay or take Johnny with him. Dave felt little tugs of guilt that it was such a relief that Mr. Harrod would be laid up for several more months. He wouldn't have to make a decision for a while.

Johnny came to the porch wearing his old pants and shirt ready to play. He saw his father seated quietly and sat down next to him. "What are you doing, Pa?"

"Nothing, just sitting here thinking," Dave told him.

"I do that sometimes. You have to just think about things some times." The boy looked at his father with a serious look on his face.

Tousling his son's hair, Dave laughed. "That's right, partner. Let's go throw a lariat until they get dinner ready."

"Great! I can almost get it thrown out and then snapped back, just like you showed me."

They walked down to the corral and spent the next half hour practicing with the lariat. Johnny picked up quickly on the different skills that Dave taught him. That was one thing he could do for his son before he left him, teach him as many skills as possible.

The next day, there was no pressing work on the ranch and they needed supplies from town. Instead of sending one of the hands, as he would normally have done, Dave decided to go himself. When he told Mrs. Harrod what he planned, Rachel overheard and asked if she could ride in with him to shop. He saw no reason not to take her. By the time, he had the horse hitched to the buckboard Rachel had come out to the barn carrying a basket.

"Ma is sending some things to Mary. I'll drop them off for Tim to give to her," Rachel explained.

"Fine, I'm going by the bank anyway." Dave held out his hand to help her climb up onto the buckboard.

It was a crisp cool end of October day. As he drove the team toward town, he tried to sort out in his mind what he would do. First stop would be the bank where he'd decided to take out a couple of hundred dollars. The idea of having the wealth of twelve thousand dollars was hard to get used to. He would get the pony for Johnny and he wanted to look in town for a nice saddle to go with it. The rest of the money he planned to use as needed and to make it last as long as possible. He would also accept Mr. Harrod's offer of some horses. They had plenty on the ranch and could easily spare a couple of mares and a stallion. He wasn't going to ask for the best one on the place, as Mr. Harrod had told him. That one would be Wayne's black stallion.

"Dave, I want to say something to you." He'd almost forgotten Rachel was with him, she had been so quiet.

He glanced quickly at her and then looked back at the road before them.

Rachel was also staring straight ahead.

"Sure, Rachel, say anything you want." Remembering their conversation when he had been in the jail, he wasn't sure he meant that.

"Well, I never did properly thank you for what you did for Pa. Randy told me about it, about how, after being gored and thrown yourself, you calmly lifted your rifle and shot the steer. And how you then told them all what to do to get Pa back home. So upset over Pa, I didn't know your leg was hurt until Ma said something. I wasn't deliberately ignoring your injury." Rachel had spoken in a quiet calm voice.

Surprised at her apology, Dave didn't know what to say. He often didn't know what to say around Rachel. "Randy made it out to be more than it really was. I just did what needed doing to help your Pa." He also spoke in the same quiet calm tone.

He decided he might as well bring up the subject of his leaving. "I know I told you I would leave as soon as roundup was over. But with your pa getting hurt,

Wayne needs me to stay until your pa's back on his feet." Dave looked out of the corner of his eye at her.

She gazed at him with a strange expression on her face.

He had no idea her thinking. "I mean to keep my word, but I feel I owe it to your folks to help out if they need me."

"When do you think that will be? When do you think Pa will be up and back to working again?"

"I'm not sure, but I don't hardly see how he could be back to riding until spring. It's a real bad break he's got." Dave glanced over at her again.

"I've never known Pa to be hurt or sick. It seems real strange to me." Her voice was subdued.

"It's hard on him for sure. He doesn't really know how to take it easy and let others do for him." Dave tugged on the reins and kept the team going straight.

"Well, thanks for helping him and Wayne out." The wind picked up and she lifted her hand to grab her hat.

Dave couldn't help but notice how pretty she looked in her pale blue dress that fit tight at the waist and then flowed into a full skirt to below her ankles. She had a matching blue ribbon tied around her hat to hold it on her head. Dave decided he better keep his eyes straight ahead, as she was just too pretty to keep looking at for too long. The memory of the brief glimpse he had of her ankle as he had helped her into the wagon was bad enough.

Dave felt that was as far as she wanted to go in the conversation so he didn't respond. Since the arrest, it was the longest conversation they had had.

When they got to town, Dave stopped first at the bank. After tying the reins to the hitching posts, he offered his hand to help Rachel descend from the wagon. The feel of her small hand in his rough calloused one sent a tingle all the way up his arm. He quickly let go of her hand and lifted her basket out of the wagon.

Rachel took the basket and walked into the bank. Dave followed her wondering if she had also felt that odd sensation at their touch.

Tim came around from behind the bank counter. "Rachel, Dave. What brings you all into town?" He greeted Rachel with a kiss on the cheek and shook hands with Dave.

Rachel handed Tim the basket. "Ma sent some baked goods for Mary. I thought you could give them to her after school is out."

Tim took the basket and placed it behind the bank counter. "Sure, we're meeting for supper."

Dave cleared his throat. "I need to do a little banking."

Rachel went to stand by the pot-bellied stove. "I'll just wait here for you to complete your business with Tim."

Dave nodded and stepped up to the bank counter. "Mr. Harrod said he had opened an account for me. I want to check on how much is in it and draw out some."

Tim pulled a large ledger up onto the counter. "Let me look up your account." He flipped through several pages and then flattened the pages out. "Here you are. David Kimbrough. You balance as of today is $12, 854.00."

Dave had heard Mr. Harrod say how much was in the account but hearing it from Tim reading from the ledge made it real. A miracle that changed his whole outlook on his future.

"I'd like to withdraw a couple hundred dollars."

Tim pulled a cash drawer out, counted out the bills, and laid them on the counter. He then carefully wrote in the ledger. "That leaves $12, 654.00. You want a statement of the transaction?"

Shaking his head, Dave picked up the money and carefully placed it into his flat wallet. "No, I trust that you will keep track of it." He turned toward Rachel. "I'm ready to go."

Rachel said goodbye to Tim, and Dave held the door for her as they exited the bank.

Dave helped her back onto the wagon seat. He again felt a heightened sense of touch as she held his hand to steady herself. "The mercantile is the next stop."

He slowly drove the wagon down the street to the front of Smithy's Mercantile. Being in town with Rachel, doing ordinary things together was more enjoyable than Dave would have ever thought, and he wanted to make the time last as long as possible.

As he reached up to help Rachel from the wagon seat this time, it seemed natural to place his hands around her small waist, lift her down, and set her gently on her feet. Though he wanted to let his hands linger around her waist, he released her and stepped back.

"Thank you, Dave. I'm going to look for some dress goods. Just let me know when you're ready to go."

Dave tipped his hat. "It shouldn't take more than half an hour to get the ranch supplies and other purchases I need." Rachel strolled into the store with Dave trailing behind. When had she grown up so completely? Her beauty took his breath away. While Rachel spent her time in the dress goods with Mrs. Smithy, Dave got Mr. Smithy to fill the ranch order.

He looked at the saddles on display while he waited. The town didn't have a saddler and Smithy kept several saddles in stock. Dave found a nice small saddle that cost more than he should have spent, but he decided to buy it.

Dave walked up to Mr. Smithy. "I want to add that small saddle to the order."

"Sure, but who out at the ranch will fit that small thing." Mr. Smithy wrote the items from Mrs. Harrod's list into the ledger book.

Dave grinned at the thought of trying to ride in the small saddle. "It's for Johnny. His birthday is coming up. And don't add it to the ledger. I want to pay for it."

"But Jake said for me to put all your purchases on the ledger." Mr. Smithy glanced up at Dave with a frown.

"I know he did, but I want to pay for this." Dave took his wallet out, removed a twenty and a five-dollar-bill, and placed them on the counter.

Mr. Smithy smiled and nodded. "I understand, Dave. It's your gift to Johnny."

Dave was glad Mr. Smithy understood. He didn't want to stand and argue with the man. After he and Mr. Smithy had loaded the wagon with the ranch supplies, he went back into the store. "You need more time?" he said to Rachel.

"No, I've got what I want. I'm ready to go."

He picked up her purchases. They made their farewells to Mr. and Mrs. Smithy and stepped out onto the boardwalk in front of the store. He placed her purchases into the wagon and wondered what she would say if he suggested they eat the noon meal at the boardinghouse.

As he was trying to make up his mind whether to ask or nor, she asked him. "Why don't we go over to Mrs. Anderson's and eat before we head back to the ranch?"

He looked down at her and saw her regarding him calmly. "All right, that would suit me fine."

Several men on horseback made their way down the street. Dave took her arm to guide her. She seemed to accept it as the natural thing for him to do. In the boardinghouse dining room, Dave let her choose the table and held the chair for her to sit.

Rachel looked up at him with a quick glance and smile. "Thank you."

Mrs. Anderson came out of the kitchen and hurried to the table. "Hello, Rachel, Dave. It's a nice surprise to see you all in here on a Monday."

Rachel set her small reticule on the table and unbuttoned the blue wool cape. "Hello, Mrs. Anderson. No, I usually only come to town on Saturdays, but Dave had to pick up some supplies at the mercantile and I needed to look for some dry goods."

Mrs. Anderson waved a hand toward the blackboard on the back wall of the dining room. "We have chicken and dumplings with dried apple pie for today."

"That sounds delicious." The way that Rachel said it, with a lilt to her voice made the plain fare sound special.

"I'll have the same."

Mrs. Anderson nodded. "I got a fresh pot of coffee. I'll bring it right out."

Dave didn't know what to say to the pretty, young woman seated across from him as the boardinghouse owner disappeared into the kitchen. It had been so long since he had sat in this same dining room with his bride, eight years ago on their anniversary. He shoved the memory back. It was in the past.

"How are things going for the ranch work with Pa being injured?" Rachel's voice was so soft that Dave barely heard her.

"It's going all right. Wayne has the experience to know what needs done. Your Pa is keeping up with what is happening, even from his sick bed."

"Yes, you and Wayne are being good about including Pa. He needs that while he is laid up."

Dave found it easier to talk with Rachel. "With the roundup over and half the herd sold, we now just need to do the winter work and make it through until spring calving begins."

Rachel tilted her head. "What work will you be doing specifically?"

She seemed to be really interested so he began to talk about the checking on the herd, taking salt and feed out onto the range, cutting firewood, checking fencing, and the other jobs that were part of the ongoing work of a ranch during winter. "There's always more to do each day than can be done. You know how it is on a ranch. The work is never really done."

Rachel laughed and nodded. "It's the same way in the house. In the winter we don't have the garden to tend but otherwise the work goes on. Meals to cook, laundry to do, rooms to clean, it can seem never ending."

Dave grinned. "Maybe because it is never ending. Do you mind it?"

"Are you asking if I enjoy living on the ranch and helping take care of the family?"

"I guess that's what I'm asking."

"No, I don't mind it. Oh, there are some things I don't enjoy doing like when it's time to butcher and put up meat. Or, the time Ma decided to try our hand at making sauerkraut. I didn't enjoy that. But I like to cook and watch those I care for eat with enjoyment."

Dave smiled. "Well, I for one enjoy you and your ma's cooking. I've put on weight in the last few months."

She frowned. "You still need to put on weight. You were skin and bone when you arrived in the spring. You look much better now."

He was pleased and surprised that she had noticed.

Mrs. Anderson arrived at their table with two large plates filled with chicken and dumplings. "There you go and if you want a refill just holler. I'll be out later with your pie." She retreated to the kitchen.

Rachel had her head down and lifted just her eyes. "Would you say a blessings for the food?"

Dave set his fork down. "Be glad to." He gave a short blessing reminiscent of Mr. Harrod's blessings for the food and then picked up his fork and began to eat.

As they were finishing their pie, Rachel said, "I want to thank you for all the help you've given Johnny with his school work. Mary said he is doing even better work than before you came."

Dave swallowed, not sure how to respond. "It's been my pleasure to help him. He's a bright boy and learns so quickly."

Rachel nodded. "Yes, he is very bright and he likes being with you. I've also noticed you teaching him how to lasso. He needs all the attention we can give him with Pa being injured. It's an unsettled time for him."

"You have given him a lot of your attention too and it shows. He's a well-mannered little boy and knows how to conduct himself. I think maybe you've had a lot to do with that." Dave was sure that his son had greatly benefited from the love and care that Rachel had given him through the years. He just wished she didn't find it so difficult to let him give the same love and care to his son. This second chance with Johnny meant too much and Dave hated that his past crowded in to mar it.

Dave didn't want the calm time with Rachel to end but they had to get back to the ranch before dark. He paid for their meal and escorted her to the wagon. Even though she could have climbed up onto the wagon without his help, he took advantage by putting his hands around her waist and lifting her up. She didn't object and even slid her hand over his as it rested on her waist. The ride back to the ranch was quiet but companionable. Dave was wishful for more.

Dave spent the rest of the week doing odd jobs that needed doing around the ranch before winter set in. Friday morning, the ground was covered by a heavy frost, Dave was shivering by the time he reached the kitchen.

Mrs. Harrod kissed his cheek. "Morning, Dave. Your face is cold. It's warmer upstairs. Would you take breakfast up to Jake for me? Maybe it will help you get warm."

"Sure." Dave gathered up the tray and climbed the stairs two at a time. His leg was completely healed and wasn't giving him any problems. Carrying in the breakfast tray, he sat it down on Mr. Harrod's lap. He then sat down in the straight back chair to visit a few minutes with his boss.

The older man was looking good except for his leg held fast in the pulley. "Morning, Dave. It's a cold morning. I can feel it from the window here by the bed. I can also see the frost out on the grass. It's heavy for the first one of the fall."

"Yeah, the first really heavy one of the season. We'll need to start making sure the water isn't freezing on the creeks."

"Time to start carrying an axe to chop it free." Mr. Harrod nodded as he took a bite of a biscuit. "By the way, you need to look in the storage shed and pull out that little pot-bellied stove and set it up in the old bunkhouse. Or, you can stay in

Mary's room for the winter. No one has stayed in the old bunkhouse through a winter for several years. We took the stove out to make more room for Jesse's family."

Dave grinned. "It was pretty cold last night and especially this morning. I'd rather set up the stove and stay put. But thanks for the offer to stay in the house."

Chuckling as he ate his breakfast, Mr. Harrod waved a fork at Dave. "I sort of guessed you'd rather stay put. Minnie would prefer you stay in the house, but if I were you, I would prefer the old bunkhouse. You need to be able to get away from all these women."

The old stove was easy to put up because the flue was still there and he only had to attach it to the stovepipe. The small stove had a cook top where he could heat water or make coffee. It had a swing feed door, large ash pit, cast iron foot rail, and draft controls. Dave built a woodbin and filled it with short pieces of wood for easy feeding of the fire. He could build a fire when he came in off the range and by the time he came back after supper the bunkhouse was warm and stayed warm until morning. Sleeping in the cave the winter before, he never felt warm. Now his life was filled with luxury.

He found time to ride over to Jud Sawyer's place and buy the paint pony. Dave arranged for Jud to bring it over on Friday as far as the springs up behind the house. He planned to stake the pony out at the springs overnight and then surprise Johnny on Saturday.

On Friday, Wayne and the other hands returned from helping Jesse with his roundup. Dave was glad to have him back. For almost four weeks, Dave had been in charge of the ranch. He was relieved to give the responsibility back to Wayne.

Saturday afternoon Jesse, Edna and the children arrived to help celebrate Johnny's birthday and to visit with Mr. Harrod. Mary and Tim came from town for the occasion. Supper was a festive time with all the family together. Johnny didn't mind being the center of attention. His grandmother made all of his favorites for supper, including a big chocolate cake with white frosting.

Dave thought it was the most impressive cake he'd ever seen. After cutting the cake and eating a big piece, Johnny opened his presents, which consisted mainly of new clothes. Dave noticed Johnny looking over at him out of the corner of his eye several times while he opened his presents. Someone knocked on the back door.

Clued in earlier by Dave, Mrs. Harrod told Johnny to answer it. When Johnny opened the door, Randy stood there. "Hey, Johnny, there's someone out here says he's waiting for you." Randy played his part to the hilt.

"For me, what do you mean?" Johnny asked with a puzzled frown.

"Come on out and see." Randy motioned.

Johnny went out onto the back porch with Dave and the others following.

Tied to the porch railing was the paint pony with the small saddle on it.

"You see, Johnny? That paint pony told me it was waiting for you," Randy told him.

The look of excitement on Johnny's face made Dave's stomach do a flip-flop, and he had a lump in his throat that wouldn't go away.

"Is it for me, truly?" Johnny looked in wonder at the pony.

"It's your birthday present from your Pa." Mrs. Harrod explained.

At the sight of his son's joy, Dave crossed his arms and hugged his chest to help him keep control. "Why don't you go see if the saddle fits?"

Johnny took one look at his father, as if to make sure it was real, then ran down to the pony, and mounted with one try. Everyone started talking and laughing.

Wayne slapped Dave on the back. "Johnny won't ever forget this birthday. His first horse that's all his own."

Dave hoped for just that, that his tenth birthday would be one his son would not forget. He couldn't take his eyes off Johnny as he rode the pony around the yard, showing off to his cousins. Finally, Dave called for the boy to come on in and let Randy put the pony away for him.

Johnny came with reluctance. He would have spent the night in the barn with the pony if Dave had let him. The others had all gone in to the kitchen ready to eat more cake. As Johnny came up on the porch where Dave waited, he put his arms around Dave's waist and hugged him. "Thanks, Pa. That's the best birthday present I ever had."

"You're welcome, son, I hope you and he can be good friends."

"What should I call the pony, Pa?"

"Whatever you want. It's your pony." Dave told him.

"I'm going to call him Paint." Johnny said without hesitation.

"Paint, that's a fine name for him. Let's go get some more of your birthday cake before it's all gone." Dave ushered him back into the house where Mrs. Harrod and the others waited.

After Johnny had eaten his second piece of cake, Dave nudged him and whispered for him to get another piece and follow him upstairs. The rest of the family was deep in conversation and barely noticed them leaving the table, all but Mrs. Harrod who evidently understood what they were doing and nodded in approval. Upstairs they went to Mr. Harrod's bedroom where he was reading a book.

"Grandpa, I brought you a piece of my birthday cake." Johnny put the plate with the cake on his grandfather's chest on top of the book.

Mr. Harrod laughed. "Well, I guess I better eat it if it's birthday cake. Now let me think how old are you? Is it eight or nine?"

"Ah, Grandpa, you know I'm ten-years-old today." Johnny responded quickly, wanting to acknowledge every year.

"Did Johnny like his present or do you have to take it back?" Mr. Harrod winked at Dave.

Before Dave could say anything, Johnny responded, "I love my present. Pa doesn't have to take it back. I named him Paint. Do you think he'll like that name, Grandpa?"

"What did the pony say when you told him?" The grandfather teased his oldest grandson.

"Grandpa, you know horses can't talk." All three of them laughed together.

Dave was ready to call it an evening, so he said goodnight and left Johnny describing all his presents to his grandfather. Dave didn't linger downstairs but went to the old bunkhouse where he lay in bed for a long time thinking about the day, and his son's reaction to the pony. He felt good about the relationship he and Johnny had developed, and he hoped it would continue to grow. He wouldn't let himself think about what would happen after he left.

It had been almost a year earlier that he'd been shot on the mountain. As Dave thought back over the events of the year, he knew that he'd changed. In a way, he'd grown up and had at last come to terms with Jenny's death. He'd at last let the past go and could now start living the rest of his life. If he'd learned anything from his past, it was that one doesn't always get what he wants, but a man just makes the best of what he has and moves on.

Chapter 22

Dave finished eating his breakfast and lingered over another cup of coffee.

Johnny stuffed half a biscuit into his mouth. "What you going to do today, Pa?"

At least, Dave thought that was what he said with his mouth so full. "I'm waiting for your Uncle Wayne to come so we can go up and talk to your grandpa."

Using the other half of his biscuit to mop up the last of the gravy on his plate, Johnny asked, "What will you talk to Grandpa about?"

"We'll talk about the work of the ranch, now that the roundup is over and winter is coming on." Dave enjoyed the quiet moment with his son. "Your grandpa wants your Uncle Wayne and me to carry out what needs to be done."

Wayne came into the kitchen from the porch. "Hey, Johnny, you heading out to school soon?"

"Yeah, Uncle Wayne. I better get going." Johnny stood and then gave his father a hug.

Dave returned the hug, as he kissed him on the forehead. "So long, son. Have a good day at school."

Johnny grabbed his coat and book bag and ran out the kitchen door.

Wayne and Dave made their way to Mr. Harrod's room. "Morning boys." Mr. Harrod put down the book he was reading.

Dave checked the pulley as he did every time he entered the bedroom.

Wayne handed his father a fresh cup of coffee he brought upstairs to him. "You thought much about the fencing up around Seeping Springs, Pa?"

"You boys do what you think best, but it would be good to get that area fenced. I've registered the springs and hold title to it but the fence would let everyone know I claim it. What do you think about a line shack up there?" Mr. Harrod sipped on the hot coffee.

Dave let Wayne take the lead in these morning talks with Mr. Harrod. Mr. Harrod guided the work by making suggestions. He rarely told them what to do directly, but if he suggested something that was the way it was usually done.

Wayne ran his fingers through his hair. "I'm not sure who to put on that job. You know most of the hands would rather do anything than build a fence."

Dave didn't mind putting up a fence. It would mean long days of hard labor for several weeks made worse by the cold weather. He was more content if he had a full day's work every day. "I can get that done for you. I'll ask Randy Goode if he'll work with me. Herb Stiller could drive the wagon with the fencing material."

"That would be great if you took that on. But Dave, you don't have to do every mean job around the place," Wayne said.

"I don't mind. Work is work as far as I'm concerned. Besides, it gives a man satisfaction to look back on a couple of miles of fencing and know that it's going to be there a while." Dave shifted in the straight wooden chair. Completing the fencing would be something tangible he could leave behind to show that he'd been there. The hard work might help him sleep without dreaming.

Mr. Harrod nodded as if pleased with the solution. "Then that's settled. Wayne, you might better send word to Smithy at the mercantile to order more wire."

Dave admired the way that Mr. Harrod managed the ranch. The older man had been one of the first ranchers in the region to put up fencing. He seemed to have an innate sense of what was the most profitable way to raise cattle. Each year he added more fencing as a way of controlling the drift of the herds and the use of the range.

❖   ❖   ❖

When Dave came in from work in the late afternoons, he stoked up the little stove in his room so it would be warm when he returned later in the evening. Then he went up to the house. With the days getting shorter and the evenings longer, he found himself spending several hours after supper at the house.

He grabbed a big armful of wood and knocked on the kitchen door with his foot.

Rachel held the door open wide. "That's a load of wood you have there."

"Thanks for getting the door, Rachel. I want to make sure you ladies have enough wood to keep that cook stove going." Carrying the logs carefully across the room, he set them down in the woodbin. He noticed that Rachel seemed more relaxed and she had spoken first which was unusual.

"I see. You have an ulterior motive for bringing in the wood. Well, fair is fair and I guess we'll have to let you stay for supper." Rachel gave him a small grin with her banter.

Johnny, seated at the table ready to eat, looked up. "Of course, Pa is staying for supper, Aunt Rachel."

She reached over and tousled his hair. "I know. I was just teasing him."

Johnny grinned and nodded. "I see."

Dave hung his coat on the hook by the back door. With the sun going down the air was cooling quickly. Mrs. Harrod took the pan of hot cornbread out of the oven and placed it on the trivet in the center of the table. Next to it was a big pot of stew filled with vegetables and pieces of beef. The rich smell of the stew and fresh baked cornbread surrounded Dave as he hurried to take his seat. After Rachel, Mrs. Harrod, and Dave joined Johnny at the table, Mrs. Harrod took Johnny and Dave's hands. Seated as he was across from Rachel, Dave reached over and gently took Rachel's hand.

Mrs. Harrod said, "Dave, would you say blessing this evening?" With Mr. Harrod not able to come to the table, it fell to Dave or Johnny to say the blessing. Dave had felt awkward at first but now he was used to praying aloud before the meal and didn't mind, especially as he got to hold Johnny and Rachel's hands.

After supper, he helped Johnny with his schoolwork. It pleased him that he could still remember his arithmetic, geography, and the other subjects. His son seemed to try harder for his father than he did for his grandmother or aunt.

With cold weather setting in, the Harrods used the front room as the family gathering place instead of the back porch. It had a fireplace at one end and a wood stove at the other. Mr. Harrod's bedroom was directly above the room, and by keeping a fire going in both the fireplace and stove, enough heat rose to the second floor to keep it warm.

Mrs. Harrod returned downstairs with the tray she had taken up for Mr. Harrod. She put the dirty dishes in the dry sink. "Johnny, was it you that brought in the wood?"

"No ma'am, it was Pa." Johnny chewed on the top of his pencil.

Mrs. Harrod came over where Dave sat. She bent and kissed Dave on the forehead. "Thank you, son. I've been concerned with how we were going to keep enough wood cut and brought in for the winter."

"Don't you worry; Johnny and I will keep the woodbins full." Dave looked over at Johnny. "Think we can do that so your Grandma doesn't have to worry?"

"Sure, Pa. That's no big chore and we can bring in the water too."

Mrs. Harrod stepped over to Johnny and kissed him on the top of the head. "You boys sure do relieve my mind."

Dave promised himself that was one concern he would take off this kind, gentle woman. Now that Mr. Harrod was incapacitated, there were several things he could do to take up the slack. He had learned one thing about his son. Dave discovered that if he did a chore with him, Johnny didn't seem to mind doing it. If Johnny were put to a task by himself, he would grumble loud and clear. Dave tried to work with Johnny when he could.

One task Dave would not help him with was the care and feeding of the paint pony. His grandpa had given Johnny clear instructions. If he wanted the privilege of his own pony, he had to be responsible for it. Johnny didn't complain about that chore. He'd fallen in love with his pony and treated it with extra special care. The main problem they had with Johnny and the pony was convincing him it didn't need oats all the time because it was getting too fat.

Dave didn't know what had changed, but since Mr. Harrod broke his leg, Rachel didn't seem as hostile to him. Maybe it had something to do with his renewal of his promise to leave after Mr. Harrod was back on his feet. Dave was glad not to have so much tension between them. With the coming of winter, they were forced to be around each other more. Every night after Johnny finished his math homework, they moved to the front room to more comfortable seats at a small study table. Johnny read aloud his reading assignment. His reward for completing his homework was that his father read to him before sending him up to bed.

Dave feared Rachel might resent his helping Johnny with his schoolwork, but instead she seemed pleased. As they sat in the living room at the study table and worked, Rachel would sit close by, doing handwork, or mending. Then she would spend part of each evening working on the quilt stretched out on the quilting frame. The frame was attached to the ceiling and when it wasn't being used it could be raised out of the way by rope pulleys.

Usually it was just the three of them because Mrs. Harrod would be upstairs with Mr. Harrod. Occasionally Dave would find his mind going in directions that would startle him. His awareness of Rachel as a woman was becoming more acute. He was sure that she had no romantic thoughts about him. He tried to force his mind to ignore the feelings he sometimes felt when he was around her. Dave found it more difficult to ignore his dreams. He was glad he woke in the dark and no one was around to see his dreams.

It had been six years since he'd been with a woman. Jenny had been his one and only, and after her death, he'd managed to suppress his desires. However he was a healthy man and constantly being around someone as attractive and feminine as Rachel awakened feelings he'd thought were long dead. It was a useless direction to let his thoughts wander. To try to protect himself, he tried never to be alone with her, but kept Johnny close by.

Rachel didn't make it easy as the appeal of her warm and kind spirit was all too often evident in how she dealt with her parents and Johnny. More and more that warm and kind spirit seemed to include him.

Rachel was pleased with how the quilt was coming. She enjoyed sitting in the front room with Dave and Johnny nearby and sewing on the quilt in the evenings. She had decided to use the pattern called, Single Irish Chain. With various shades of blue, a white background, and black border, it made a bold design.

Pa had been in bed for almost two months when one morning she responded to a knock on the back door. It was the doctor for his weekly visit. "Good morning, sir. Come in out of the cold. Can I get you a cup of coffee? Ma has gone to Wayne's house for the morning. It's the first real break she has had from the care of Pa. She left me in charge." She took his coat and hat.

"Morning, Miss Rachel. Yes, winter is on its way. It's cold out there. I'll take that coffee. How is our patient?" The older man sat down at the table.

Rachel poured a cup and sat it in front of the doctor. "He's trying real hard to be a good patient. But Pa is definitely getting restless."

"That's not surprising. As he heals and starts to feel better, he'll want to get out of bed." Doc drank the cup of coffee quickly and stood. "I'd better go up and check on Jake."

"I'll come with you." Rachel climbed the stairs to her father's room with the doctor behind her. She tapped lightly on the door of the bedroom. "Pa, Doc is here."

"Come in, Frederick. Sorry you had to drive out in this weather." Jake Harrod lay in the bed where he had been for the last ten weeks.

"Let's see how your leg is healing. Rachel, will you help me unwrap this bandage."

Rachel was getting used to helping the doctor. At least now, the wound around the broken bone was almost healed. When the leg was unwrapped, she stepped back so Doc could get a closer look.

"What do you think, Frederick? Can I be getting out of this bed?" Jake Harrod looked at the doctor hopefully.

"I know it's hard, Jake. The flesh is healed but the bone will need several more months to completely heal. If you don't stay in bed with this pulley, you may end up hardly able to walk." He spoke calmly but with a certainty.

Jake gave a deep sigh. "I don't like it but I also don't want to be crippled. I guess I can take it."

Rachel reached over and took her father's hand. "It'll pass quickly, Pa. It's already been over two months."

"I'll be back to check on you next week." Doc shook hands with Jake, picked up his bag, and went down the stairs.

"I'll see Doc out, then I'll bring you some dinner." Rachel quickly followed the doctor. When she got downstairs, she found her mother had returned from Wayne's place. She and Dave were seated at the table with cups of coffee.

Doc sat his bag down on a chair and stood behind it. "I'm glad you're here, Minnie. I need to talk to you about Jake."

"Jake isn't worse?"

"No, Minnie, he's not worse. In fact, he is healing well. However, that's part of the problem. He's starting to feel so much better and wants to get out of bed. But you got to tell the family not to expect Jake's full recover until spring and to prepare themselves for a winter of trying to keep him comfortable. Spend as much time with him as possible to help keep his mind occupied. I have to get going. I'll see you all next week." The doctor put on his coat and hat, picked up his bag, and left.

Ma started toward the stairs. "I'm going up to your pa. Would you mind getting the cornbread out of the oven in about fifteen minutes?"

Rachel went over to the stove to stir the chicken and vegetable stew that simmered. She glanced over at Dave where he sat at the table. He looked so serious and handsome. "Pa's going to be all right. He just needs time."

Startled, Dave looked up at her. "I'm sure he is."

"You looked so serious. I thought maybe you were concerned about him." She took bowls down from the cabinet, and set them on the table.

"I know it's hard on Mr. Harrod. But I was just remembering back to last winter when I had to heal from the bullet wound alone in the cave."

"I can't imagine what that was like. Pa is better off than he realizes. I know he's impatient with his slow healing, but he's never impatient with any of the family. It makes it easier to care for him."

"Yes, he's a blessed man with two strong sons and two beautiful daughters, plus some wonderful grandchildren."

Rachel could feel the heat of a blush rising on her cheeks. She liked the sound of his voice as he said she was beautiful. "We are the blessed ones, having a Pa and Ma as we do."

"Is that why you've stayed here on the ranch instead of going back east to school like Mary did?" Dave leaned forward with his arms relaxed on the table.

Rachel needed to check the cornbread but she didn't want to interrupt the conversation with Dave. They had so few times when it was just the two of them. "I love living here on the ranch. I always have. I love the work with the cattle, riding the horses, and yes, even the cooking and cleaning. I guess I'm just a simple country girl." Rachel smiled at her confession.

Dave returned her smile. "You may be a country girl, but there's nothing simple about you."

Rachel looked into his handsome face and soft brown eyes, and felt something turn over within her. Almost frightened at the strength of the feeling, she turned back to the stove and took the cornbread out of the oven. She had never had such a strong reaction to a man as she did at this moment. Was she starting to care for Dave as more than her brother-in-law? What would she do if she did come to care for him as a man, someone to love? He was just going to leave again.

Chapter 23

Dave fell into the routine of spending Sunday morning visiting with Mr. Harrod while the family went to church services. The time spent with just the two of them helped to broaden and deepen an already good friendship. Dave found himself sharing many of the things from his past and talking about the possibility of starting a ranch in the mountains in the future. Mr. Harrod encouraged him to talk through possible plans for buildings and grazing. However, two areas Dave never shared were the promise he'd made to Rachel to leave without taking Johnny, and the strange thoughts and feelings he found himself having about Rachel.

When she sat sewing the quilt while he and Johnny played chess, he always sat so he could see her. It was all he could do some evenings not to go over and stroke her hair, which she wore down more often in the winter. Dave watched the thick light brown hair flowing to her waist, and found himself wondering what it would be like to run his fingers through it.

Mary and Tim, Jesse and Wayne with their families all came for dinner the first Sunday of December. It was a cold day but sunny and clear. After they ate, the children bundled up in their coats, knitted hats, and ran outside to play. The rest of the family including Dave moved to the front room to visit.

Mary sat next to her mother with Tim standing behind her. "I have something to tell you all. Tim and I have discussed it and we've decided to wait until summer to marry." She had everyone's attention. "I want Pa to walk me down the aisle. Tim has been so kind and good to me. He's willing to wait."

Jesse took his wife's hand. "When would you get married?"

"I talked to Doc and he said Pa should be just fine by June. So instead of a winter wedding with only a couple of weeks off school, we'll marry in June after school lets out for the summer." Mary reached up and put her hand on Tim's.

"Are you in agreement, Tim?" Mrs. Harrod asked looking up at the slim young man her daughter had chosen for her husband.

"I won't lie and say I'm not disappointed by the postponement, but I understand that it's important to Mary for her father to walk her down the aisle." Tim grinned at Mary. "If I get to marry this wonderful woman, I don't mind how long I have to wait."

Dave understood both Tim's disappointment and his willingness to wait. Mary was a wonderful, beautiful Christian woman that any man would be proud to marry. He had always respected her serene outlook on life and he suspected she was the smartest of the Harrod children.

Rachel shifted in her seat and cleared her throat. "Since we're all here together, why don't we talk about what we're going to do about Christmas with Pa still in bed."

Mrs. Harrod nodded. "That a good idea. I asked Doc about letting Jake off the pulley for a few hours so you boys could bring him downstairs to be with the family, but he's afraid to chance disturbing the leg. What do you think, Dave? Do you think Doc is right?"

Dave looked at the kindly face of the woman who was the nearest thing to a mother he had since losing his own mother at age ten. "I think Doc is right. Mr. Harrod's leg is healing well for now. If it can continue for another two or three months, he should be able to walk without any problems. I'm sorry."

"Don't be sorry, Dave. I think you're right. This is just one Christmas we will have to have Jake upstairs and the rest of us downstairs." Mrs. Harrod had accepted what had to be.

Wayne wasn't ready to accept that his father would have to be separated from the rest of the family for most of the holiday festivities. "Wait a minute, Ma. What if we carried Pa down the stairs in his bed, pulley and all? What do you think, Dave?"

Dave didn't like it that he had to disappoint these people who had come to mean so much to him. "I don't advise it. There would be no way to carry the bed down and keep the pressure on the leg constant. There's no telling the damage it might do."

Rachel stood and went over to sit by her brother. She put her arm through his. "I think Dave is right and we shouldn't chance it. We will just need to have a parade of us going up and down stairs to make sure Pa's not alone. We'll get past this Christmas, then Pa will get back on his feet by spring. It won't be long."

Grateful for Rachel's support, Dave felt better about speaking the truth. He also wanted Mr. Harrod to be a part of family activities, but he would rather see his friend walking without difficulties.

Mary stood and smoothed her dress. "Speaking of a parade up to see Pa, Tim and I need to go tell him about our decision to postpone the wedding."

Dave guessed Mr. Harrod would be pleased with their decision.

During the next few days Dave overheard different ones in the family talking about getting presents for each other. He needed to think about presents for the family too. He had no trouble deciding what to get the men in the family, including the little boys. One winter he'd worked on a ranch down on the border and had learned leather tooling from an old Mexican man. Pedro had worked on beautiful boots, saddles, and belts, which the owner had then sold sharing some of the profit with the old man. Dave had hung around Pedro until he taught him to tool leather.

Dave didn't have the tools or time to make boots, so he decided to make each of the men and boys a belt for a total of eight. Searching in the storage room in the barn he found some tools and borrowed them. The owner of the livery stable in town sold him some leather. He designed each belt with a different pattern. The hardest part was finding buckles and getting belt sizes without letting anyone know what he was doing. After he returned to his room each evening, he added wood to the fire in the stove and worked for several hours on the belts.

With Johnny feeling free to wander in and out of the old bunkhouse, he could only work on the belts after the boy went to bed. Dave spent much of his time while working on the belts trying to think of something to get the women. He'd gone into town twice to look in the general store but nothing seemed appropriate. Hattie was easy to figure out. He'd heard Hattie tell Rachel about a dollhouse one of her friends at school had and how much she liked it. Using scraps of wood he found around the place, he began to build her a two-story dollhouse.

Randy helped him complete the dollhouse. The young cowhand had never seen anything like it. He was intrigued with trying to get every minute detail correct.

A week before Christmas, Mrs. Harrod asked Dave to bring in some trunks from the storage room in the barn. They were full of decorations for the Christmas tree.

He sat at the kitchen table drinking another cup of coffee before heading over to Jud Sawyer's place to pick up a hog Jud had butchered for them. Dave was running out of time to find presents for the women. Mrs. Harrod poured herself a cup of tea, and then sat down at the table with him.

He decided to ask her what to get for Rachel and Mary. "Mrs. Harrod, I need some help with a problem."

"Why sure, if I can. I'll be glad to help you."

Dave laughed at the serious expression she gave. "It's not anything really big, but I can't figure out anything to get Rachel or Mary for Christmas. Can you give me an idea of something they would like?"

She smiled back at him. "Dave, you don't need to worry about getting any presents unless you want to give them."

"I know, but I really would like to get them a gift, I just can't seem to come up with anything."

"Well, they always want anything to fix up with like most women. A new ribbon or comb for their hair would be nice, especially for Mary. Just whatever you want to give will be appreciated." She assured him as she poured him more coffee.

"What about you? What would you appreciate for Christmas?" He picked up his cup and waited for her answer.

"My goodness, Dave, just having you here is my present." She patted him on the arm. "Although, there's something you could give me that I would appreciate more than any gift."

She had Dave curious.

"You know Christmas is on Sunday this year. A wonderful present for me would be for you to go to church with us. I know you're not a regular church goer, and that's your right to choose, but you asked what I would like, and that's it."

Not prepared for what she really wanted, Dave looked at his coffee cup and didn't know what to say. It wasn't that he didn't believe in God or was against going to church with her. It was more that he was so out of the practice. He hadn't realized that she felt so strongly about it. Neither she nor any of the family had said anything to him about the fact that he was the only one in the family that didn't go to church services.

Mrs. Harrod reached over and patted his hand again. "Don't worry about it, Dave. It's just something I wish for, but I don't have a right to put any pressure on you. I just remember how good I felt when you and Jenny would always come to church services with us, and I saw all my family there together." She leaned forward and folded her hands on the table. "I know it's been hard for you since Jenny passed away. It just broke my heart that first Sunday you were here. I saw you through the church window at her grave by yourself. Jake and I both wanted to get up and go out to you, but we knew you needed to be alone with her."

Dave looked up at her amazed. "You all saw me? You never said anything."

"No, we felt if you wanted to talk about it, you would." She spoke softly and gently.

"It's hard for me to talk about. It was almost like I couldn't let her go until that Sunday." Dave stared at her work-roughened hands and remembered that she also had to let her daughter go.

"I know. It's been hard for all of us, but much more for you. We at least had each other, but you went through it all alone."

Her concern and the tears in her eyes touched Dave. He knew they were for him and not for the loss of her oldest daughter. "I realize now that I didn't have to do it alone. I could have stayed here, as you all asked me to, but at the time, I didn't know how to do it any other way." The sound of the grief was there in his voice.

"I know. I think Jake and I have understood that. But I'm not so sure Rachel or Johnny understood that you just did the best you could at the time."

Dave looked up at her and slowly and softly told her the truth. "If we could only go back and do different. If I could, I wouldn't have left, but I would have stayed to help raise my son." Dave felt tears welling up in his own eyes. "But I missed my chance and I'll never have it again."

Taking his hand in both of hers, Mrs. Harrod shook her head, "No, Dave, you haven't missed your chance. You're here now and that's what counts. Johnny still has a lot of growing up to do and he needs you to help him."

Just then they heard the bell from Mr. Harrod's room. Mrs. Harrod gave Dave a quick hug, kissed him on the forehead, and then was gone up the stairs.

Dave carried the cups to the sink and then headed out to ride to Jud Sawyers. As he rode, a cold wind blew, leaving him cold but he ignored it. The conversation with Mrs. Harrod had taken an unexpected turn. What she'd asked for as a Christmas gift was such a small thing. He could easily give her the gift she wanted.

By the time he got to the Sawyer's place, the sunshine was gone and the clouds had the heavy look of snow. Jud was at his barn and glad to see someone. The Sawyer place wasn't very big or prosperous looking. Dave couldn't decide if it was a ranch or a farm. Jud couldn't seem to make up his mind either. He was the only one around that kept hogs, and he supplied all the ham and bacon that the Harrods needed. After Dave told Jud all the local news and how Mr. Harrod was progressing, they got around to packing the meat and tying it on the back of Dave's packhorse. Jud insisted Dave come in for coffee and stew before he started the cold ride back to the Lazy H.

Dave greeted Mrs. Sawyer who was a short roly-poly woman with a round face that seemed always to be smiling. As Dave sat at the table and ate a bowl of stew and cornbread, he noticed different pieces of lace and embroidery on a shelf in the kitchen. He asked about it because it looked like much more lace than one woman would use.

Mrs. Sawyer said, "Oh, my yes, I do have a lot of pieces. I've been planning to take them in to the general store. Mrs. Smithy sells them for me, but I just never got around to it."

"Would you mind if I looked at them?" Dave stood and took a closer glance at the pieces of lace.

"Go right ahead. Some of these lace collars make nice Christmas presents," she said.

That was exactly what Dave was thinking. As he gingerly touched the delicate lace with his work-calloused hands, he decided he would buy each of the five women in the Harrod family a piece of lace. Seeing that he was serious, Mrs. Sawyer got down another box that had other finished pieces.

One piece was a beautiful lace tablecloth. Dave decided to get that for Mary's wedding present. He picked out a lace collar for each of the women and a small one for Hattie. Mrs. Sawyer insisted on wrapping each piece carefully in brown paper. As she finished wrapping the lace, Dave spotted some little wooden flutes on another shelf.

Jud looked almost embarrassed as he admitted that he'd carved them for Mr. Smithy to sell. Dave added the flutes to his purchases, one for each of the children.

With hesitation Mrs. Sawyer quoted a price of five dollars.

Dave shook his head. "That is not a fair price at all." He thought she was going to cry so he quickly said. "I won't take all of these gifts for less than twenty dollars."

She placed her hand over her heart. "Oh, that's way too much."

Dave grinned. "That's my final offer."

With a shy smile, she took the twenty-dollar bill. "God bless you, Dave."

He bent down and kissed the little short woman on the cheek. "Merry Christmas."

Jud wiped his eyes. "Let me go help you get that into your saddlebags."

By the time they had his horses out of the barn, it had started to snow.

Jud stood with his hands in his pockets. "Come back any time and have a Merry Christmas."

Dave waved and led the packhorse loaded with meat down the lane bowing his head against the snow. He felt relieved to have found something to give the women for Christmas. He just hoped they would like his choices.

The snow was coming in flurries blown by the wind and in places, it started to cover the ground. Dave decided instead of riding directly to the ranch, he would swing by the school and ride on in with Johnny. He was concerned about how heavy the snow would get since this could be the first major storm of the winter.

Even though it was early in the afternoon when he rode up to the school building, Mary had dismissed the students and was sending them home. As Dave dismounted, he heard a shout behind him and turned to find Jesse riding up.

"Hey, Dave, you ride in to make sure Johnny gets home?" Jesse dismounted.

"I didn't know how bad this storm might get. I guess you're here to ride with Hattie."

"I'm glad I had to be in town today. I don't like her riding by herself in weather like this. Usually I send one of the hands to meet her halfway, but today I can ride back the whole way with her."

Mary came out of the schoolhouse with her coat, hat, and gloves on and Johnny and Hattie behind her similarly wrapped up against the cold.

"Get your ponies out of the barn and be quick about it." Mary told the children.

She walked up to Jesse and Dave. "I'm glad to see you two. I worried about them starting out with this snow coming down so heavy."

"It worked for me to be here to ride with Hattie. What about tomorrow? Will you have school?" Jesse asked.

Mary looked up at the clouds and wiped some of the snowflakes away from her face. "I don't know. It's not so hard for the children here in town to make it. You all decide for yourselves. I don't want to take a chance on them having a problem. We only have two more days until we stop for Christmas anyway. It won't hurt either Johnny or Hattie to miss school."

"Well, if I do send Hattie to school tomorrow, I'll probably have one of the hands ride the whole way with her, so don't worry about it." Jesse reassured his sister.

Johnny and Hattie rode from the little barn at the back of the schoolhouse ready to start home. They were excited by the snow and getting out of school early.

Mary pulled her scarf tighter. "Dave, tell Ma I'll be home on Friday. Tim is taking the train on Thursday to go visit his folks. I'll wait until after he leaves to come out."

"If the weather looks too bad either I or one of the hands will come in for you," Dave told her.

"That will be helpful. Thanks, Dave."

Jesse kissed Mary on the check and then mounted his horse. "We're planning to be at Ma and Pa's place on Saturday. You know how Ma likes for everyone to be together for Christmas Day. We'll see you then."

Jesse and Hattie started toward the north, and Dave and Johnny rode toward the west.

The two children waved and yelled good-by until they were out of earshot as if they would never see each other again.

Dave shook his head in wonder at the ways kids found to have fun.

By the time they made it to the ranch, the snow blew so thickly it was hard to see the road.

As they guided their horses into the barn to unsaddle, they found Randy saddling up ready to go and meet Johnny.

"Sure glad you're here Johnny. Your Grandma is worried about you." Randy took the saddle off his horse.

Dave started unsaddling. "Run on up to the house, Son, so your grandma will know you're here. I'll take care of Paint for you."

"All right, Pa. You going to come on up to the house soon?"

"It may be a little while. I'll help Randy take care of the horses and then I need to check some things. Tell you what, you make sure the woodbins are full, and after supper we'll play some chess." Dave wanted to get his packages to the bunkhouse without anyone seeing them.

The snow continued to fall most of the night, but the next day dawned cold and clear. Knowing that Mary would have school, Johnny rode into town. Randy followed him just to make sure he had no problems.

Dave headed out with Wayne to check the cattle. Most of the cattle would find shelter in some of the breaks and canyons, but there was always a danger they would drift before the wind and bunch up against a fence. The storm had not been severe enough for the cattle to freeze, but they still had to be checked on for possible problems.

As he and Wayne rode back toward the barn, he saw Rachel riding out across the range. She often took her horse out to exercise him and to get some fresh air for herself. On impulse, Dave waved at Wayne and followed Rachel. He had to admit that she could ride.

She stopped at the top of a rise where she could look out over the grassland toward the setting sun. In the distance, was the river that ran through the rangeland.

Dave rode up beside her and sat quietly on his horse, watching the sun as it turned the sky red.

Rachel shifted in her saddle and looked at him. "Are you watching over me?"

He grinned. "Sort of, do you mind?"

"No, I appreciate the thoughtfulness of it."

"Well, with this snow on the ground and some ice, you never know what might happen. I just want you to be safe." He really did want her to be safe. And it was nice to sit on their horses and look out over the land at the sunset.

Rachel gave a shiver. "Maybe we should head back to the barn. I need to help Ma with supper."

Dave took his gloves off and laid his hand over hers as they rested on the pommel. They were cold to the touch. "Here put my gloves on."

Before she could protest, he picked her hand up and slipped on the glove, which was too big. He then slipped on the other one.

"Let's head back." He turned his horse and led the way toward the barn. They needed to start back before he gave in to the almost overpowering desire to lean over and kiss her.

❖ ❖ ❖

On Thursday, Dave rode to town to get some supplies for Mrs. Harrod. She and Rachel had baked all week and had run out of certain items. Dave didn't quite understand why they would need so much food for just one day, but the women seemed to have a plan of baking that only they understood. While he was in town, Dave made some last minute purchases of his own.

Early on Saturday of Christmas Eve, Wayne with his two boys, and Dave with Johnny, took a wagon down by the creek bottom to cut a spruce tree. Wayne and Dave had already decided on one for the family Christmas tree. After letting even little Matt have a swing with the ax, they cut down the tree and loaded it on the wagon.

Jesse and his family arrived as they got back to the house and helped to set the tree upright in the living room. The Harrod tradition was to decorate the tree together as a family before supper on Christmas Eve. Through out the evening they made a game out of putting the presents under the tree as secretly as possible. With so many people in the house, it was hard to do anything without someone watching.

All of the cowhands had family or friends with whom they planned to spend the day except for the youngest. Randy had no family and Mrs. Harrod invited him to spend Christmas Eve and Christmas Day with the family.

By the time everyone went to bed the pile of gifts under the tree spilled out on the rug. Little David slept with Johnny and Hattie slept with Rachel at their grandparent's house. Jesse and Edna, with Billy had gone over to Wayne's house.

Dave doubted the children would get much sleep. They were too excited. He waited up until he thought everyone was asleep and then quietly took his presents in through the front door to place under the Christmas tree. The faint glow from the fire in the wood stove gave him plenty of light to see what he was doing. Getting the dollhouse in without making any noise was the hardest part. When he had everything placed to his satisfaction, he put more wood in the stove and went back to his room to try for a few hours of sleep.

It was still dark when Dave woke. After dressing in the cold room, he went to the house. Mrs. Harrod was already in the kitchen with the coffee made. Dave took an armful of wood in, as was his habit now.

"Merry Christmas, son. I hope you got some sleep." Mrs. Harrod greeted him as she poured him a cup of coffee. "I'm making pancakes and we will probably eat in shifts. So why don't you and I go ahead and have our breakfast."

"Sounds good to me. It seems I'm always hungry these days."

"Well, I notice that you put away a lot of food but you're still too thin. I don't know where all that food goes." Mrs. Harrod set two plates of pancakes on the table with fried bacon and scrambled eggs as side dishes.

Dave laughed. "If you don't mind, I'll keep on putting the grub away. With your cooking I'm sure I'll put on weight one of these days."

They were on their second cup of coffee when Mary and Rachel came down.

Mrs. Harrod prepared a tray for Mr. Harrod. Dave volunteered to take it up so the women could concentrate on the cooking they had started for the Christmas dinner. He'd barely made it to Mr. Harrod's room when he saw the children running toward the stairs in their bare feet.

Each child was allowed to open one present before breakfast, and then the whole family would open gifts when they returned from church services.

Dave doubted the children would pay much attention to the sermon.

By the time Dave took Mr. Harrod's breakfast tray back downstairs to the kitchen, Jesse, Edna, Wayne, and Nancy had arrived so Billy and Matt could pick out their one present.

Dave went back to his room to ready his surprise for Mrs. Harrod.

Randy brought the double-seated buggy up by the back porch behind Jesse's buggy in readiness for the family to go to church together. Dave walked across the yard to the house.

Randy stood by the horses grinning at Dave.

Dave nodded and winked as he passed on his way to the back porch. Squaring his shoulders and taking a deep breath, he opened the door and stepped into the kitchen.

Jesse and Wayne were helping their wives into their coats.

Mrs. Harrod had just come down the stairs with Mary and Rachel behind her. As she walked into the kitchen pulling on her gloves, she looked up to find everyone standing like statues staring at Dave. He was dressed in a black broadcloth suit with a white shirt and black string tie.

Dave took Mrs. Harrod's coat down from its hook and walked over holding it ready for her.

"Oh my, Dave," was all she said as she slipped into the coat.

He held out his arm and she slipped her hand through it.

"Merry Christmas, Ma. I hope you like your present."

"I love my present. Thank you, son." Her eyes were shinning as Dave, ignoring the others, escorted her out to the buggy.

The rest of the family followed in silence, including Johnny who grinned from ear to ear at the surprise his father had sprung on them.

Dave made sure Mrs. Harrod was comfortably seated in the front seat of the buggy and then helped Mary, Rachel, and Johnny into the back seat. Jesse and Wayne and their families climbed into Jesse's big buggy. Dave started the horses toward the church with Mrs. Harrod's arm through his.

Randy was already heading toward the house to visit with Mr. Harrod, which Dave had arranged with him.

On arrival at the white church building, Dave escorted Mrs. Harrod inside as everyone greeted each other. He let her guide him to the family pew because he'd never been in the building. Later he didn't remember much about the service. In one way, he felt uncomfortable, but in another sense, he felt warmed by the gathering of the family around him in this place.

It brought back memories of attending services with Jenny, not in a painful way, but simply as good memories. He was conscious of the other family members and especially of Rachel. During the singing of the hymns, he could hear her strong clear soprano voice above the other voices. It surprised him how many of the hymns he remembered. He enjoyed singing bass along with Jesse and Wayne, who were in the pew behind him with their families.

Dave looked over at Mrs. Harrod and noticed tears running down her face in spite of her smile. Had his coming to church with her given her that much joy? Humbled that so little a thing could have that affect, he made the decision that he would attend Sunday worship services with the family for the rest of the time he was at the ranch.

The ride back to the house was noisy. Everyone seemed released from the spell Dave's going to church service had put upon them. The children were especially high spirited, since they knew that once they got to the house they could open the rest of the presents. The rest of the day passed with everyone in high spirits and enjoying the huge meal that the women served in the middle of the afternoon.

Everyone expressed delight at the gifts Dave gave. Seeing their appreciation made him glad for the effort. For several hours, Dave was able to forget that he'd given his word to Rachel to leave. He allowed himself to enjoy the family and to watch the children as they delighted in their presents. Even Randy was like a kid in his reaction to the gifts the others had thoughtfully given him. Dave suspected that the young cowhand hadn't had many Christmases with family.

As Dave thought back on the Christmas Day the year before, which he'd spent alone in the cave, he wasn't sure which seemed more unreal. The contrast was so great that he felt one of them must be a dream. But that night as he looked once more at his Christmas gift from Johnny, he knew this was the one he wanted to be real.

Johnny had surprised him with a drawing of his mare. Dave hadn't realized that Johnny was so talented. Dave stood it on top of the chest of drawers next to the pictures of Johnny he'd gotten on his birthday.

Chapter 24

After Christmas, winter settled over the land with a seriousness that encouraged people to stay close to home. Mary was able to have school for the children who lived in town through the winter storms, but for several weeks, the children who usually rode in from the ranches were unable to get through the snowdrifts. Johnny would have enjoyed his unexpected vacation more except his grandparents insisted that he spend most of his days studying. Dave sympathized with him, but knew that the grandparents were right.

Dave stomped into the old bunkhouse not sure he would ever be warm again. Someone on this cold, snowy February day had lit a fire in the pot-bellied stove. He suspected it was Rachel. Relieved at the warmth he removed his boots and shucked his wet pants, shirt, and union suit. Riding through the day in the falling snow, it had been impossible to stay dry much less warm. Pulling dry clothes out of the bureau, he gave a silent thanks to Mrs. Harrod and Rachel who always made sure he had clean clothes.

Stamping back into his boots, he heard the ringing of the supper bell. On such a winter evening, it felt good to anticipate a hot meal and warmth of company. After shrugging into his heavy coat and gloves, he pulled his hat on snug against the cold north wind that whipped between the old bunkhouse and the ranch house. This warmth of family wasn't going to last, but for now it was enough.

Dave gathered an armload of wood and entered the heat of the kitchen. The smell of fresh baked bread blended with the savory aroma of roast beef with gravy that bubbled on the stove in a big Dutch oven. The kitchen was crowded with the addition of Wayne and his family. A chorus of greetings welcomed Dave as he offloaded the wood into the bin and then removed his coat, hat, and gloves.

Rachel took his things before he could step over to the hooks on the wall where coats and scarves crowded each other hanging beneath the shelf upon which sat the numerous hats and gloves of the family.

Mrs. Harrod patted Dave's arm. "You're just in time to set this pot on the table. Put it in front of my place and I'll dish up everyone's plate."

"Yes, ma'am." Dave lifted the heavy Dutch oven filled with roast beef and vegetables and carefully placed it on the table. He licked his lips in anticipation of the meal.

After the blessing everyone got busy talking and eating. The hubbub was especially intense as Wayne's two little ones added to the noise with their high-pitched, childish voices.

Wayne said something to Dave who just cupped his ear and shook his head.

"I asked did you spot any newborn calves today?" The bellow of Wayne's voice seemed to startle everyone into quietness.

Dave shook his head and grinned. "None today but I did see a lot of wolf tracks."

Wayne grabbed another piece of bread. "Good. It's not too early to find some but they have more of a chance of survival if they come a month from now. The wolves have come down from the hills and can cause a lot of damage. You're probably as good a shot with a rifle as anyone on the ranch. How about you taking on tracking and eliminating the wolf pack before we lose more beef?"

Dave didn't particularly like the job, but he knew it needed to be done. "Sure, I can do that for you."

For the next week Dave trailed and shot wolves. He skinned them and then he and Randy worked in the shed at curing the hides. It would have been warmer in the barn but the smell bothered the horses. It was with relief when he was able to finally tell Wayne that the wolves were no longer a threat to the livestock, although they had to keep an eye out for lone wolves that could still travel onto the ranch.

The last day of February was clear and cold and Dave spent the morning shoeing some horses with Randy's help. He had the foreleg of the black gelding he had been riding pressed between his legs as he carefully tapped the new horseshoe on. When he looked up he saw Doc's buggy coming up the lane.

Tipping his head toward the approaching buggy, he mumbled between the nails held between his lips. "Go take care of Doc's horse."

Randy let go of the gelding's bridle and walked to meet Doc. "Sure a cold day to be out and about, Doc. Go on in the house. I'll take care of your horse." After Doc climbed down and went into the house, Randy led the horse and buggy into the barn.

In a few minutes Rachel came hurrying across the yard. "Doc wants you to come help him, Dave. When you get to a stopping place."

Dave released the gelding's leg and stood straight to undo the kink in his back. He had been bending over most of the morning. "Just finished. After I wash up I'll be there. Do you know what Doc wants?"

Dave hardly knew what Rachel was saying, he was so busy noticing how pretty she looked with the sunshine seeming to illuminate her face with a glow that he felt as a shock throughout his body. He shook his head to get his thoughts back on what she was saying.

Rachel frowned. "He wants you to help take the pulley off Pa's leg. Do you think he's ready for that?"

Taking a deep breath, Dave tried to look at her beautiful brown eyes with one of confidence. "If Doc thinks your pa is ready then I'm sure he is. He won't be doing a jig for a few months but he should be walking by spring."

Rachel walked close to Dave as they headed to the house. "Thanks for the reassurance. I worry so about what all this has done to Pa."

Dave placed his hand on the small of her back to let her go through the kitchen doorway ahead of him. He could feel the warmth of her body through the wool dress and shawl that she was wearing. "He's doing fine and by summer you won't even know he had been injured.'

It was with reluctance that Dave removed his hand from her back. After washing his hands at the sink, he climbed the stairs to Harrod's bedroom where he found Mrs. Harrod and Doc gathered around Mr. Harrod in his bed.

Doc moved around to the other side of the bed and looked across at Dave. "I've told Jake and Minnie that I think his leg is as healed as it can get and is ready to be released from the pulley. We'll let him have a few days just getting used to the leg being out of traction before I let him try to walk."

Dave walked up to the side of the bed and grinned at Mr. Harrod. "Just tell me what to do to help."

Mr. Harrod grimaced. "Well, first thing is don't look so cheerful about this. I figure it's going to hurt like the dickens."

Doc pointed to the sack full of oats. "If you will hold the weight, I will detach the pulley from the leg."

Dave moved to the end of the bed, carefully lifted the bag, and held it while Doc untied the pulley lines from the nail they had driven through the thighbone.

Once the pulley lines were clear, Dave set the bag of feed into the hall along with the lines and pulley.

Doc mixed some white powder with water and lifted it to Mr. Harrod's lips. "What we got to do to get the nail removed is going to be very painful. It will go better if you're more relaxed."

Mr. Harrod made a face. "Yuke. That stuff tastes so nasty."

Mrs. Harrod held her husband's hand. "How long until it takes effect?"

Dave caught Mrs. Harrod eye with a glance. "I'd feel better if you would take Rachel and wait downstairs. You two being here just makes me nervous and won't help Mr. Harrod."

Squeezing his wife's hand Mr. Harrod spoke with the firmness of the head of household. "You take Rachel and wait downstairs. Doc will call you as soon as you can be of help. Make a fresh pot of coffee so he can have a cup before he leaves."

She leaned down and kissed her husband on the lips. "All right, Jake. Now you relax and let Doc get on with it."

Rachel looked as if she was about to say something, but her mother grabbed her arm and propelled her toward the hall. "Come on sweetheart. Dave is right. We don't need to be here."

Dave was relieved to see the women leave and turned to Doc. "Now what do we do?"

Doc smoothed his mustache. "Thanks for suggesting they leave. This will go easier without having to worry about them suffering through watching you in pain, Jake."

Mr. Harrod shifted his good leg and his eyelids were starting to droop. "I'll rest my eyes a minute and then you can get to it."

Doc smiled. "Dave, he should be out of it in a couple of minutes. I'm going to wash the area around the nail and the nail itself with carbolic acid. Then I need you to hold the leg still while I grab the nail with this pair of pliers and work it loose. As soon as I have it loose, I will try to jerk it through in one move. The wound will bleed but I hope not bad and I can just put a bandage on it without having to stitch it up."

Gripping Mr. Harrod's thigh above the nail and below the knee, Dave bore down with his weight and anchored the leg to the bed.

Doc fastened the pliers on the nail and worked it back and forth with a steady pressure. "It's starting to rotate. On the count of three really grip hard as I jerk the nail out."

Knowing that he would be leaving bruise marks, Dave gripped the leg hard.

Softly Doc counted. "One, two, three." Mr. Harrod groaned but didn't open his eyes.

Dave felt the pull on the leg bone but the nail slipped out. Only a thin trail of blood trickled down from each side of the thigh where the nail had been.

Setting the pliers and the nail onto the tray on the bed stand, Doc sighed. "Glad that's done. Now I'll clean the wound and put on a fresh bandage." After Doc had cleaned the wound with more carbolic acid, Dave lifted the leg so Doc could wrap the bandage around the leg.

Dave wiped his brow with his shirtsleeve. "Hope we don't have to do something like this again."

Doc tied off the bandage. "It has been an interesting medical case. I may write it up for a medical journal after I see how Jake does in a month or so. Please tell Minnie and Rachel to come on up. I know they are anxious."

Dave went to the top of the stairs and spotted both Mrs. Harrod and Rachel waiting at the bottom. "You can come up now. It's done."

The two women hurried up the stairs and into the bedroom.

Doc closed his case and picked up a towel to drape over the tray to hide the bloody nail. "Minnie, it is so important to keep Jake off his leg for a few more days. I'll be back out to check on it. Then we will start him to getting up to walk. Change the bandage morning and evening until it is healing and then just keep it clean."

Mrs. Harrod leaned up and kissed the older man on the cheek. "Thank you so much, Frederick. You have been such a support through all of this."

"Thank Dave. If he hadn't been here I would have had no choice but to take the leg off. Jake will walk on two legs because of Dave's knowledge and help."

Dave felt heat rising up his neck. He didn't want any thanks for helping his friend. Not after all they had done for him.

Placing her hand on his arm, she smiled. "We know, Frederick. And I give a prayer of thanks for Dave every day."

Dave glanced at Rachel and she was giving him a look that darkened her eyes and left him wanting to lose himself in their depth.

The next couple of weeks brought steady progress. Mr. Harrod was anxious to get back on his feet, but just being free of the confinement of the pulley seemed to bring relief. Then Doc allowed him to sit in a chair in his room and to walk a bit on crutches. As eager as he was to get going again, five months in bed had left him weak.

Though angry with himself for thinking such a thing, Dave wished Mr. Harrod had taken longer to heal. He knew how long and confining the winter had been for his friend, but he had promised Rachel he would leave when her father was back on his feet.

Dave recoiled from even thinking about what leaving Johnny was going to be like. He'd always managed his life with just a few rules, but one hard and fast rule was that a man kept his word.

The winter faded toward the coming of spring and the spirits of the whole family rose as Mr. Harrod started making rapid progress toward recovery. The first day he was able to come downstairs and eat supper with the family was a cause for celebration.

Feeling almost physically ill, Dave could hardly force himself to eat. He excused himself early and retreated to his room, leaving puzzled looks behind him.

Dave started to go back to the old bunkhouse soon after supper now that Mr. Harrod was able to spend the evenings with the family in the front room. It seemed to Dave it would be easier if he stopped spending so much time with Johnny. He felt it would be easier for Johnny after he was gone.

The family seemed puzzled by his behavior. As he offered no explanation, they didn't feel free to ask. Dave often noticed Mrs. Harrod giving him a questioning look.

But the look that was hardest to take was the one of hurt on Johnny's face when Dave refused to play chess with him, but instead told him to ask his grandfather.

Dave didn't know how to go about leaving. He felt close to despair, but he had no one he could talk to about his dilemma.

Toward the end of March, Mr. Harrod recovered sufficiently that he rode out for a few hours with Wayne to look over the herd. The older man tired easily and walked with a decided limp. For his friend's sake, Dave hoped the older man just needed time to build up his strength.

Dave couldn't put off leaving any longer and be true to his word. He decided he would tell Wayne, and Mr. and Mrs. Harrod first and then tell Johnny by himself.

The next day Jesse came over to talk about the spring roundup. They sat at the kitchen table at the end of the noon meal, Dave asked if he could say something to them.

"My goodness, Dave, you don't have to ask. Say whatever you like," Mr. Harrod said.

With all of them looking at him, he cleared his throat. "I've decided it's time I left and started looking for a place of my own."

"Left? What do you mean?" Wayne's brow furrowed up in question.

"I plan to leave next week and go back to the mountains. There's some land there that if I can get it, I mean to start a ranch of my own." So far, it had not been so hard to say, as he'd feared.

Mr. Harrod looked at him as if mulling over what he'd said. "I can understand your wanting a place of your own and this is probably the best time of year to start out. I won't deny that we will miss you and Johnny something awful."

Out of the corner of his eye, Dave glanced at Rachel and then quickly looked away. He felt he would not be able to say it. By forcing himself he said, "I'll not be taking Johnny with me. He's better off here and if you'll let him, he'll stay."

"Let him? Of course we'll let him, but are you sure you want to do that?" As he spoke, Mr. Harrod had put his hand on top of his wife's hand.

"It's not a question of what I want, but of what's best for Johnny. I don't want him to get hurt, and I can't be sure I could protect him if he came with me."

Mrs. Harrod spoke so softly they had to strain to hear her. "Hurt, Dave, hurt for Johnny will be you leaving him again."

Dave felt something twist inside him. "I know he'll feel bad for a while, but he'll soon forget me. I think this is best for him."

Mr. Harrod looked at him hard as he asked, "You are planning to tell him ahead of time, aren't you?"

Getting up from the table, Dave looked at their serious faces. "I'll tell him this evening."

Before anyone could say anything else, Dave turned and left the kitchen. He headed for the corral and saddled a horse. Riding out he had no direction in mind, he just wanted to ride away from the terrible feeling he had inside of himself. But it rode with him.

Never one to put off doing the mean jobs he decided to ride toward town. He waited for Johnny to come along the road toward the ranch on his way home from school. Dave had never felt so desolate in his life as he did watching his son ride up to him on the little paint pony.

At first Johnny was calling to him and grinning, but as he got closer he wore a serious look on his face.

"Hey, Pa, what's wrong?"

"Nothing is wrong," Dave replied, with a mouth that was as dry as cotton. "Let's go check on the swimming hole on our way to the ranch."

"All right, Pa."

They reached the side of the creek and dismounted to let the horses drink.

"Let's sit down for a minute and talk, son."

"What do you want to talk about?" Johnny had such a look of trust that it made his heart hurt.

"I got something to say to you that I don't know if you will understand or not." Dave wasn't sure he understood why they had to have such pain in caring for one another.

Johnny sat on the ground looking up at his father with the large brown eyes so like his mother. "You're going away aren't you? When are you going?"

Dave could not have been more surprised. How Johnny knew he didn't know. "Yes, I'm leaving next week. I promised you if I had to leave I would tell you."

"Why do you have to leave, Pa? I know Grandpa and Grandma would let you stay."

"I know they will, but I need to leave and go find a place for myself. Your grandpa's ranch is a good place and I'm glad you can grow up here, but I need to find my own land and get started building my own ranch." Dave hoped Johnny wasn't going to ask many more questions. He felt close to breaking down and all he really wanted to do was take his son in his arms and hold him.

"Pa, why can't I go with you? Don't you still like me, Pa?" Johnny now had tears running down his cheeks.

"Like you? Johnny, I like you best of anyone I know, and even more, I love you best of anyone I know. But son, I can't take you with me. It's just not the right thing for you." Dave's voice was raw with emotion he couldn't hide anymore.

"Oh, Pa!" Johnny was suddenly in his arms with his head buried in Dave's chest. He had his arms wrapped around Dave as if he never intended to let go.

How long he sat there holding his son he didn't know, but eventually he realized they needed to go on to the ranch or the folks would start to worry.

"Come on, son, we better get going." Dave got up and helped Johnny back on his pony. The ride back to the ranch was silent.

Dave didn't want to go in for supper, but he knew it was useless to put off being around the others. Supper was a quiet affair. Dave hadn't realized how much Johnny usually talked at mealtime. But this evening he was quiet.

Rachel was also quiet and kept looking at Dave with eyes that were very sad.

Dave wanted to say to her that she should be happy; she was getting what she wanted.

After supper, before Dave could get up from the table, Mr. Harrod got up. "Wait here, Dave. I've something I want to show you." He went into the front room and returned shortly with a big flat wooden box. Opening it, he pulled out several maps of the western regions.

Dave had never seen anything like them, but he remembered the family making mention that Mr. Harrod had been an Army surveyor before he'd married and settled down to ranching.

"I'm interested in this mountain valley you told me about, Dave. See if you can locate the area. These maps are old, but when I've talked with travelers I've added landmarks and trails." He spread the maps out on the kitchen table Mrs. Harrod and Rachel had hastily cleared.

They all sat around the table waiting for Dave to figure out the map and locate where he intended to build his ranch.

"Here's Junction and it's due north of there. I know there are some trails through here, but nothing is indicated." Dave was fascinated with the map. He wasn't the only one, as he traced the area north of Junction, Johnny's head kept getting in the way.

"Johnny, if you don't back off a ways your Pa won't ever find the right spot." Mr. Harrod pulled his grandson back.

"Here's Elkhead and the road that goes north there. So it's got to be down in this area." Dave pointed to an area that had nothing marked on it.

Mr. Harrod pulled out some paper and a pencil. "Describe the terrain in the area and let's see if I can draw you a map of the region that will fill in this old army one."

They spent the next hour with Dave giving a detailed description and Mr. Harrod marking it down. Dave painted a word picture for them of where he planned to stake out a place of his own.

He described the upper valley, and how many head of cattle he thought it would support, and the lower valley where the searchers had first spotted him and where he would move the herd for the winters. The approximate location of the cave was marked and the area he wanted to build his cabin.

The high mountains and the pass were harder for him to pin point in terms of distance. The terrain had been so rugged and steep. The trail where he'd met the bear was even harder to place with exactness.

Mrs. Harrod asked, "Jake, how far is it from here? How long a trip would it be?"

Mr. Harrod scratched his head. "Well, let's see. The railroad is north of us here and the road is good to Junction I'm told. I've never been on it, of course. On horseback, I would say a man could cover the distance from Rock Corner to Junction in about a week. From your description, Dave, I would say it would take another full day to get to the mountain valley. Is that about right?"

Dave looked at the map. "I think that's right. On horseback, it will probably take a little over a week to get to the area. I'll probably stop in Junction and buy supplies so that will slow me down some."

"Now, Minnie, by wagon it would take longer, unless you went north here and got the train to Junction. That would cut a few days off the trip. I see that as an advantage for you, Dave. Having the railroad that close will help you get your cattle shipped." Mr. Harrod already talked as if Dave had a working ranch. He was glad Mr. Harrod had thought to pull out the maps. It had seemed to ease some of the tension.

"I'll get a piece of soft hide tomorrow and copy this map for you. It's easier to pack and will last longer than paper. As you can, add to it and before long you'll have this whole area mapped out." Mr. Harrod told him as he started rolling up the piece of leather.

"My goodness, Johnny, it's way past your bedtime. You've got school tomorrow!" Mrs. Harrod exclaimed.

Johnny's face fell. It was as if in his interest and listening to his father's description of the land, he had forgotten momentarily why they were looking at the maps in the first place.

He wrapped his arms tightly around Dave's neck. "You'll be here for breakfast in the morning?"

"Yes, Johnny, I'll be here in the morning."

"Goodnight, Pa," Johnny said, as he again hugged him hard.

Returning the hug Dave kissed his son on the forehead. "Goodnight, son."

Johnny released his hold on Dave's neck and without giving the others their usual kisses ran out of the kitchen and up the stairs.

Rachel stood, said goodnight softly, and slowly climbed the stairs behind Johnny.

Dave wanted to follow and take both of them in his arms. Instead, he quickly said his goodnights and went back to his place in the old bunkhouse. It was Rachel's face as much as Johnny's that he kept seeing, as he lay for hours before sleep would come.

Chapter 25

The next few days passed quickly. Dave kept finding work around the ranch he wanted to do before he left. He did repairs on the barn and house. Mrs. Harrod had been waiting for one of the hands to get around to plowing the garden for her. So Dave spent the morning plowing it and got it ready with neat rows for the seeds to be planted.

After washing up on the porch, he went into the kitchen for the noon meal. Mrs. Harrod met him with a hug and a kiss on the cheek. "Thanks for plowing my garden, Son."

He was glad to have done something that seemed to please her so much.

Wayne came in with Mr. Harrod and sat down for dinner. "Nancy is in the middle of a sewing project and told me to eat with you all."

Mrs. Harrod ruffled his hair as if he were still her little boy. "Good. I like to have you at my table."

As they lingered over coffee, Dave cleared his throat. "I picked out a stallion and two mares to take with me. They're in the barn. After you see which horses I chose, you can let me know what I owe you for them."

Mr. Harrod shook his head and with a calm look said, "There is not a question of payment and whichever ones you chose is fine."

"But—" Dave started to protest.

"End of discussion." Mr. Harrod took a sip of coffee then set the cup on the table. "But I would like to talk to you about selling you a small herd of cattle next spring."

Wayne grinned at Dave. "We would just as soon drive a herd to the west as north to the railroad. I've been over that trail so many times it's boring."

"Thanks. I'd like to plan on that. I can spend this first summer and winter getting a cabin and barn built. By late spring I should be ready to start stocking the land with a herd of cattle."

Mrs. Harrod rose from her place at the table and started stacking the dirty dishes. "Dave, I've got several pots and pans to send with you for your kitchen. What else do you need? We have enough to share."

Dave hadn't thought much about what he would take but he could tell the Harrod's had other ideas. Every day they were putting tools, kitchen utensils, bedding, and other items that Dave would need to get started, in a corner of his room. He'd assumed he would have to purchase everything or do without. But as Wayne had jokingly told him, they had been wanting to get rid of the stuff for years.

The word spread that Dave was leaving and he was surprised how many people in the community seemed genuinely sorry to see him go. His last Sunday it was difficult to get away after the church service because of all the people who wanted to wish him well on his journey. The expressions of regret at his leaving touched Dave.

Jesse and Edna, with the children, and Mary and Tim from town had spent Sunday with the family and had said their good-byes. It seemed to make the reality of what he was doing sink home even harder. Dave tried not to think about what it was going to be like to actually ride away from the ranch.

That evening he sat on the back porch with Mrs. Harrod. He hadn't wanted to go across to his room and to bed with his dark thoughts and even darker dreams for company. Johnny had already been sent to bed since the hour was getting late. Rachel had gone up to read awhile. Mr. Harrod had gone out to the barn to check on a sick horse before turning in for the night. It was unusual for Dave to find himself alone with Mrs. Harrod.

As they sat talking, Mrs. Harrod stopped rocking in her chair. "May I ask you something personal, Dave? Something I probably don't have the right to ask?"

Dave was curious what she wanted to know. "Sure, you ask me whatever you want. I'll do my best to answer."

"Dave, have you thought about marrying again? It's been six and a half years now."

Of anything she might have asked, that wasn't what Dave would have guessed. "Not really. I mean, I would like to have someone someday, but I haven't really thought about it."

"Is it because of Jenny? Do you feel you need to be loyal to her?" Mrs. Harrod's voice was serious.

Dave realized she was leading up to something she felt strongly about. "Last year, before coming here, I would have said yes, but not anymore. Now I feel she would want me to marry, not only to find a mother for Johnny, but also to provide for me."

Mrs. Harrod nodded her head. "That's the way I see it, but I wasn't sure how you felt. Have you thought about anyone in particular?"

Dave looked down at his hands and then back at Mrs. Harrod's kind face. He wasn't sure he should answer or not. "I've thought about someone, but I don't think it's possible."

"Would you mind telling me about it?"

He decided he might as well say it. "The only woman I've thought about in that way since Jenny has been Rachel."

To his surprise, she smiled and nodded. "I thought so."

"You knew? But how? I've never said anything about what I've been feeling."

Laughing, Mrs. Harrod reached over and patted his hand. "You didn't have to say anything. I can see it in both of your eyes when you look at each other."

"What do you mean? Are you saying that you think Rachel has feelings for me?" Dave could not believe she was serious.

"Of course she does. Didn't you know? For the last year, she has grown more and more in love with you. But she'll never say anything until you do."

Dave respected Mrs. Harrod, but he knew she must be wrong about this. There hadn't been any hints from Rachel as far as he had discerned.

Out of curiosity he asked, "Are you saying it would be all right with you if we got married and she came to the mountains with me?"

He couldn't believe he was really asking her something that he'd never even allowed himself to think about as more than a vague desire. Dave had felt himself physically attracted to Rachel for months, and if he was honest, he knew that it was more than a physical attraction. He was drawn to her quiet, gentle manner. Her patience and service with everyone in the family was mature beyond her age. Even though they had had a rocky beginning when he first arrived, he understood it. Other than Johnny, it was Rachel that he looked for whenever he came to the house.

"If that's what both of you want, you would have our blessings. I think you could make each other happy." Mrs. Harrod spoke matter-of-factly and he realized she'd thought a lot about it.

"But Rachel has never said anything to indicate she felt that way about me," Dave protested.

"She may not have expressed it in words, but she certainly has in her behavior. It's been obvious to me for some time," Mrs. Harrod said with certainty.

Dave was about to ask her just what it was in Rachel's behavior that had led her to such a conclusion, when Mr. Harrod came walking up from the barn. Dave didn't feel free to share the conversation with him.

Dave was amazed he'd had such a talk with Mrs. Harrod. Thoroughly confused, he said his good nights and went to his room. He spent a dreamed filled night tossing and turning, haunted by Rachel and Johnny.

Johnny was always haunting him. The boy didn't say much, but he followed Dave at every opportunity he got. Dave would have felt better if Johnny had talked about it, or even gotten angry with him. Instead, his son just looked at him with sad hurt eyes. Several times Dave was tempted to tell him to pack and go with him. Then Dave would remember the bounty hunters, who had appeared the September before, and his promise to Rachel. Why was doing what was best for Johnny so hurtful to them both?

The day before he had set to leave was a strange one. Large thunderstorms had blown through the countryside all day. The air felt as if charged with some sort of force. The animals were all uneasy. Dave wished that Johnny would ride in from school on the little paint pony.

Dave was finishing some repairs to the garden fence for Mrs. Harrod when he heard the bell from the back porch begin to ring. He looked up to see a particularly ominous wall of greenish gray clouds moving in fast from the west.

Mr. Harrod shouted for everyone to go to the root cellar.

Dave dropped his tools and started toward the house in a run all the while looking at the clouds. He saw what had caused Mr. Harrod to start yelling. A tornado was definitely forming and dipping down from the clouds to the ground. He ran faster toward the back of the house and the root cellar. The tornado grew and appeared to be heading directly toward them. There wasn't anything they could do except to get out of its way.

Randy was already holding the door open as Dave got to the root cellar. Mr. Harrod was trying to get Mrs. Harrod and Rachel to go down the steps.

Dave heard Rachel screaming at her father. "But Pa, we've got to find Johnny!"

"There's no time. Get down the steps. I'll go look for him." Mr. Harrod was still trying to get Rachel to go down the steps, as Randy struggled to hold the door against the rising wind.

Dave glanced back. The twisting funnel was bearing down on them. Johnny was out there unprotected. No time to look for him. The storm was coming too fast. Gritting his teeth and not worrying about being too gentle, he shoved Mr. Harrod down the steps, forcing Mrs. Harrod and Rachel into the cellar.

"Randy, get in and help me close the door." Dave and Randy both clamored down the short steps and pulled the door shut above them. The next several minutes were ones of noise, dust, and trying to hold the door shut against the pull of the wind. It took both Dave and Randy's full strength. The noise gradually abated and the pull of the door against their arms stopped.

Cautiously, Dave opened the cellar door. The rain was descending in torrents, but the wind had died down considerably. Dave tried to see beyond the ranch house to track the tornado's path. Within minutes, the rain slowed to a gentle sprinkle. To the west, the sun was breaking through the clouds.

Dave helped the others up the steps and out of the cellar. The women were frantic with worry, especially for Johnny who would have been riding along the road from town.

Wandering to the front of the house, it took Dave and the others a moment to realize that the reason they could see Wayne's house so clearly was because the big barn was now just a pile of rubble. Horses and chickens were running frantically about the yard.

Rachel grabbed Dave's arm. "Oh Dave! What about Johnny?"

That was also Dave's thought.

He laid his hand over her hand on his arm and tried to give her a reassurance that he wasn't feeling. "Don't worry, Rachel. He has to be all right. We'll catch some of these horses and start looking."

Nancy and the two little boys came out of their house and ran up the road. Mr. and Mrs. Harrod started toward them. Before they could meet, Wayne and several riders came in from the south.

Wayne jumped off his horse and grabbed his wife and boys in one big embrace.

Dave yelled at Cody. "Bring your horse over and let me ride him."

Rachel asked, "What are you going to do?"

"I'm going to look for Johnny." Dave took the reins from Cody.

She ran toward Wayne's horse. "I'm coming with you." She swung into the saddle before Dave was mounted.

Dave was too worried about Johnny to protest, but with a wave to the others, mounted the horse and led the way down the lane to the road.

The signs of the tornado's passing were everywhere. They had to guide the horses carefully around the debris in the road. Dave saw several dead cows.

They had traveled no more than a mile when Dave spotted a small crumpled figure by the side of the road. He pulled up his horse and swung down. Terrified at what he might find, he ran to the prone figure. Taking Johnny up in his arms and holding him carefully, Dave was relieved to find him still breathing.

"How bad is he hurt?" Rachel knelt by Dave.

"He's breathing and I don't think anything is broken. He has a bad bruise on his forehead. Maybe he just got knocked out," Dave said with relief.

"If anything happened to Johnny, I couldn't stand it." Rachel slowly brushed back the hair from Johnny's forehead. She'd tears flowing down her cheeks. "I don't understand how you can bear to leave him."

Dave looked up at her with surprise. "But I thought that was what you wanted. You told me that was the best thing for me to do for Johnny's sake."

Rachel looked stricken as she responded, "Is that why you're planning to leave without him? Because of the things I said to you at the jail?"

"Yes, I gave you my word I would go and leave Johnny here with you so he would be safe." Dave held the unconscious boy close as he looked at her.

"Dave, forgive me for ever saying such things and for the way I have acted ever since you got here last year," Rachel said with a little sob. "I was so afraid of losing Johnny that I wasn't thinking very straight. I didn't know what kind of man you had become. The more I've come to know you, the more I realize that I was wrong. Johnny needs his father."

Dave was puzzled. "What are you trying to tell me?"

"I'm telling you that I don't want you to leave. If you do leave, you must take Johnny with you. Pa explained to me the need of a man to have his own place. Wayne and Pa would love for you to stay here and work with them, but it wouldn't be the same as having your own place." She brushed some of the tears away. "I saw how you talked about building a ranch in the mountains. For you there's something special that pulls you back there."

Dave could hardly take in the hope she offered. "Do you mean it, about Johnny coming with me?"

Stroking his arm gently, she smiled through her tears, "If you don't, I don't want you to leave."

A light started to appear in the black hole of despair Dave had been lost in for the last six months. Not fully believing what she was saying, he asked, "What about my promise I gave you?"

"I had no right to ask such a thing of you. I didn't realize it at the time, but I should never have let you give me your word to leave and not take Johnny. If you need to hear it, I'm saying it. I'm releasing you from your word. From now on you do what you feel is right for you and your son."

He fought the emotions that were surging almost overwhelming him. It was as if a dam had crumpled and waves of joy and relief were about to sweep him away.

"Rachel, you don't know what this means to me," he said softly as he looked into her eyes, holding his son close. Fight as hard as he could he couldn't stop a tear as it escaped out of the corner of his eye.

Rachel reached up and gently brushed it away. "Yes, I think I do now. I'm just sorry I was the cause of so much pain for you."

Dave thought of taking Johnny with him and knew that wasn't enough. Remembering what Mrs. Harrod had told him about her suspicion of Rachel's feelings he took a deep breath and took a chance.

"What about you, Rachel? Would you be willing to come with us?" Hurrying on before she could answer, he said, "I know it's going to be hard. I don't have much to give you. But I love you and the thought of leaving you behind has been as much a hurt to me as the thought of leaving Johnny."

Dave waited without breathing for her response. She searched his face as looking for reassurance that he meant what he said. Slowly she smiled and placed her hand on his cheek. "Yes, Dave, I'll come with you to the mountains or anywhere you're willing to take me."

Still holding his unconscious son in his arm, he pulled Rachel close to him, kissing her softly on the forehead.

The boy gave a moan and struggled in his father's arms and their attention shifted from each other to Johnny.

He glanced up at them with a confused look. "Hey, Pa, where did you come from? What happened?"

Relieved beyond words that his son was conscious and talking, Dave hugged him and laughed. "A tornado tried to get you, but you beat it. How are you feeling?"

"My head hurts. I must have fallen off Paint. Where is he?" The boy struggled to sit up as he looked around for his pony.

"Don't worry, Son. We're going to get you back to the ranch, then I'll go roundup your pony." Dave turned to Rachel. "I think we have some things to talk about. Let's get Johnny to the ranch and see what needs done there. Maybe this evening we can talk."

"Yes, I think that we both have a lot to say to each other. But you're right, for now let's get Johnny home. Ma and Pa will be worried sick." Rachel reluctantly let go of Dave's hand.

Chapter 26

It didn't take long to get back to the ranch. Mr. and Mrs. Harrod's relief at having Johnny safe was evident. Dave spent the rest of the day assessing the damage to the buildings and livestock and making sure that everyone was safe.

The tornado had skipped across the countryside, repeatedly rising back up into the sky only to dip down to earth again. Everywhere it had touched down destruction was left behind. It had spared the house and old bunkhouse, but had demolished the barn and then had skipped over Wayne's house, taking part of his roof. For days after the tornado hit, they found dead cattle along its path.

The church building was destroyed with nothing left behind but its foundation and the front steps, perfectly intact. The storm just missed Rock Corner, and instead traveled south of town.

Up at Jesse's place they were not even aware of the tornado's passing until Mr. Harrod sent a rider to tell them what happened at the ranch and to make sure Jesse and his family were all right.

At supper that evening, Dave told the Harrods he was going to put off leaving for a few more days so he could help get things back in shape. There was obvious relief on the part of the Harrods and Johnny.

After supper, Mrs. Harrod put her grandson to bed early. He didn't protest since he was feeling the results of his fall from the pony. The boy had several bruises and a big lump on his forehead. He didn't complain about anything except a slight headache and his concern for his pony.

Mr. and Mrs. Harrod soon excused themselves and went to bed, leaving Dave and Rachel alone sitting on the back porch. Dave found himself strangely shy with her, not knowing what to say or where to start. Rachel helped him by reaching over and putting her hand in his.

"Rachel, did you mean what you said this afternoon, about going with me?" He looked down into her soft brown eyes.

"Yes, Dave, I meant it," she replied simply.

"I guess we need to make some plans. The first thing is to tell Johnny and your folks. And then for you to decide when you want us to get married." He could not believe what he was saying .

Rachel smiled and cocked her head. "Are you asking me to marry you, Dave Kimbrough?"

"Well, yes. We can't go to the mountains together unless we get married, can we?" Dave had assumed that was part of it.

"No, we can't." Rachel responded. "But it takes time to plan a wedding and then to leave for a new place. Are you willing to wait?"

Dave had not thought about organizing a wedding or packing for Johnny and Rachel's going with him. It didn't matter how much time it took if he could have them with him.

"You tell me what I need to do. I'm willing to do whatever it takes," Dave replied.

"Then let's tell the family in the morning." Rachel grinned at him. "Unless you want to wait, what about in two weeks? That should be enough time to get everything done and be packed. We will need to get on to the mountains as soon as possible to have a cabin built before winter sets in."

Her understanding of the urgency to get to the mountains made it easier for them to start planning what needed to be done. He was making the right decision in marrying Rachel. She would be more than a wife. She would be his partner in building a new life. There was no concern about what Johnny would think of the idea. He would be thrilled that his two favorite people were going to spend their life together with him. The Harrods would regret Rachel and Johnny going so far but from what Mrs. Harrod had said to him, Dave knew they would give their blessings.

Dave and Rachel talked long into the night. They soon had plans for the wedding and what to pack. When Dave realized how late it was, he stood and pulled Rachel into his arms. The strength with which she had her arms around his neck gave him a reassurance that what was happening was real and not his imagination.

"I love you, Rachel, more than you can know," he whispered in her ear.

As they stood close together, bathed in the moonlight, she took his face in her hands and looked intently into his eyes. "I love you, too, with all my heart. And I promise you, Dave Kimbrough, that I will do everything in my power to make you as happy as a man can be." She slowly pulled his head down and softly kissed him on the lips. Then without another word, she backed out of his arms and went quickly into the house, leaving him standing on the porch in wonder.

The next morning broke clear and bright. It matched Dave's mood as he walked across the yard to the house for breakfast. When he went into the kitchen, he surprised Mrs. Harrod with a big hug and a kiss on the cheek.

"My goodness, Dave, you seem in good spirits this morning."

As he sat at the table, Dave grinned at her and Mr. Harrod, who was already settled at the table. "It's a great morning and I'm hungry as a bear."

Mrs. Harrod filled his coffee cup. "Well, I'm glad to hear it. You have been kind of picking at your food the last few weeks. Let me pull the biscuits out of the oven and get Rachel and Johnny down here so we can eat."

Before she could call them, Rachel and Johnny came into the kitchen. She had on a bright yellow dress. A matching bow held her long brown hair back as it flowed in waves to her waist. She gave Dave a radiant smile of love.

Dave knew he'd never seen her look more beautiful.

Instead of sitting in her usual place, she sat down by Dave in Johnny's place.

Johnny looked from his father and back to Rachel. Without a word, he slipped into Rachel's place.

Taking Rachel's hand under the table, Dave cleared his throat. "We have something we want to tell you all."

Mrs. Harrod set the plate of hot biscuits on the table and sat, looking at her husband with a question.

Mr. Harrod shrugged his shoulders at her and turned to Dave. "What is it, son?"

Dave looked at Rachel, who smiled shyly back and nodded. "Rachel and I have been talking. We've decided to get married."

Mr. and Mrs. Harrod both burst into smiles.

Mrs. Harrod reached over and gave Rachel a hug. "I'm so happy for you, sweetheart. When did you decide this?" she asked. "When are you getting married?"

Before they could answer her, Mr. Harrod asked, "What does this mean in terms of your starting your own place?"

Dave looked at his son, who had not said anything yet. "If it's all right with you all, we want to get married in about two weeks. Then we plan to take Johnny and head for the mountains to start building a cabin."

Dave had said what Johnny waited to hear. He jumped up from the table and ran to his father, throwing himself into his arms. "Do you mean it, Pa? You're taking me and Aunt Rachel with you?"

Dave felt a lightness of heart that he'd not had since before Jenny's death. He held his son with one arm and wrapped the other around Rachel's shoulders. "If you want to, you can come with us."

"You mean to live with you from now on at your new ranch?"

"That's right. It's what I have always wanted, but I wasn't sure it was best for you. Now I know that it is. We want you with us if that's what you want." Dave wasn't prepared for Johnny's response.

He started to cry and buried his head in the curve of Dave's neck.

"Oh, yes, Pa. I want to come with you," he said in a muffled voice.

Dave wrapped his arms around his son. "It's settled then, you're coming with us. Rachel and I will get married and then the three of us will leave for the mountains."

He looked up to see Rachel smiling at them with tears running down her face. "Don't cry, Rachel, it's all right." He couldn't bear to see her tears.

"I know. I'm just so happy for you and Johnny."

Dave wiped the tears from his son's face. "Now, Johnny, go sit down and let's eat breakfast. We got a lot to do in the next few weeks. We need to decide what to take and get it packed. And we want to help your grandpa get a new barn built."

Mrs. Harrod brushed a corner of her eye. "And we have a wedding to plan. Oh, Dave, Rachel, I'm so happy."

At the sound of a knock at the kitchen door, Dave saw Cody standing on the porch with his hat in his hand. "Excuse me, folks, but I thought you would want to know."

"What is it, Cody?" Mr. Harrod asked.

"Well, when I got up this morning and checked on the horses we rounded up yesterday, after the tornado, Johnny's little paint pony had wandered up to the corral."

Johnny was out of the kitchen running toward the corral, almost before Cody had finished what he was saying. No one even tried to call him back.

"Thanks for letting us know, Cody. Is the pony hurt?" Mr. Harrod asked.

"No, sir. Oh, he has a few little cuts, but nothing serious," Cody replied, then excusing himself, he went back toward the barn.

Even though they had work to do to get the ranch cleaned up from the results of the tornado, they lingered over their breakfast and talked of Dave and Rachel's plans.

Rachel frowned and turned to her father. "Pa, do you think the church building can be rebuilt in time for the wedding?"

Mr. Harrod placed his hand over his daughter's. "Your pa will make sure that it is. There's a lot of things I would like to give you, honey, that I can't do. But having the church building ready for you is something I can do."

Mrs. Harrod nodded. "Why don't you go into town this morning and order the lumber and post an announcement that we will have a gathering to raise the church building next Saturday. That way folks can plan on it."

Dave squeezed Rachel's hand. "That is something I can work on,too. I don't know much about planning a wedding but I'll help get the church ready and make sure the preacher is there."

Mr. Harrod glanced at his wife. "We're real pleased about you all getting married."

She smiled. "And I'm not really surprised."

The next two weeks passed quickly. Dave spent much time in deciding what to take to the mountains, besides helping to build a new barn. Since Johnny and Rachel were coming with him, Dave changed his thinking about what he would need in their new home. Before he had thought only in terms of the work of building a ranch and the tools he would need, now he was also considering what he would need to make a home comfortable for his new bride and son.

The stack of items to pack was soon too large for one wagon. After talking it over with Mr. Harrod, Dave made the decision to ask Randy if he would be willing to come work with him. Randy would be a great help building a cabin.

Without hesitation, Randy responded that he was more than willing.

Dave would drive one wagonload filled with supplies and Randy the other one loaded with the furniture the family gave Rachel as a wedding present. They planned to leave a couple of days after the wedding.

After talking with Mr. Harrod and Wayne, it was decided that Dave would spend the summer, fall, and winter getting the place ready with corrals, a barn, and fences to receive a small herd of cattle. Wayne would deliver the herd in the spring. Having the money in the bank to carry out his plans was a novelty that Dave was learning to enjoy.

When the rest of the family had been told of their wedding plans all responded with good wishes. The women began immediately to plan the wedding and to start getting together what they felt Rachel would need to be comfortable in her new home.

Mary teased her about jumping the gun on her wedding plans. Mary had set her wedding for the middle of the summer. Rachel's one regret was that she would not be there to celebrate her sister's wedding. But it was a regret over ridden by the joy of her own plans.

The Saturday after the tornado had destroyed the church building, the people gathered at the site, and began the process of cleaning up and rebuilding. With different ranches donating timber and labor, it was quickly finished by the date that Rachel and Dave had set for the wedding.

A week later, standing at the front of the small church building with Wayne and Johnny beside him, Dave felt stiff in his black broadcloth suit and new white shirt. If getting a haircut and dressing up pleased his bride to be then he was willing to put up with it.

Dave felt like his head was spinning from all the activities of the last two weeks getting ready for this day. The church building had been completed the week before but still smelled of fresh lumber and paint. Dave had to admit that it looked nice with bunches of wildflowers in vases around the front.

Mary as maiden of honor stood across from him and was dressed in a deep blue silk dress that showed off her lovely features. She gave him a smile of encouragement.

Wayne as best man stood behind him in his Sunday suit.

Johnny was squirming standing next to him in a new suit that his grandmother had made just for this occasion.

Just as Dave began to think Rachel had changed her mind she appeared at the door at the back of the church with her arm hooked around her father's. Dave took a deep breath and stood tall as he focused only on the beautiful sight of his bride to be.

Rachel wore her mother's white wedding dress trimmed in black velvet at the neckline, waist, and just before the full lace flounce at the hem. A round neckline framed in lace showed the barest skin to her collarbone. Deep lace ruffles finished the three quarter length sleeves. A full skirt fell from the small tight fitting waist. Her long hair was pulled back and up, gathered with a ribbon, and then curled to allow a sea of ringlets to cascade down her back. A lace veil that hung down her back to her hips only covered half her face. He could see her eyes sparkling and the smile she gave him was like the sun coming out. She seemed to be gliding toward him.

As the preacher said words that Dave would not remember, he looked out the window, past Rachel, at the cemetery were he'd buried his first love. Jenny's spirit seemed to be near by and Dave felt a sense of approval for what was taking place. The memories of his life with Jenny would always be there, but they would be memories that stayed where they belonged—in the past. He would not be taking a ghost with him as he started his life with Rachel to whom he now gave his pledge of love.

He turned his gaze away from the view out the window and looked into the face of one who promised to love and live with him for the rest of her life.

He heard the preacher say, "You may now kiss the bride."

Taking Rachel's face between his hands, he gently kissed her. The final edges of darkness, that had been a part of his life for so many years, were gone. A bright light of hope flooded forever the black hole at the center of his being.

THE END

Other Titles by A J Hawke Available on Amazon:

CABIN ON PINTO CREEK By A J Hawke

Elisha Evans is out of luck. By the age of twenty-five, he'd planned to have his own ranch. Instead, he's forced to beg for a job, destroying his dreams of having a family he can provide for and protect. Betrayal and loss bring him to a cabin on Pinto Creek in the high Colorado Rockies. Just before winter hits, he finds a broken-down wagon in the snow with precious cargo inside. Perhaps, his luck is about to change.

Susana Jamison doesn't feel so lucky. Despite being rescued by Elisha, she is challenged to the limit of her strength, both physically and spiritually, when faced with the brutal conditions of frontier living and the dangers she encounters. Can she hold on to her faith in the midst of this desperate situation, especially when she's forced to marry a man she's doesn't love?

An inspirational historical western romance, Cabin On Pinto Creek is the first in the Cedar Ridge Chronicles.

CAUGHT BETWEEN TWO WORLDS By A J Hawke

Single parent Flint Tucker had no intention of leaving his three-year-old daughter on the ranch in Colorado with his parents. Not even for the dark haired beauty found on a mountain trail. So how did he end up in New York working for Stephanie Wellbourne?

Stephanie Wellbourne needs help trying to save her position as CEO of her late father's corporation. She's sure Flint Tucker is just the man for the job if she can get him to stay in New York. Why is he not enticed by her wealth and position?

How can a man from a ranch in Colorado and an Upper Manhattan career woman find love when they are CAUGHT BETWEEN TWO WORLDS?

An Inspirational Contemporary Romance